"Billie!" a woman called from the house next door.

That voice. It *couldn't* be.

Adam glanced at the little girl, who was still holding the softball that had broken his window. "Over here, Mom!" she yelled. "Next door!"

"Billie, there you are—"

Adam turned slowly as the woman came around the hedge. She stopped dead when she saw him.

She looked as fresh and inviting as a Carolina sunrise. A flowing skirt and pale blouse hid all but the outline of her body. Her hair had been pulled away from her face, and her bangs hung low, almost to her lashes.

From this distance, he couldn't see her eyes, but he knew the color—hazel. Brown and green and gold. Wide, and slightly tipped at the corners. A band squeezed his chest, making it difficult to breathe.

"Hello, Adam," she said quietly. "I see you've met my daughter...."

Dear Reader,

Last year, I requested that you send me your opinions on the books that we publish—and on romances in general. Thank you so much for the many thoughtful comments. For the next couple of months, I'd like to share with you quotes from those letters. This seems very appropriate now, while we are in the midst of the THAT SPECIAL WOMAN! promotion. Each one of our readers is a special woman, as heroic as the heroines in our books.

This August has some wonderful books coming your way. *More Than He Bargained For* by Carole Halston, a warm, poignant story, is the THAT SPECIAL WOMAN! selection. Debbie Macomber also brings us the first book in her FROM THIS DAY FORWARD series—*Groom Wanted*. MORGAN'S MERCENARIES, Lindsay McKenna's action-packed trio concludes this month with *Commando*. And don't miss books from other favorite authors: Marie Ferrarella, Susan Mallery and Christine Rimmer.

I hope you enjoy this book, and all of the stories to come! Have a wonderful August!

Sincerely,

Tara Gavin
Senior Editor
Silhouette Books

Quote of the Month: "Romance books provide the escape that is needed from the sometimes crazy and hard-to-live-in world. It takes me away for that three or four hours a day to a place no one else can come into. That is why I read romances. Because sometimes there is not a happy ending, and going to a place where there is can uplift the spirit that really needs it."

—J. Majeski
New Jersey

SUSAN MALLERY

A DAD FOR BILLIE

Silhouette®

SPECIAL EDITION®

Published by Silhouette Books New York

America's Publisher of Contemporary Romance

To Terry, with love and thanks. Your accepting nature has taught me to be more understanding of those around me—including myself. Your self-belief has convinced me that in addition to being my strongest critic, I must also be my own best fan. Your determination to succeed reminds me to keep striving for my own goals. They say that while we can't choose our family, we can choose our friends. This time, dear friend, I chose well.

SILHOUETTE BOOKS
300 East 42nd St., New York, N.Y. 10017

A DAD FOR BILLIE

Copyright © 1993 by Susan W. Macias

All rights reserved. Except for use in any review, the reproduction or utilization of this work in whole or in part in any form by any electronic, mechanical or other means, now known or hereafter invented, including xerography, photocopying and recording, or in any information storage or retrieval system, is forbidden without the permission of the publisher, Silhouette Books, 300 E. 42nd St., New York, N.Y. 10017

ISBN: 0-373-09834-0

First Silhouette Books printing August 1993

All the characters in this book have no existence outside the imagination of the author and have no relation whatsoever to anyone bearing the same name or names. They are not even distantly inspired by any individual known or unknown to the author, and all incidents are pure invention.

®: Trademark used under license and registered in the United States Patent and Trademark Office and in other countries.

Printed in the U.S.A.

Books by Susan Mallery

Silhouette Special Edition

Tender Loving Care #717
More Than Friends #802
A Dad for Billie #834

SUSAN MALLERY

has always been an incurable romantic. Growing up, she spent long hours weaving complicated fantasies about dashing heroes and witty heroines. She was shocked to discover not everyone carried around this sort of magical world. Taking a chance, she gave up a promising career in accounting to devote herself to writing full-time. She lives in Southern California with her husband—"the most wonderful man in the world. You can ask my critique group." Susan also writes historical romances under the name Susan Macias.

Billie Barrington — Pitcher

Ht. 4ft. 3inches   w. 58 lbs.

Throws Right — Bats Right

Born: January 14
Home: Orchard, South Carolina

will be drafted by:
The San Francisco Giants
? ? ?

Orchard Division 2
Childrens League
8 wins
2 Losses

Awarded most improved pitcher

drawn by Kailie Van Fleet

Chapter One

*C*rash!

Adam Barrington glanced up as a softball flew through his window, arced in a perfect half circle across the room, then *thunked* onto the center of his desk. As it rolled over the loose papers and spread sheets, he put out his left hand. The ball dropped off the side of the desk and directly into his palm.

Except for the tinkle of falling shards of glass, the room was silent. Adam leaned back in his chair and waited.

It didn't take long. About thirty seconds later a small face appeared at the broken window. A red baseball cap hid the child's hair and shadowed the eyes.

"You caught my ball."

"You broke my window." He rose to his feet and approached the mess.

"Yeah. I see." The kid glanced at the remaining bits of glass and the other intact panes. "What if I tell you it wasn't my fault?"

"Was it?"

There was a heavy sigh. "Probably. I mean I'm not playing catch with anyone, so I can't say someone else threw it. This window costs a lot. More than my allowance for a month, I bet." Another sigh. "My mom's gonna kill me for sure."

Adam fought back a grin. "Wait there. I'll be right out and we can discuss reimbursement."

The child slumped visibly. "It's never good when adults say *discuss,* then a big word you can't understand."

He chuckled as he walked through the hall and out the front door. The kid stood on the wide expanse of lawn beside the window and stared glumly at the shattered pane. At first Adam had assumed he was a boy, but as the child turned and pulled off the baseball cap, he saw "he" was a "she."

Short dark hair clung to her head; bangs, mangled by the cap, stuck out in uneven spikes. Wide and somber brown eyes watched him like a prisoner waiting for execution. Shorts and a grubby T-shirt covered a sturdy tanned body. She was somewhere between six and ten, he guessed. He'd never had much experience estimating children's ages.

"It looks bad," the girl said. "I'll pay for it, I swear. And even if you don't believe me, my mom will make sure. She's big on me assuming the 'proper responsibility.'" The last two words came out in a stern falsetto.

"I can't say I blame her, if you go around breaking people's windows."

"Well, I don't." The girl planted her hands on her hips.

"You broke mine."

"It was an accident."

"Somehow you strike me as the kind of child who has a lot of accidents."

Her lower lip thrust out mutinously. "I do not!" The lip curled up. "Okay. Some. A few. But not *lots.*"

For the second time in as many minutes, Adam had to fight the urge to grin. "What's your name?"

"Billie."

"I'm Adam." He thrust out his hand. They shook solemnly. He gave her the softball. "I haven't seen you before, Billie. Are you from the neighborhood?"

"No. San Francisco. We just moved here. It's a long drive. How come you don't talk funny? I mean, you kinda do, but not like that lady in the store. But she was nice. She gave me candy."

Billie pulled a half-eaten sugar stick out of her shorts pocket. After picking off a loose thread, she stuck it into her mouth.

"Well?" she asked, after a moment.

"This is South Carolina, Billie. As far as we're concerned, you're the one who talks funny."

"I do not!" She gave the candy a last lick, then thrust it back into her pocket. "Can we play catch until my mom comes out? She'll want to apologize for my reptile behavior. Are you mad? We'll be neighbors. I don't want you to hate me or anything. I'm basically a good kid." She grinned, an impish light dancing in her wide brown eyes. "At least that's what my mom says when she doesn't know I'm listening. Do you have any kids? Mom didn't know if there were any on the street. I prefer boys. Mom says she's glad I'm a girl, but I don't know if it's so great. Have you ever had to wear a dress and then keep *clean?* Yuk." She pulled the baseball cap over her head.

Adam blinked several times. He didn't know where to begin. Reptile behavior? It seemed easier to focus on the obvious. "Neighbors?"

She pointed to the house next door. The Southwick place. "We're moving in. The furniture's not here yet, so we might have to camp out—on the floor."

He glanced over his shoulder at the house in question. The two-story structure, a smaller version of his own home, stood where it had for eighty years. In the last couple of months the old tenants had moved out and a string of workmen had taken over. The outside had been painted, the inside as well. Carpeting had been replaced and an electrician had fixed several old circuits. It hadn't been sold, that he knew. The only real estate office in town used his bank, as did the local escrow company. New tenants, he told himself. Another family. He didn't mind. It's not as if he'd for a moment thought Jane might move back. Her parents had retired to Galveston and she had—

He frowned as he realized he didn't know what she'd done. But it didn't matter. They'd been old news for a long time.

"Are you ready?" Billie asked.

"Ready for what?"

"To play catch. Mom'll be right out. She's trying to figure out what furniture goes where. If it ever gets here. I won't throw hard."

She tossed the ball with an easy underhand.

He caught it instinctively and threw it back. "Young lady, you do not have to worry about throwing too hard for me."

"I don't know. I'm the pitcher on my softball team. I have a mean curve ball."

Adam glanced at the broken window. "That I believe. How many wild pitches last year?"

She wrinkled her nose. "We won our division."

"How many?"

"I don't remember."

"Let me guess. Not some or a few, but a lot?"

She laughed. The sound reminded him of something, but before he could place it, she threw the ball, harder this time. "Yeah, a lot. Coach says I'll develop more accuracy as I mature."

"I hope that's soon. I have a lot of windows."

Billie tugged the cap over her eyes, and bent in a crouch. "Here she is, ladies and gentlemen, the National League's first female pitcher. Not only has she pitched a record six shutouts in a row, but her batting average is close to five hundred." She cupped her hands over her mouth and breathed heavily to sound like background crowd noise. "She's pitching to her favorite catcher, a champion in his own right, Mr. Adam—" She paused and looked expectant.

"Barrington. Adam Barrington."

"Adam Barrington, one of the old-timers. He can still catch a mean curve ball."

"I'm honored," he said dryly.

She wound up and threw. The curve ball started out steadily enough, then lost its speed and direction. He lunged to the right, but it rolled past him and into the bushes.

"I gotta work on that curve," she said.

"Try the backyard."

"Why?"

With a flick of his wrist, he sent the ball toward her. "There's a screen of bushes and trees between you and my windows."

She wrinkled her nose. "I don't usually—"

"Bil-lie."

The woman's call came from the house next door. Adam stiffened. That voice. It couldn't be. He glanced at Billie.

"Moms." She shrugged. "They always know when you're having fun. Over here," she yelled. "Next door."

"Billie, there you are. We need to go into town and use the phone."

He turned slowly. The woman came around the hedge and stopped dead when she saw him. Her gaze darted between him and the child. Twilight had fallen upon the steamy South Carolina day, turning bright sky dark, softening the light. Sweat beaded on his brow and coated his back, but she looked as fresh and inviting as a Carolina sunrise. A loose flowing skirt and pale blouse hid all but the general outline of her body. Hair, true brown without a hint of red, had been pulled away from her face into a braid. Her bangs hung low, almost to her lashes.

From this distance he couldn't see her eyes, but he knew the color—hazel. Brown and green and gold. Wide and slightly tipped at the corners. He glanced back at Billie, still holding the softball. A band squeezed his chest, making it tough to breathe.

"Hello, Adam," the woman said quietly, slowly moving past the hedge and onto the lawn. "I see you've met my daughter."

Her daughter? The band tightened. He dropped his gaze to her left hand. No ring. So she'd married and divorced. He wasn't surprised.

Billie frowned at her. "How'd you know his name?"

"I grew up in this house, honey. I told you that."

Billie looked at him. "You lived next door to my mom?"

He couldn't speak. Slowly his gaze was drawn back to the woman. A longing swept over him. Hard and powerful, it crashed through his body, the need like an undertow pulling him down. But on its heels burned a rage so hot, the longing evaporated into mist and blew away. His hands tightened into fists at his sides. How dare she come back?

The depth of feeling startled him. He forced himself to take a deep breath, then release it slowly. It had been over for years, he reminded himself. His body relaxed; the fists uncurled. He felt nothing. That had been his choice then; it still was.

Emotions flickered across Adam's face. They passed so quickly, Jane didn't have time to label them. No doubt he was as stunned as she. Despite her expectations—*she* had known she was moving back to Orchard—this wasn't the meeting she'd planned.

"Hello, Jane."

How calmly he spoke, she thought, wondering if he could hear the pounding of her heart. His momentary loss of control had been squashed; she stared at the handsome but unreadable face of Orchard, South Carolina's leading citizen. Adam Barrington, bank president, favored son and brother.

He hadn't changed much. Still a hair over six feet, still lean yet strong, still sophisticated. Even in twill shorts and a T-shirt, he looked like an ad for a men's magazine. The caption would read something along the lines of "The Executive at Home." But in this picture there was no happy family. She'd asked. He hadn't married.

He continued to look at her, seeing she could only guess what. But she couldn't read *him*. Was he angry? He had every right to be. Her mind screamed at her to turn and run back to the safety of her house. It would only be a temporary solution; they were neighbors. The truth would come out eventually. Small Southern towns were notoriously bad at keeping secrets. For now she was safe. If he'd known, if he'd suspected—even Adam Barrington wouldn't have been able to stay that controlled.

On the long drive from San Francisco to South Carolina via southern Texas, she'd had many opportunities to plan the right thing to say when they met for the first time in years. Perhaps a casual conversation at the bank when she opened her account or an accidental meeting picking up the Saturday morning papers on fresh-cut green lawns. In every scenario, she'd imagined herself as detached, distant but friendly and well-groomed. Hot, wrinkled and frazzled didn't fit the picture at all!

"It's been a long time," she said, forcing herself to smile and walk those last few feet until she stood directly in front of him. She thought about offering her hand, but that seemed too strange. And as for a welcoming hug—he didn't look all that welcoming.

"How many years?" he asked.

"Nine," she said immediately, then cursed herself for her rapid response. He would probably think she'd counted the days. That she'd missed him and regretted her impulsiveness. She had, dammit, but he didn't need to know.

"So you guys were friends?" Billie asked, her head moving back and forth as she watched them intently. "Like you played baseball together?"

Jane forced herself to look away from Adam's mesmerizing gaze. Those brown eyes had always had a power over her, she thought as she brushed her damp palms against her skirt. Tall oak trees shielded them from the main road and the curious stares of neighbors. Word of her return had already begun to spread. At least no one would witness this awkward reunion.

"We dated," she admitted.

Billie paused, then continued to toss the ball in the air and catch it. "Oh." Her disappointment was obvious. At eight, her daughter had yet to find boys interesting for anything other than beating in sports.

"Briefly," Adam added.

He called two years brief?

"What happened?" Billie asked.

"Your mother went away."

Again the words were spoken with no emotion. He was telling a story that didn't matter to him anymore. If it ever had. The abridged version of life with Jane and Adam. Short, sweet, and while missing the point completely, it did convey the basic facts if not the mood of the whole event. A finality. It had been over for a long time.

"You're moving back?" he asked.

"That's the plan." She smiled brightly, not daring to meet his eyes. God knows what he would read there. The pocket on his T-shirt became fascinating. "My parents have settled down in Galveston, and the tenants living in the house here decided not to renew their lease. I, ah, there was a job opening at the junior high, so here we are."

"You're a teacher?"

"English!" Billie made a gagging noise. "The worst. You should see the books she's always trying to get me to read."

"You only like stories with blood and killing. That's not literature or even suited for children. There are lots of classics that—" She stopped and shrugged. "It's an old argument."

"Who's winning?" Adam asked.

Jane smiled at her daughter and pulled on the bill of her cap. "She is, but I'm determined to hang in there."

"You never told me you wanted to be a teacher."

She searched his face. The familiar lines, high cheekbones, strong, square jaw, hadn't changed much. He'd been a man when she'd left. He would find differences in her though: the last time he'd seen her, she'd only been a girl. Legally a woman, but at heart, emotionally, still very young. Time had changed her, both inside and out.

"I did. Several times. You didn't listen."

The lines of the jaw she'd been admiring tightened with her words. Fire flashed in his brown eyes. A wavy lock of hair fell over his forehead, the only wayward thing about him. "I listened. You were the one who—"

He stopped and looked at Billie. Her daughter stood openmouthed.

"Who what?" Billie asked.

He shook his head, withdrawing from the heated conversation. "It doesn't matter. The repairmen have been fixing up the house for weeks. I'm sure you'll be pleased with their work."

Who what? Jane asked silently, repeating her daughter's question. Left? She'd admit to that. Left badly? Ditto. To understand why, he might do well to look to himself.

"Everything looks terrific," she said. Billie tossed her the softball. She caught it, then threw it back. "The upstairs bathrooms have been remodeled."

"That was a couple of years ago," he said.

Part of her marveled at the surface calm of their conversation. She wanted him to say something, do something, not just stand there like a polite acquaintance. He would have gone on with his life, might even have forgiven her, but forgotten—no way. Neither of them had. So he would pretend it didn't matter, and she would pretend not to feel guilty. A fair exchange, she thought. Except for one small eight-year-old problem.

"It's been great to see you, Adam," she said, ready to make her escape. "Billie and I have to get to town. It's late and the furniture company swore they'd be delivering today. If they're not, we have to make other arrangements."

He glanced at his watch. "The office will be closed."

"The headquarters are on the West Coast. They'll still be open."

"Uhh, Mom?" Billie stared at the ground and shuffled her feet. That didn't signal good news.

"What have you lost, forgotten or broken now?"

"A window."

Jane thought about the small amount of money they had to last them the summer. She wouldn't start teaching until September and her first paycheck wasn't due until almost the end of that month. Please, God, let the window be a small one, she thought as she turned to face her house. Maybe they could board it up for a few months. If it was on the side that faced Adam's yard, all the better.

"Where?"

"There."

But Billie wasn't pointing in their yard. Instead her small tanned arm thrust up toward the front of Adam's house.

"No," Jane said. "Not—"

"Yup. I was playing ball and it got away from me."

She glanced at Adam. He was studying her with that damned inscrutable expression of his. "All those times I ignored my mother when she told me to act like a lady are being paid back in spades. Sorry."

"No harm done," he said. "Except for the glass, of course."

"Of course." Was he making a joke? The great Adam Barrington risking humor? That wasn't fair, she reminded herself. He'd always been witty and charming. She'd been the one out of her element.

"It's over here." Billie walked ahead of them, past the front porch and stepped close to the bed of flowers in front of the freshly painted white mansion.

"Don't step on the . . . roses," she called as her daughter planted a tennis shoe squarely on a peach-colored blossom.

"Tell me those aren't still Charlene's favorites," she murmured half to herself.

"They are." Adam kept pace with her, stopping at her side when they reached the scene of the crime.

"See," Billie said, almost proudly. "It would have been a perfect pitch."

"Yeah. All that's missing is the batter, the catcher, a few other players and the umpire." Jane glanced up at Adam. He looked down at her. If she hadn't been so tired and out of sorts, she might have thought there was a smile tugging at the corner of his mouth, that the straight line didn't look quite as straight as it had a minute ago.

"It's just this one pane." Billie jumped up and pointed. Her landing crushed the rest of the rosebush. "Ow. It scratched me."

"Self-defense on the part of the plant. Let me see." Jane bent down and brushed the skin. "You'll live."

"I'm bleeding," Billie said with a whine in her voice.

"One drop. You won't miss it. Besides, you killed that rose."

Billie stepped onto the grass and stared at the squashed bush. "Oh. Sorry." She grabbed a stem, careful to hold it between thorns, and tried to straighten the broken plant. The stalk drooped to the ground. Crushed petals littered the soil. "It's a goner."

Jane rose and looked at Adam. "I mean this in the nicest possible way, but tell me that Charlene is dead. Because if she isn't, I'm about to be."

This time he did smile. The slow curve revealed perfect white teeth. Her heart fluttered madly against her ribs. She'd forgotten about his smile and how it made her feel that swooning was a lost art form.

"Charlene is alive and well," he said, his eyes crinkling in the corners. "She'll be out for blood when she finds out about this. You know how she feels about her roses."

"There's already been blood." Billie marched up to them and pointed at her leg. "You guys are adults. I'm a kid. You're supposed to get worried when kids bleed. And what about infection? You're always making me wash my hands."

A single drop rolled down and stained her sock.

"All right, let's deal with the medical emergency." Adam crouched down and pulled a handkerchief out of his pocket. He moistened the corner and blotted the tiny puncture. "It's stopped bleeding. You should be able to keep the leg."

"Good." Billie held on to his shoulder for balance. "It's going to be hard enough making the major leagues as a girl. With only one leg, I'd never have a chance." She glanced at the sky. "It's getting dark, Mom. Where are we spending the night?"

"In town. Come on, honey, I've got to go call the furniture company. Adam, I—"

His smile had faded and in its place was the distant coolness of a stranger. For a minute or two he'd forgotten, as she had. It had been like the old days, before she'd left town. Before she'd done the unforgivable.

She would apologize. Not now. It was too soon and she didn't want an audience, not even her daughter. Later, perhaps after he'd had time to digest the fact that they were going to be neighbors. In his present mood he'd deny there was anything to discuss, maybe even refuse to listen to her.

If only he'd admit he felt something. Anger, hurt, regret. She'd carried her burden of guilt around for so long, she felt weary and overwhelmed by the weight. Even if he hated her, it would be a start.

"I'll get you the money for the window and the rose-bush. My purse is in the house. I really do have to make that phone call. May I bring it by tomorrow?"

"Use mine," he said, staring at something over her head. He'd stuffed his hands into his pockets, as if to keep her from seeing the tight fists. But the outline of his knuckles pressed against the twill material of his shorts. Below, the muscles of his tanned thighs bulged against the skin. He still jogged; she could tell from the lean, powerful silhouette of his legs.

"Your what?"

"Phone, Mom. Geez." Billie stuffed her softball into her oversize pocket.

"I couldn't. It's long-distance."

"Of course you could," he said. "It'll save you the drive into town."

"It's only a mile."

She didn't want to go into that house. Too many memories waited there. It had been bad enough next door, but at least all the old furniture was gone and the walls had been painted and repapered. In Adam's house, things would be the same. Already the sun was setting and the scent of night-blooming jasmine filled the air. If she closed her eyes, she would be able to remember everything. She kept her eyes open.

"You're very kind," she said at last, because there was nothing else to say without admitting the truth. She'd come home for a number of reasons. The fact that the past stood in the way of most of them was something she'd have to get over. "After I make my call, we'll talk about the window."

"I picked out a bedroom that overlooks your house, Adam," Billie said, fishing her ball out of her pocket and starting toward the front door. "Maybe we could set up walkie-talkies, you know, like a secret club." She glanced at her mother. "No girls allowed."

When Billie threw the ball to him, he half turned as if he was going to toss it to Jane next. He caught himself and returned the pitch to Billie.

Jane thought about pointing out to Billie that she *was* a girl, but knew better. "Honey, I don't think Adam is interested in your 'boys only' club. He has a business to run and a life that doesn't have room for your wild ideas. And you're a little young to be calling him by his first name."

"He said I could."

"I said she could."

They spoke together.

Jane stared at the tall man and the short little girl. Their feet braced against the thick grass. Fists pressed into hips in identical stances of defiance. Billie had turned her cap backward so that the bill stuck out behind her and the band mashed her bangs against her forehead. Wide brown eyes, the color of thick mud—the color of Adam's—stared back at her.

Like father, like daughter.

He hadn't guessed. She'd have to tell him . . . eventually. But what was she going to say? It had been almost nine years since she'd left Orchard and Adam. Nine years in which they'd never spoken or corresponded. The control she'd always hated had been polished to perfection. He'd barely shown a flicker of emotion when she'd walked up to him. But that was about to change. She was done hiding. As soon as they were settled and she was sure the time was right, she'd share her guilty secret: he was Billie's father.

Chapter Two

"Fine." Jane raised her hands in defeat. "If Adam doesn't mind, then call him what you want." She glanced at him. "I'm giving you fair warning, when Billie decides she likes someone, his life ceases to be his own."

Adam looked down at the young girl standing next to him. He shouldn't indulge her on general principle; she was her mother's daughter. But he couldn't find it in himself to turn away from her engaging grin.

"All right!" Billie said, holding up her free hand. "Gimme five."

He hit her palm with his own, then walked up the stairs onto the porch. "The phone is this way."

"Wow! A swing! I've never seen one like that." Billie dashed across the porch to the old-fashioned swing hanging from the rafters. The worn chains groaned in protest when she threw herself on the seat. One forceful push against the wooden floor set the seat in motion. "This is totally cool. Mom, can we get one?"

"Maybe in a few months."

"Come try it."

"I've been on a swing before." Jane stared at the ground, looking at neither Billie nor Adam.

He understood her reluctance. The anger threatened again, slicing and hacking at his wall of self-control. That swing. That damn swing. He should have taken it down years ago. From the corner of his eye, he saw Jane glance at him. The quick darting look, the worry darkening her eyes and drawing the color from her skin, pleased him. If she hadn't—

But she had. And he'd stopped caring a long time ago.

"This way," he said, holding open the front door. Jane walked past him. A subtle fragrance licked against him. Elegant, yet welcoming, it left the taste of longing on his tongue. He wasn't as immune as he'd like to be, but he would never let on.

Billie slid off the swing and followed. "Can I come over and use it?"

"Sure. Anytime."

"Great." She stepped into the foyer and whistled. "This is some place. Wow! Stairs! Can I slide down the banister?"

She darted across the hall. Jane moved after her. By the time she reached Billie, the girl had one foot on the first stair.

"No you don't," she said, holding her firmly by the arm. "No playing on banisters, no softballs in the house. You know the rules." She plucked the ball from her daughter's hand and tossed him an apologetic smile. "We grow them wild out West."

"I think I can handle it." He stuffed his hands into his pockets. "How about lemonade and chocolate cake?"

Billie shrugged out of her mother's grasp and walked sedately to his side. "I'm always hungry."

"Why doesn't that surprise me?" He motioned to the study. "The phone's in there. On the desk. We'll be in the kitchen. You still remember where that is, don't you?"

"Yes." She glanced at her daughter. "Don't get into trouble."

"Who me?" Billie looked up at him. "She's always doing that. Telling me to stay out of trouble."

Jane moved into his office. The last rays of sun filtered through the lace curtains on the windows beside the front door and caught the thick braid hanging down her back. The tail, tied in a peach-colored ribbon, ended several inches below her shoulder blades. He knew from experience that her hair, when loosed and brushed smooth, would tumble clear to her waist. Satin, he remembered. Living satin, all warm and sweet smelling. It could drive a man out of his mind.

The hand still in his pocket clenched tighter. The iron control he prided himself on kept him from groaning aloud or following her to touch the thick braid to see if it was as he remembered.

"So how long have you lived in this house?" Billie asked.

"What?" He forced himself to turn away from Jane and glance down at her daughter. "Oh, all my life." He led the way through the foyer and down a long wide hallway toward the kitchen.

"We've moved a lot. Mom says the first year I was born, we lived in a house, but I don't remember that. It's always been apartments. I like having other kids to play with, but I really need a yard. The landlord used to get mad when I practiced pitching in the hallway. It rains a lot in San Francisco. Does it rain here? Is it always this hot? Hey, you've got some old pictures here. Do you know people this old?"

She stopped in front of a display of antique photographs hanging over a narrow writing desk. Adam retraced his steps until he stood behind her. "They're of my family. We've lived in Orchard since the early 1800s."

"Who's he?" She pointed at a small grainy photo of a man in uniform.

"My great-great—I can never remember exactly how many greats—grandfather. He was a major during the war."

"The war?"

He touched the frame, then took her hand and led her down the rest of the hall and into the kitchen. "The War of Northern Aggression."

"I never heard of it." She paused in the middle of the room. "This is big. You've got two stoves. Is one broken?"

"No. My parents used to do a lot of entertaining. Why don't you sit here." He pulled out a stool next to the long center island, then lifted her up.

"Where are your parents now?"

He took a glass from the cupboard beside the double sink and set it in front of her. "They died."

"I'm sorry." Billie removed her cap and brushed her bangs flat. "Does it make you sad?"

"It was a long time ago."

"I had a friend at school. His mom died and he cried a lot. I told him he could share mine, but it didn't help. At least he still has his dad."

"I was a little older than your friend when I lost my parents," he said as he uncovered the cake and reached for a knife. "Nineteen. And I have a brother and sister."

"Older or younger?"

"Both younger."

"I wanted a brother, but Mom said it wasn't a good time." She turned on the stool and grinned when it spun. "Do you have kids?"

"No."

"A wife?"

He sliced off a generous piece of chocolate cake and slid it onto a plate. "No. Eat your cake."

She wrinkled her nose. "That's a grown-up way to say stop asking questions, huh?"

"Yes." He winked.

She giggled and dug in. "Mmm. This is great." A crumb fell off her fork and onto her chest. She tried to brush it away and succeeded in smearing a dark streak down her T-shirt.

He poured them each a drink, then pulled up another stool and watched her eat. There were flashes of Jane in her. The shape of her eyes, the gift of humor. But the rest of her personality had to come from her father. Jane had been sweet as a child, but never outgoing.

What had happened? he wondered. Billie hadn't mentioned anything about her father, although he knew it usually took two to produce a baby. It seemed odd that there wasn't a man around to take care of this little girl.

"Did you stop and visit with your grandparents on the way out?" he asked.

"Uh-huh. Texas. They live next to the water." She took a drink of lemonade. "It's nice there. I like the beach. Where are your brother and sister?"

"Dani lives in Atlanta. She's married and has a little girl about four years younger than you. Ty has a construction company in the next town."

"Dani's a girl, right? Short for Daniella?"

He nodded.

Billie licked a dab of icing off the corner of her mouth. "Mom knows her. I think they were friends a long time ago. Is there a tree house in the backyard? She talked about that on the drive out. My mom went to school here and everything."

"I know." So Jane had mentioned his sister but not him? No surprise in that. After the last time he saw her—

He forced away the memory, refused to acknowledge the coldness that had swept over him or the overpowering scent of flowers and burning candles.

"There's icing." She pointed to the chocolate ribbon left on her plate. "Want to split it?"

"You go ahead."

"Okay." She swept her finger across the gooey confection, then stuck it in her mouth. "Yummy."

It seemed easier to concentrate on Billie and ignore the past. He didn't believe in thinking about things that couldn't be changed. Choices had been made a long time ago. It didn't matter anymore.

"What are those for?" She pointed to the copper pots hanging on the far wall.

"Cooking."

"I've never seen pans that color before."

"Adam, who are you entertaining in the kitchen? I declare, you'll give our family a bad name."

Charlene Belle Standing, of *the* Carolina Standings as she referred to her family, swept into the kitchen. A bright purple caftan fell in soft folds to the floor. Several bracelets jingled on each wrist. Her hair, still a bright shade of red, had been twisted into an old-fashioned chignon. She was close to sixty, looked forty and acted like she was twenty-five. Or fifteen.

"My, my. And you are?"

Adam rose to his feet. "Charlene, this is Billie. Billie, my favorite aunt, Miss Charlene Standing."

Her blue eyes snapped at him. "I'm your only aunt, Adam. If I'm not your favorite, then I've been doing something terribly wrong." She moved closer to Billie and stopped on the far side of the island. Diamond rings on three fingers of each hand gleamed in the overhead light. "Child, you look so familiar, but we haven't met. I would have remembered."

For the first time since he'd met her, Billie was tongue-tied. She stared at the older woman.

"She's Jane's daughter. You remember Jane Southwick? She lived next door."

Charlene raised one arched brow. "I see. That explains it. You have your mother's eyes. A different color perhaps, but the shape's the same. Pretty eyes, I always thought."

He waited for her to make a comment on his introduction, to call him on his choice of descriptions for Jane. He could have said she was his old girlfriend, or at least a friend of the family.

"Is your hair really that color?" Billie blurted out at last.

"Obviously your tact must come from the other side of the family. Jane was always the most well-mannered child."

Billie grinned, undaunted. "I'm more trouble than I'm worth, but she loves me, anyway."

Charlene moved around the island until she was standing next to Billie's stool. She leaned close and took the girl's face in her hands.

"I was raised by wolves, you know," Charlene said.

"Really?" Billie's eyes widened to the size of saucers.

"When I was three, they stole me and kept me in the woods."

"Charlene," Adam said, his voice heavy with warning.

"Hush. I'm bonding with the child. That's what people do these days." She smiled. "You understand, don't you, Billie?"

"Sure."

Charlene kissed her cheek. "We are going to be great friends."

"Okay. Do you play baseball?"

"No, but I love the young men in their uniforms, and I bet heavily on our local team."

He fought the beginnings of a headache. "Charlene, don't start anything here. Remember what happened the last time Dani brought her kids? You taught her six-year-old to play poker. Dani was unamused and I suspect Jane will feel the same way."

"He's a sweet boy," Charlene said to Billie as she sat on Adam's vacant stool. "But a worrier. It comes from raising his younger siblings."

"What are siblings?"

"Brothers and sisters. Adam went to Harvard."

"I've been to Texas."

"There are Standings in Dallas, I believe. They run cattle or oil. I can't keep them straight." She slipped off several of her bracelets and spread them on the island. "Do you like any of these, Billie? They're pretty, don't you think?"

"I guess."

Billie cast him a worried glance. He knew she wouldn't want to offend her new friend, but was less enthused about the jewelry than she wanted to let on. Now if Charlene had opened a box of baseball trading cards he was sure that would have been another story.

"Adam, I got through to the moving company. They won't be able—" Jane walked into the kitchen. Her gaze moved past him to the gaudily dressed woman next to her daughter. "Charlene?"

"Jane!"

His aunt stood up and held open her arms. Jane flew into her embrace. "Charlene, I've missed you so much."

"It's your own fault for leaving, child." The tears in her eyes and the catch in her voice took away the sting of the words.

Adam stood awkwardly on the fringe of the reunion. Charlene and Jane had always been close; of course they'd be happy to see each other. It didn't matter to *him*. He didn't feel anything, not even regret.

"Have you met Billie?" Jane brushed her cheeks.

"I have met your daughter. There's a lot of her father in her, isn't there?"

Jane stiffened slightly. "Some," she said cautiously.

Adam wondered if that meant she didn't like her ex-husband. Stupid question, he told himself. If she still liked the guy, they'd be together. Unless he'd left her. He wanted to ask what had happened, why she was alone. But he couldn't. Questions like that might make her think he was interested.

"Charlene told me she was raised by wolves," Billie announced.

Jane stared at her friend. "You didn't."

"It's the truth. As God is my witness."

Jane looked over her shoulder at Adam and rolled her eyes. "I can't believe she's still using that old line. You'd think after all this time she could be more creative."

Adam was tempted to smile back at her, to share the memory. His control instinct wouldn't let him. They had nothing left to share. Her grin quivered, then faded altogether. She turned back, hunching her shoulders against an invisible weight.

"What did the furniture company have to say?" he asked.

"The truck broke down in Nevada and won't be here until Monday."

"Monday," Charlene said. "You mean you're in that big house next door without a stick of furniture?"

"We brought a few things with us," Jane said.

"Not beds. Not food." Billie swiveled on her stool. "Can we stay in a hotel with cable this time, Mom? I hate these channels with nothing good on. Do you know that in one place they didn't have the sports channel?"

"You're not going to a hotel," Charlene said. "There are plenty of extra rooms right here."

Adam glared at his aunt. "I'm sure they'd be more comfortable in a place of their own."

"He's right. We wouldn't want to impose." Jane spoke without facing him.

"Why?" Billie asked. "I like Adam and he likes us. Charlene can teach me to play poker."

"Poker?" Jane stared at Charlene who was suddenly interested in slipping her bracelets back on. "Charlene, you can't teach a child—"

"I never said that. It was Adam. He's always accusing me of things that aren't true. I might be a little unconventional—"

"A little," Adam growled. "The town eccentric is more like it."

"That's not fair. Orchard is a backwater town. It's not my fault if I've had more experiences than the average local citizen."

"Experiences? Is that what you call it when you get on the CB and invite truckers to stop by and sample your—"

"Adam!" Charlene stood and straightened to her full height. She was barely over five feet. He wasn't the least bit intimidated. "There are children present."

"Just me," Billie said.

"Why don't you wait on the lawn?" Jane handed her daughter the softball.

"But I wanna listen. You *always* send me out when it gets good."

"When you're a grown-up, you can send your children from the room. It's one of the privileges of adulthood. Now scoot."

Billie pulled on her cap, then left the room. Her footsteps dragged audibly on the bare wood floor.

"I'm leaving," she yelled from the foyer. "I'll be outside. Alone. In the dark."

"Have fun," Jane called. "And stay away from the windows."

"Don't tell me," Charlene said.

"Yup. We're here five minutes and she's already broken one."

"Definitely takes after her father." Charlene smiled.

"What does that mean?" Jane asked quickly.

She put her arm around Jane's shoulders. "Only that you never broke windows when you were a girl. You were always too much of a lady."

Jane opened her mouth, as if she was going to protest, then shook her head. "I give up. It's late, we drove almost five hundred miles today. I adore you." She kissed Charlene's cheek. "But I can't make heads or tails of anything right now. Do not, under any circumstances, teach my daughter to play poker. Adam." She gave him a weary smile. "Thanks for the use of your phone. I'll get you the money for the window and the—" she glanced at Charlene "—the other thing tomorrow."

The overhead light cast shadows on her face and darkened the rings under her eyes. Lines of fatigue deepened the hollows of her cheeks. A few strands of hair had escaped from the braid. One wisp drifted near the corner of her mouth. He fought the urge to brush it away, to reach out and feel the silky smoothness of her skin. The anger was well under control, but the want— He'd always known it was the most dangerous emotion.

"I insist you stay here," Charlene said. "And Adam agrees with me."

Jane was looking at him. The need to punish her—hurt her as he had been hurt—boiled up inside. His silence would be telling enough. She would know he didn't want her here. But he wouldn't risk letting her think she still mattered. Better to let her stay.

"That's what neighbors do here," he said. "You'll have a whole wing to yourselves."

"I don't want to impose." Two bright spots of color stained her cheeks.

"No imposition." Even to his own ears his voice sounded strained. "Sally comes in five days a week. She always keeps the guest rooms ready."

"But—"

"No buts." Charlene linked her arm through Jane's. "It's all arranged. Let's go get that darling daughter of yours and collect your suitcases. I see you've kept your hair long. I like it. Maybe we can go to the salon together and you can get a trim. I hate to criticize, dear, but Billie's hair is quite atrocious. You might want to have a little talk with her about the merits of acting like a lady..."

Their voices faded as they walked toward the front door. Adam forced himself to relax. Jane and Billie would only be here for a couple of nights. It was a big house; they could easily avoid each other. And if they didn't—

He shrugged. *He* didn't have a problem with Jane Southwick now or ever. Nine years ago she'd shown him the truth about relationships in general and theirs in particular. Loving someone meant being left. He'd learned his lesson well. He'd offered his heart to a young woman once and she'd returned it broken and bleeding. That part of him was safely locked away, and no ghost from the past was going to find the key.

"You haven't told him, have you?"

Jane glanced around the cheerful guest room, but there was nowhere to hide. She finished putting out Billie's nightgown, then checked to make sure the door to the bathroom was tightly closed. The sounds of her daughter's off-key singing and the splashing of water against the side of the tub continued uninterrupted. All the activity was supposed to give her time to compose herself. It wasn't working.

"You know," Jane said, glancing up at her friend.

"How could I not?" Charlene stepped over to the bed and sat on the corner. "The eyes, her personality, the way she stands. A blind man could see it."

The hard lump in her stomach doubled in size. Jane felt herself grow pale.

"I meant that as an expression, dear," the older woman said hastily. "Nothing more."

"Good. Because Adam—"

"Men don't look for things like that." Charlene took her hand and tugged, forcing Jane to sit on the bedspread, next to her. "Start from the beginning."

Jane folded her hands in her lap. "I've made a mess of everything."

"That sounds the tiniest bit exaggerated."

"I left here nine years ago, had Adam's baby and never told him." She paused and drew in a breath. "Now I'm back and I've brought home his child. What would you call it?"

"Fine Southern drama." Charlene's blue eyes glittered with suppressed laughter. She sobered quickly. "Sorry, dear. I understand your concern, but you are back, and you're going to tell him about Billie, and everything will be fine."

Jane twisted her fingers together. "I'm not going to tell him."

"What?"

"I mean, I am, but not just yet."

The lump grew again, pressing against her ribs and making it difficult to breathe. Dear God, she prayed, then paused. What to ask for? Forgiveness? She could use a strong dose of that. Common sense? That went without saying. Show me the right thing for my daughter, she thought. But would God listen? Would anyone? After what she'd done?

No one had told her guilt tasted so empty. That the hollowness would linger on her tongue, as though the emptiness was too much for her heart to bear, and the excess would seep out into her body, stealing joy and promise.

Charlene touched her arm. "Then why are you here if not to tell Adam about his daughter?"

"I am. I will. I thought—" She squeezed her eyes shut, but that didn't block out the past. "I thought it would be so easy. I'd show up, tell Adam I was sorry and he'd forgive me. Then I'd introduce Billie and we'd live as neighbors. Like a TV sitcom." She paused, feeling overwhelmed. "I've been a fool. It's not going to be like that. It can't be. I should never have come."

"If your furniture is being delivered Monday, then it's a little late for second thoughts."

Despite herself, Jane smiled. "Always practical. And this from a woman who still claims to be raised by wolves."

Charlene straightened. "I *was* raised by wolves."

"You got lost in the woods for a day. The family dog was with you. That's hardly being raised by wolves."

A smile twitched at one corner of Charlene's mouth. "Dogs are related to wolves. And you're avoiding the real issue."

"I know."

Jane rose and walked to the window of the guest room. The sultry night air drifted past the curtains, carried lazily by a sleepy breeze. Familiar fragrances brought back memories. Jasmine for evenings, flower blossoms for day. The scents clung to her skin, a sticky residue from the humidity. So different from the life she had built, yet so right.

"I'm proud of what I've accomplished," she said, leaning on the window frame. "It was tough at first, financially, I mean. Billie was a good baby, but any infant is expensive."

The evening noises began, the screeching and chirps sounding like an orchestra being tuned.

"I couldn't go back to college until Billie started school three years ago," she continued. "But I never gave up the dream of teaching. I got my credential a couple of months ago. My parents offered me their house here, then I got the job at Orchard Junior High. It seemed like a sign. And a chance."

"To let Billie meet her father?"

Jane touched the lace curtains. Behind her, Charlene waited silently.

"Yes," she admitted at last. "It's what Billie wants more than anything. A father. But I hadn't counted on what it would be like coming here, seeing him, the house, knowing that I'd never escape. I owe her, I owe them both. And all I want to do is turn around and run back to San Francisco."

"What does this have to do with telling or not telling Adam?"

She released the curtain and turned to face the older woman. "I don't want to compound my mistakes. If I tell him and he's not interested in being a father, she'll be hurt worse than before."

Charlene frowned. "You can't hide the truth forever. This is Orchard, dear. Small Southern towns are notoriously bad at keeping secrets."

"I know, and I'll tell him. In my own time. But first, I want to know he wants her. I want to be sure that he won't punish *her* for the mistakes I've made."

"We don't always have the luxury of time."

"I know. I'm so afraid."

"Because you've kept him from his daughter for eight years?"

The dart hit home. She crossed her arms over her chest. "I didn't feel like I had any other choice at the time."

"You could have come home. Adam would have taken care of you."

"I didn't want that. I'd always been the quiet one, the obedient child." She tucked her hands in her pocket. "Adam was always ready to guide me. To tell me what was right for me, whether I wanted the information or not. I was afraid of him—of us." She shrugged. "I ran. Foolishly. And when I couldn't run anymore, I stopped. Only to find out I was pregnant."

"You could have come back then."

Jane remembered the cool fog of her first San Francisco morning. It had taken her almost a month to make her way across the country. As her stomach had churned with the lingering effects of nausea, and the tears left cold trails down her cheeks, she'd imagined going home. She'd humiliated Adam in the most devastating way possible, but if she told him about the baby, he would have taken her back.

For several hours, she'd stood staring out at the ocean. Her fear of going home, of giving up like her mother, had been greater than her fear of going forward. She'd left Orchard to prove to herself she had the strength to make it on her own. Returning at the first sign of trouble would have meant losing forever.

"My pride wouldn't let me come back," she said.

"Pride makes a cold bedfellow."

So Charlene wasn't going to accept the half truth. "I wasn't sure I mattered to him," she said softly, confessing the most painful secret of all. "I didn't want to be an obligation."

"He loved you."

"Did he?" She stared over her friend's head at a landscape hanging above the bed. The warm colors—the reds and yellows of the flowers, the mossy green of the trees—blended perfectly with the wallpaper. "Or did he know I'd be easily trained? A perfect banker's wife. Quiet, malleable, well mannered. Sometimes I thought he had a list that he checked whenever he met a woman. I was the most suitable."

"It wasn't that way." The older woman frowned. "You make him sound unfeeling. Adam is a passionate man."

Jane dropped her gaze to the hardwood floor. "I suppose with Billie as proof, I'd be silly to deny that." But her memories blurred about that night and the others like it. She'd been so young—too young. And too much in love. "I would have given him my soul. He was more interested in a hostess."

Charlene shook her head. "You're remembering him with the eyes of a child. Perhaps Adam had offered you *his* soul and you didn't notice."

"I loved him. I would have noticed."

Charlene watched her closely. The wrinkles around her eyes and mouth had been formed by smiles rather than displeasure. Heavy makeup and the brightly colored hair couldn't disguise her softhearted nature. "Tell me about Billie."

Jane chuckled. "I'd like to tell you I've done a fine job with her, but I can't take the credit. Billie is . . . Billie."

"Her father's daughter?"

"Sometimes," she admitted, remembering the first time her child had looked at her with Adam's defiant gaze. The pain had been unexpected but she welcomed the connection with the man she had once loved. "I see him in her eyes." She moved to the bed and resumed her seat. "But Billie is so full of life and Adam—he's not *anything*. It's as if I'm an old acquaintance who has shown up for a weekend visit."

"What did you expect?"

Jane glanced down at Charlene's hands clasped in her lap. A few more age spots marred the pale skin, some wrinkles bunched at the knuckles, but other than that, these were the hands she remembered from her youth. The shiny rings glittered, the bracelets tinkled and rattled.

"I thought he'd hate me," she said at last, voicing the fear that had dogged her since leaving the West Coast.

"For nine years? Everyone has to let go sometime. Change. You did. Perhaps he did as well."

"He never married."

"That's true." Charlene glanced at her. "But he has been involved with several women. Adam is many things, but not a saint. Or a martyr. He didn't wait for you, Jane. That I am sure of."

"I know."

The lie sat heavily on her tongue. Logically, she *knew* he hadn't, but there had been a tiny piece inside her heart, the spot where dreams hid. Every year Charlene had sent a letter in her Christmas card to Jane's mother. Every year there had been no mention of Adam marrying. It didn't mean anything, she told herself, even as she dared to wonder if it did.

"You'll want me to keep quiet for now?" Charlene asked, smoothing a hand over her hair.

"I just need a little time."

"Don't take too long. He'll figure it out on his own, and if he doesn't, someone from town will. Better for him and Billie if he hears it from you."

Jane again fought the guilt that filled her with empty sadness. "There's a lot at stake. I could lose Billie."

"Never that." The older woman smiled. "She'll always be your daughter. And there's so much you could gain. Adam—"

"Mo-om, I'm shriveling up in here," Billie called from the bathroom.

"I'm coming." She picked up the nightgown and walked into the bathroom. "All clean?"

"I'm a prune."

Billie stepped out of the tub and into the fluffy towel Jane held for her. She wrapped the terry cloth around her child's body and began to rub. The scent of soap and freshly cleaned little girl tickled her nose.

"I love you, honey," she said, giving her a squeeze.

Billie eyed her suspiciously. "I heard you talking to someone. You aren't planning anything awful, are you? Not like those singing lessons?"

"No singing lessons," she promised.

"Good. Then I love you, too."

"Little girls shouldn't barter their affection. May I come in?" Charlene hovered outside the door.

"Sure." Billie brushed her bangs out of her eyes. "I wasn't bartering, I was checking. She always wants me to do girl stuff. Yuk."

"Perhaps because you are a girl," Charlene said.

"It's not my fault." Jane handed Billie the nightgown. She pulled it over her head and wiggled until it dropped past her knees. "Look at this. There's a kitten on it!" She pointed at the offending appliqué. "I've told her a thousand times I want pajamas."

"This was a gift from your grandmother," Jane said, reaching for a comb.

"Let me." Charlene took the comb and settled on the lid of the toilet. After positioning Billie between her knees, she began to tame her short cut. "I am so looking forward to you discovering boys."

"Why?" Billie sounded suspicious.

Jane turned away to hide her grin.

"One day you'll look up and the boy you thought was a terrific—" She glanced at Jane.

"Catcher," she supplied helpfully.

"Catcher . . . will be a charming, handsome young man."

"Not to me." Billie cocked her head. "You're not married. Mom told me."

"I am not like most women. I prefer my men—"

"Charlene," Jane warned.

"I was just going to say that I prefer them appreciative."

"I don't understand," Billie said. She yawned and rubbed her eyes.

"You will," Charlene said. "One day." She leaned forward and kissed her cheek. "I'm so pleased you're here. Both of you."

"We can still be friends, even if you don't know much about baseball." Billie wrapped her arms around Charlene's neck. Jane saw her friend hug her back.

"Thank you," Charlene whispered, her voice hoarse with emotion. "Now, off to sleep."

Jane settled her daughter in the big bed, handed her her worn teddy bear and plugged in the night-light she'd carted clear across the country. She and Charlene kissed her, then moved quietly into the hall.

"She's darling," Charlene said as Jane closed the door. "And you look as tired as she did. It's late. We'll talk tomorrow."

Jane thanked her, walked to her door and pushed it open.

"Jane?"

"Yes?"

"I will keep quiet about—" she motioned toward Billie's room "—everything. At least until you figure out the real reason you came back."

Chapter Three

"Hi. You're up. I thought I'd be the only one. Mom's still in the shower. What's for breakfast?"

Adam bent the corner of his paper and stared at Billie as she bounced around the kitchen. Today's outfit was an exact duplicate of yesterday's except her T-shirt and shorts hadn't had time to get dirty. Yet. The red baseball cap covered most of her hair, the bill had been tugged down to her brows. A softball bulged from the oversize pocket of her denim shorts.

"You wanna play catch later? Mom says we have errands in town. Shopping, that kind of stuff. Oh, and to see about glass for the window. Did I tell you I was sorry about that?"

He shook his head. "No."

"I am. Really." She stopped in front of the table. "Whatcha reading?"

"The paper."

"Did the Giants win?"

"Who?"

"The San Francisco Giants. They're my favorite team."

He set down the financial section and flipped through until he found the sports page. "Here."

Billie sat next to him at the bleached oak table. "Thanks." She peered at his cup. "Do I get coffee?"

"No."

"Toast?"

He pushed his plate toward her and picked up the paper. "Milk?"

"It's in the refrigerator." He scanned the columns until he found the article he'd been reading. Lack of sleep made his eyes burn. The house had been still. Jane and Billie's rooms were far enough away that he couldn't hear them, but he'd known they were there. Despite reading the most boring financial newsletter he could find, despite the shot of Scotch and the cold shower close to midnight, he'd been awake until dawn. That was the hell of it. He could force his mind to forget, but his body was less willing to cooperate.

There was a dragging noise behind him. He tried to ignore it. It was the "whoops" followed by mad scrambling and "I got it, don't worry" that caused him to look up.

Billie stood on top of a stool. One foot rested on the seat, the other on the counter. A glass balanced precariously in her grasp.

"What the— What are you doing?"

"Getting a glass. Mom told me not to bother you. She said we have to be quiet and stay out of the way." She climbed down. "I'm pretty sure I can stay out of the way, but the quiet part is gonna be tough."

"No kidding." He gave up and tossed the paper onto the table. "What do you normally eat for breakfast?"

She grinned. "Donuts?" she asked hopefully.

"Not a chance. How about cereal?"

"What kind you got?"

He opened the cupboard and scanned the contents. All the boxes contained sensible multigrain products. He glanced at Billie. "Somehow I don't think you'll approve of the selection."

"Then toast is fine."

She picked up a slice and nibbled on the corner. Her mouth twisted into a grimace as she tasted the marmalade.

He chuckled out loud, surprising her and himself. "I'll make you fresh. There's peanut butter in the fridge. Or honey."

"Great." She crossed to the fridge.

"Oh, and grab that bowl of fruit salad and the milk. Are we hitting all the major food groups here?"

"All of 'em except donuts."

"That isn't a major food group."

"Okay, a minor food group. But it's still my favorite."

Billie held the bowl of fruit and the milk in her arms, then bent over and reached for the peanut butter. Milk sloshed onto the floor and three grapes slipped from the bowl to land in the puddle. She straightened, the peanut butter jar clutched in her free hand, then used her hip to shut the door. He waited, but she remained oblivious to the mess on the floor.

They assembled breakfast together. Billie spread a thick layer of peanut butter on her toast, then looked around. "You got any bananas?"

"I think so. Why?"

"To put on the bread. It's yummy."

His stomach lurched. "I'll pass. You go ahead."

She handed him the fruit to cut, then she mashed the slices onto the flattened toast. While he poured the milk, she dished out two bowls of fruit. They each got a serving, as did the table. Only a couple of chunks hit the floor. He stepped around them and resumed his seat.

"Good, huh?" A milk moustache outlined the top of her mouth. Crumbs stuck to the peanut butter on her cheek.

Ignoring her engaging grin would require a man stronger than himself. "Yeah, it's good." He folded the newspaper and set it on the extra chair.

They chatted through their meal. Billie discussed the school she'd left behind and her friends. Although she must miss them, her outgoing nature would make it easy to settle in.

"There's a couple of softball leagues in town," he said. "Perhaps I could have a word with the coaches and see if there's any room for another player."

The last bit of her toast fell back to the plate untasted. Big brown eyes got bigger. "You'd do that? For me? After I broke your window?"

Adam cleared his throat. "It's no trouble. Besides, I have a lot more glass to worry about. If you're off playing on a team, I'll rest easier."

"You're the best."

She flew out of her seat and around the table, then flung herself against him. Thin arms, small but surprisingly strong, tightened around his neck. She smelled of soap and milk and peanut butter. The kiss on his cheek was sticky and wet, but he didn't pull back. Little girls and their dreams were out of the realm of his expertise but there was something about Billie that would be easy to get used to.

"I promise I'll never break a window again," she said.

"That's some promise."

She giggled. "Okay. I'll *try* never to break a window again."

"Better." He laughed.

"You're up early."

Adam stiffened at the sound of a new voice and glanced up. Jane hesitated in the doorway to the kitchen. Her eyes flickered from Billie, still standing next to him, to the table and back.

"We had breakfast together," her daughter said. "Adam helped. And he's going to see if I can play softball this

summer. Isn't that cool? I'm gonna go tell Charlene." She
turned to run out the back door. With her hand on the knob,
she paused. "Is this the way?"

"Her house is down the path about two minutes. There's
only one. You can't miss it," he said.

"Bye. Oh, morning, Mom." The door slammed shut behind her.

"All that energy first thing in the morning." Jane offered a tentative smile. "I'll just grab a cup of coffee, then
leave you in peace."

"There's no need to rush off on my account." Even to his
own ears, the words sounded stiff. He wanted her out of his
sight—out of his life—as soon as possible, but he'd be
damned if he'd allow her to figure that out. "Help yourself
to breakfast."

"I'm not hungry." Jane walked over to the coffeepot and
poured herself a cup. "You've made a friend for life."

The sundress she wore fit tightly across her back, then
flared out to fall in soft folds just at her knees. The bright
magenta fabric added a glow to the light tan on her shoulders and arms. Once again, her hair had been pulled back
in a thick braid. The slightly damp rope gleamed in the light.

He hated the way his fingers curled, as if to encircle the
braid. His gaze drifted down past the curve of her calves to
bare feet with painted toenails. With a suddenness that surprised him, his mind filled with a picture from another time,
so long ago. She'd been getting ready for a date with him.
He'd dropped by unexpectedly and had caught her in the
middle of her preparations. Fat pink curlers had covered her
head. A ratty shirt, stolen from her father's closet, concealed her body to mid-thigh. She sat on the floor, her long
legs bent, a tissue woven between her toes. Even now he
could inhale the acrid scent of nail polish, see the tongue
sticking out of the corner of her mouth as she concentrated, hear the shriek when she'd looked up and seen him
watching her.

Her blush had climbed clear to her hairline, then dipped to the cleavage showing in the V of the white shirt. She tried to run from him, but he caught her easily. His body heated at the memory. Her protest had died amid roving hands and joined mouths. Later that night she'd been beautiful. A woman. But what he remembered was the teenager in curlers, shy but eager, trying desperately to please. He'd wanted more, he'd realized that day. Had wanted it all. So that had been the night he'd made his decision. It had changed everything.

The hiss from the coffeemaker as she replaced the pot recalled him to the present.

"My desire to get Billie on a softball team is purely selfish," he said. "Just looking out for my property."

"I'll take care of that window today. I know you're working, so I'll go to the hardware store."

"Working?" He frowned. "It's Saturday."

"I know. But you usually worked... I thought you'd still." She turned to face him, her eyes averted. "My mistake."

"One of many." He tried to call the words back, but it was too late. The first crack in the armor, he thought. There wouldn't be another. She couldn't get to him anymore. "When we were—" He paused and searched for the correct phrase. He didn't like the one that came to mind, so he tried another tack. "It was never my intention to continue that schedule. I did what I had to in order to get the bank healthy. While I don't keep what people refer to as 'banker's hours', I do only put in the usual forty or so." Another crack. There, in the sharpness of his voice. Jane set her coffee on the counter and walked toward him.

"Adam, I'm sorry."

"There's no need to apologize."

"You must feel—"

"Nothing." He cut her off before she could voice what he was doing his damnedest to ignore. "Not a thing. I don't want your apologies. I don't want—" A burst of anger struck the side of his soul. The blow caught him off guard. He took a deep breath. "Let it go. I did."

"I don't believe you." Her hazel eyes searched his face.

He made himself sit quietly, forced the lid down on his anger and secured the lock. "That's your problem." He glanced at his watch. "I've got a couple of appointments in town. Feel free to use the phone and call whomever you need."

"The phone?"

"To let people know you arrived safely. Or if Billie needs to speak to anyone."

"I spoke to my parents yesterday. Who would Billie call?"

She was making it difficult. He rose. "Your ex-husband. Billie has a father, does she not?"

"Oh." Jane twisted her fingers together. "Oh, that. I ... there's no one to call."

"You have sole custody?"

Jane paled visibly and backed up a step. "Yes," she whispered. "I think so."

"Think? What do the divorce papers say?"

"Why are you asking this?"

"I want to know if a strange man is going to show up on my doorstep."

"There's no one. Billie and I are alone." She took another step away and bumped into the counter.

"I see." Her statement didn't please him, he told himself. Jane could have married six times since she'd left and it wouldn't matter to him. Why would he care that she'd probably left some other man the way she'd left him?

"We'll be fine," Jane said, crossing her arms over her chest. "There's the car to unpack and the house to clean. Don't worry about us. Billie and I have lots to do."

"She's a great kid."

For the first time since entering the kitchen, Jane looked at ease. "Really? You think so?" She smiled. "I know she thinks the world of you."

"She's just happy I didn't take off a layer of her hide for breaking the window."

"Billie knows you'd never hit her."

"How would she know a thing like that?"

"She's very wise about people."

"That's a good skill for someone her age."

Her arms dropped to her sides. "I wish I'd had it. I always saw what was on the surface. I never thought to look for more."

She was trying to tell him something, but what? "And now?"

Her eyes darkened as the gold fled. She moistened her lips. "I'm getting better. It comes with age."

"You don't look much older." He took a step toward her. The involuntary movement sent alarms ringing through his head. Being attracted to Jane would make his bid to forget the past that much harder. He didn't want to remember what he'd lost; it had taken too long to let go.

Feel nothing. It was the only thing that worked. But his feet continued to move closer, until he stood in front of her. The need to punish was lost as the rise and fall of her breasts, the bare feet inches from his own, again reminded him of that afternoon. She'd only worn panties under her father's shirt. Did the sundress allow much more? She'd filled out in her time away, not much, but enough. He smiled as he remembered her shyness the first time he'd touched her breasts. Her reluctance had been explained when she'd finally confessed that they were much smaller than Bobbi Sue's, with whom she shared a locker in gym class.

Adam had murmured he didn't care about seeing Bobbi Sue, dressed or naked. That Jane was the one driving him crazy. She'd allowed him to release the catch on her bra and had arched in pleasure when he touched her pale virgin skin.

He raised one hand toward her face. There weren't any lines to show the passage of time. Her cheek looked as smooth and soft as he remembered. She watched him fearlessly, until her eyes drifted closed.

No! He tightened his hand into a fist, then turned away. No more remembering. The past held nothing for him. It couldn't. He didn't want her.

"I'm late," he said, and left the room without once looking back.

Jane measured out the correct length and cut the shelf paper. One cupboard down, three to go. She brushed her bangs off her forehead. The muggy afternoon heat sapped most of her energy. After a morning in town, during which the replacement window for Adam's house had been ordered, Charlene had offered to take Billie for a swim at the club's pool. Jane had been invited to tag along, but thought she'd better start getting the house ready. It was Saturday, the furniture would arrive Monday. There wasn't a lot of time. Besides, with Billie gone, she'd work faster.

Unfortunately she also had time to think. About Adam. About that morning. One more mark against her, one more measure of guilt.

She'd lied. Not outright, of course. But a lie by omission remained a lie. He thought she was divorced. That she'd met and loved and married another. That Billie had a father somewhere out there. What would he say when he found out the truth?

There couldn't have been another man. Despite the miles and years between them, she hadn't been able to forget. Her daughter—his daughter—was a daily reminder. She couldn't move on until she'd let go of the past. So why did doing the right thing have to be so tough? The answer was easy: Adam.

He'd been so unaffected. Except for that brief moment, when he'd almost touched her face, he'd acted like a stranger. A well-mannered host offering refuge to distant, but unknown relatives. Not by a flicker of a lash did he let on that they'd once meant something to each other. How she wanted to blast him from his damn, cool self-possession. And she could do it. But for Billie's sake, she needed to bide her time.

Jane smoothed the paper onto the shelf. Charlene had warned her that he hadn't waited. But he also hadn't married. It was probably because she'd taught him not to trust anyone.

The back door slammed and Billie bounced into the room.

"We're back."

"How was it?"

"Great. I met tons of kids at the pool. The girls are kinda dopey, but I talked to some boys about the softball team." Billie dropped her towel onto the counter and raised up on tiptoes to offer a kiss. "They didn't believe me when I told them I was a pitcher."

"So she threatened to beat one of them up." Charlene entered the room. "I declare, we'll have our hands full trying to tame this one."

"I don't need taming." Billie thrust out her lower lip. "He said he didn't fight girls, but I knew he was scared." She assumed a fighter's stance, feet spread, fists raised. One strap of her bathing suit slipped down her shoulder.

Charlene ruffled her hair. "She's a tiger. And she dove off the high board."

"I'm impressed." Jane measured the next shelf. "Anything broken or lost?"

"Nah." Billie climbed onto the counter and wiggled to get comfortable. "Besides, Charlene told me that lots of kids break things. Adam kicked a football into his mom's chandelier when he was in high school."

Jane smiled. "I'd forgotten that, but now that you mention it, we could hear the screaming all the way over here."

Charlene inspected her work. "Sometimes it's easy to forget Adam wasn't always the responsible man he's become." The older woman lifted Billie down from the counter. "You need a bath, young lady."

"But I just went swimming. I can't be dirty."

"The pool isn't clean, it's wet."

"Mo-om."

Jane raised her hands in the air. "I'm staying out of this one, kid. You're on your own."

Charlene led her to the back door. "Let's go out to dinner tonight. They serve fried chicken at Millie's diner on Saturday, and Billie told me you rarely make it at home."

"I hate cleaning up afterward. I'd love to go to Millie's. Is the food still terrific?"

"This is Orchard. We don't take kindly to change."

Billie tugged on Charlene's hand. "Can Adam go with us?"

"No, dear. He's going out tonight with...a friend." She glanced at Jane, her shrug apologetic. "It seemed to be a sudden decision."

"Okay," Billie said. "But we can bring some back, in case Adam doesn't like his dinner."

They left together, with Billie still complaining about the bath. Jane cut the shelf paper, then slipped it into the space. She didn't care that Adam was going out on a date; it wasn't her business. If his cool response was to be believed, her return to Orchard hadn't affected him at all.

That couldn't be true, she thought, sagging against the shelf. But it was. If he'd come after her all those years ago, if he'd forced her to listen to him, given her a sign he cared, that she was more to him than a convenience, she might have been convinced to stay. He had let her go without a word.

Like it or not, they were going to be neighbors. He couldn't avoid her forever. Even if he didn't care about her, he had to be angry about the past, about what had happened. When he learned the truth about his daughter, the daughter that had been kept from him—

Jane bit her lower lip. She'd only seen Adam truly enraged once. The collections manager at the bank had tried to intimidate a delinquent widow by using physical force. When Adam found out, he'd been a man possessed. The rage in his eyes, the barely controlled violence in his stance, the deadly quiet voice he'd used to fire the employee, had frightened her and had made her wonder if she knew him at all.

Looking back through the eyes of an adult, she realized he had kept himself from her. The essence of what he was— the promising oldest son forced to grow up before his time— had remained hidden. She'd been no match for him. Even his carefully reined-in passion had frightened her virgin body. No wonder he'd let her go without a word. What had there been to say?

She opened another package of shelf paper and unrolled it along the counter. The easiest thing would be for her to go along with him and play her own game of pretending nothing had happened. But that wasn't an option for her. She had to think of Billie and protect her. Until they had put the past behind them, they couldn't face the present. Until he had dealt with his anger, she couldn't trust him with his daughter.

Jane sat at the window seat in the guest room. In the trees, morning birds called to one another and their young. It wasn't yet seven, but already the humid heat threatened. Another Southern Sunday, she thought, pulling her light, cotton robe closer around her body.

Last night Adam had stayed out late. She'd waited up as long as she could, but exhaustion had forced her to bed.

This morning she'd rushed to the window and had caught a glimpse of him jogging off. He had to come back sometime, and she'd be waiting. They still had a lot to discuss, and avoiding each other wasn't going to make it go away.

After washing up in the bathroom, she pulled on shorts and a blouse. She would dress for church after her talk with Adam. She checked to make sure Billie was still asleep. Her child lay curled up like a possum. The light sheet covered everything but the tip of her head. Jane silently shut the door and made her way down the stairs.

The house echoed with morning stillness. Underfoot, the hardwood floors felt cool and smooth. Adam had pulled up the old wool carpets and replaced them with scatter rugs. Most of the furnishings remained the same, but yesterday she'd caught sight of a complex entertainment unit in the game room. While he'd kept the family portraits and photographs, the darker paintings had been exchanged for bright moderns and a few lithographs. An original cartoon cell hung in the hallway outside her bedroom. The changes in the house were minor, but no less important for their subtlety.

Reaching the bottom stair, she sat down and waited. It had been almost an hour. He *had* to return soon. So what was she going to say? How far was she willing to push him? Telling herself that dealing with his anger herself was better than risking it spilling over to Billie was one thing. Facing Adam in a rage was quite another.

The girl he'd known before would never have defied him. If he'd told her he didn't want to talk about something, she would have never mentioned it again. That girl had been lost somewhere between Billie's birth and the present.

The back door slammed and jerked her out of her reverie. Here goes nothing, she thought grimly as she rose and brushed her damp palms against her shorts. She walked through the dining room and into the kitchen. And stopped.

Adam stood with his back to her. His bare back. Since he'd last jogged out of sight, he'd removed his T-shirt. Sweat glistened on his skin, the sheen defining the rippling muscles clenching and releasing like thick ropes. One hand held the refrigerator door open. He reached in and pulled out a bottle of juice. He shook the container, then raised it to his lips. As he drank, her throat tightened and swallowed. A bead of moisture dripped from the bottle onto his chest and was lost from view. Her gaze drifted down, past the flat midsection rising and lowering with each deep breath, past the bulge indicating his gender, to long, powerful legs. She knew the exact moment he became aware of her presence. The sudden tension of his body forced her to look up.

He hadn't shaved. Stubble darkened his jaw and outlined the firm line of his mouth. A smattering of hair, damp and matted from the run, arrowed toward his waist. Her breathing grew ragged. Not from exertion, but from apprehension. She had initiated this meeting, it was up to her to tell him what she wanted. But her tight throat wouldn't allow speech.

Adam closed the refrigerator and set the bottle on the counter. After grabbing his T-shirt off the chair, he wiped his face and chest.

"What do you want?"

He stood with his hands on his hips. The elastic of his shorts dipped scandalously low; he looked every inch a dangerous man. Billie had the same way of standing, of looking defiant and angry. But Billie was only eight, still a child. Adam was—Adam was the girl's father.

"I ordered a replacement for the window," she blurted out.

His mouth twisted with irritation, but he didn't speak.

"I wanted you to know. It should be here Monday. They'll install it and everything."

"Fine."

He stood there, perhaps sensing there was more, or waiting for her to leave. Those eyes, she thought, at last letting her gaze meet his. Those damn eyes. He still made her feel young and foolish. At seventeen, the six years difference in their ages had loomed between them like an uncrossable bridge. He'd been forced into adulthood by the death of his parents and the responsibility of his siblings. She'd been forced into adulthood by her own actions.

"I'm sorry," she said at last.

"Did Billie break something else?"

"No. I'm sorry for—" She clasped her hands together to stop their trembling. "Dammit, Adam, say something."

"Such as?"

"Why are you so calm about this? I waltz in here after being gone almost nine years and it's like nothing happened."

He shook his head impatiently. "I don't have time for reminiscing. I'm not interested in the past. It's done with. Let it go. I have."

"You're lying."

"And you're beating a dead horse."

He moved to walk past her. She touched his arm to stop him. Her fingers brushed against hot, damp skin. A current leapt between them and she jerked back, half expecting to see smoke. He froze in mid-stride, caught between her and the counter.

"What do you want?" he asked, shifting until one hip braced against the cupboard. The T-shirt hung over one shoulder.

She stared at the hem of the garment, studying the tiny stitches as if the answer lay hidden in the weave or the design.

"I'm moving in next door."

"So?"

"There's no way to avoid—"

"The hell there isn't. I don't want to be friends. I don't, as a rule, socialize with my neighbors. So your living there doesn't matter to me."

She told herself his disinterest came from pain, but a part of her wondered if she was wrong. Was Charlene speaking the truth? Had Adam recovered from what had happened? Did she not matter anymore?

"Billie likes you."

"And I like her. I'll be friends with the kid. I don't need to deal with you for that."

If only it were that simple.

"So the past means nothing?" she asked. She knew she was really asking if *she* meant nothing.

He shifted. Again she risked raising her gaze to his. The brown irises had darkened to black. The lines bracketing his mouth deepened.

"What do you want from me, Jane? You want me to tell you I still think about you? I can't, because I don't. It's over. I've moved on."

"I'm not asking if you think about—" this was harder than she'd thought "—me. I understand that we've both moved on. But I won't believe you've forgotten what happened. How it made you feel. Or what I did."

He looked away then, staring past her to something she couldn't see. The curse he mumbled made her flinch.

"It doesn't matter," he said. "I don't care."

"I don't believe that."

He shrugged. "Believe what you want."

What was the old saying? In for a penny, in for a pound. "You once asked me to marry you."

He laughed harshly, the sound carrying more irritation than humor. "Hell of a coincidence. You once said yes." His arms folded over his chest. "Don't push me. I still don't understand what you're looking for, but I'm the wrong man. You don't want to get me angry, and that's about five seconds from happening."

"At last," she said, stepping closer, feeling her own temper rise. "The fine, upstanding Adam Barrington. Banker, model citizen. You mean there's someone inside? Someone real, with feelings? Is that a crack in the old wall there? I'm not completely at fault, you know. You let me go, damn you. Why? Why didn't you come after me?"

Jane covered her mouth. That wasn't what she'd planned to say at all. But it was too late.

"Let you go?" He spoke quietly, with a barely controlled rage. The muscles in his arms bulged with the effort of his restraint. His eyes burned with a hot fire that had nothing to do with passion and everything to do with rage. "You walked out on me. Not a word or a note. Just a church full of people and a bride who didn't bother to show up."

Chapter Four

Adam straightened his arms at his sides and balled his hands into fists. His muscles trembled at the effort to restrain himself. His angry words, so filled with frustration and hurt, hung between them, echoing silently against the kitchen walls.

Damn her for forcing him to give it all away. Control, he told himself. Get control. But it was useless. Hot emotion tumbled through his body, swept on by heated blood. It bubbled and rolled within him, building with speed and pressure until the explosion became inevitable.

"It wasn't like that," she said, speaking so softly he had to strain to hear her. "I never meant it to happen that way. I thought—"

He swore loudly, the vulgar word cutting off her apology. "You thought?" he asked sarcastically, his rage burning the last of his civility. "What did you think? That no one would notice? That I'd get over being publicly humiliated?

That your running away wouldn't be the topic of conversation around town for months?''

She lowered her head. She'd pulled her long hair back in a loose braid. Bangs hung down her forehead, but her neck and ears were exposed. A dull red flush climbed from the neck of her T-shirt to her hairline.

"I'm sorry," she whispered.

"Sorry? Is that the best you can do? There was nothing, Jane. Not one damn word. I'd seen you drive up with your mother. You were in the church. Then you disappeared. What the hell happened?''

She opened her mouth to answer. He cut her off. "Don't bother." He turned away and faced the cupboards. If he continued to look at her, he wasn't sure what might happen. "We all waited for almost an hour. I heard the people talking. I told myself there was a problem with the dress, or that you'd broken a heel."

He didn't have to try to remember that afternoon. The sounds and smells enveloped him like the clammy mist of summer fog. She'd insisted that the church be filled with roses. White roses. That scent had haunted his sleep for months.

He pressed his palms against the counter, as if the tile could cool his heated blood. He'd thought he'd forgotten it all, but the past broke through the wall of his control, swept across his emotions, unleashing the potential for destruction. Again his fingers curled toward his palms as if he could squeeze out the memories. Or the person who had caused them.

"Adam, I'm sorry," she said, interrupting his struggle to maintain a semblance of composure. "So very sorry. It was never about you. You've got to believe that. It was about me."

"You've got that right." He spun to face her. "You ran away. It was a childish thing to do. I'm the one who had to deal with the aftermath of your behavior and make up some

story about what had happened when I didn't have a clue.
I'm the one who sent the notes of apology, returned the gifts
and paid the bill for a reception that didn't happen.''

She raised her head. Unshed tears glistened in her hazel
eyes. She blinked frantically, but it didn't help. A single drop
rolled down her cheek. At one time her distress would have
moved him. He would have gathered her in his arms and
murmured words of comfort. Not anymore.

"Typical," he said, shaking his head. "The going gets
tough and you cry. You haven't grown up at all."

"That's not fair."

"Don't talk to me about fair. What do you know about
it? Did you ever give any thought to what you left behind?
You squawk about my not coming after you. Lady, even if
I'd wanted to, I didn't have the time. Someone had to handle damage control. I know all you were interested in was
seeing how easily you could wrap me around your little finger, but I had—and, no thanks to you—still have a position to think of in this community. I do business with most
of the town. I was putting my sister and brother through
college. Did you ever stop to think that the fine people of
Orchard might not want to trust their money to a bank
president who'd been stood up at the altar? That they might
begin to wonder if there was some flaw only you knew
about?"

Despite the embarrassment staining her cheeks, she paled.
"They wouldn't have."

"Think again."

She raised her arm as if offering an apology. "I didn't
know."

He glared at her and she dropped her arm to her side.
"You didn't bother to find out," he said. "All you could
think of was yourself."

"It wasn't like that. I tried to tell you—"

"When? I was standing there in the front of the church.
Like a fool. When I figured out something was wrong, I was

pretty much a captive audience. If you were trying to get my attention, you got it. But you didn't have the guts to stay and talk. That's what gets me the most. Not one word of warning."

"I did try to talk to you. Before the wedding. You wouldn't listen."

He reached for the T-shirt hanging over his shoulder and pulled it down. She jerked her head at the movement, as if she'd suspected he would hit her. Her reaction inflamed him. Despite her actions, he'd never given her reason to fear him.

"I listened but all we talked about was the wedding," he said, his jaw tight with suppressed emotion. "Do you want pale pink or blush for the napkins?" He raised his voice mockingly. "Wild rice or steamed potatoes?"

"If you disliked my conversation so much, why did you want to marry me?"

He folded his arms over his chest. "Everybody's entitled to one mistake."

She closed her eyes and swallowed. Another tear rolled down her cheek. "And I'm yours?"

"You said it, lady, not me."

She looked at him. "I didn't do it on purpose."

"Is that supposed to make it better? That you acted out of ignorance?"

She shook her head. "Of course not. I'm just saying that I was very young."

"I guess that works as well as any excuse." He fingered the shirt in his hands. "It's my fault, I suppose. I'm the one who tried to make you more than you could be."

She flinched as if he'd slapped her. "I knew you'd be angry, but I never really expected you'd hate me so much."

"You're not worth hating." He looked over her head. "I don't care anymore."

She reached out her hand again and this time touched his bare forearm. The physical side of him—that masculine self that had never been able to get enough of her—reacted to the slight touch. Awareness quivered as the imprint of each finger burned into his skin. It wouldn't take much, he acknowledged, despising the weakness inside and her for causing it.

With a slow gesture, too deliberate to be ignored, he pulled away from the contact. Jane bit her lower lip and stepped back. It wasn't even close to a draw, he thought. He'd hurt her, but nothing like what she'd done to him, all those years ago.

"If you could just let me explain," she said, twisting her fingers together. "I never meant to—"

"I don't give a damn about your explanations. Or you."

Her hazel eyes studied him. Tears threatened again, but she brushed them away impatiently. "You're too angry to not care, Adam. Your temper gives you away."

One point for her, he thought grimly. "All right. I care enough not to want you in my life. How's that?"

She turned and walked toward the hallway. When she reached the door, she looked back over her shoulder. "Be careful what you throw away, Adam. You may find you need it after all."

After she fled into the quiet morning, he stood alone in the kitchen, drawing deep breaths into his body. Once lost, the control was difficult to recapture. Random thoughts raced through his mind. Memories from the past—lost dreams, half-forgotten moments. He'd offered her all he had and she'd turned him down flat. Publicly. Now she expected exoneration for her behavior. Hell would freeze over before he'd ever—

"Was that a discussion you'd want her daughter to hear?"

"What?" He spun toward the back door.

Charlene stood in the pantry. "I could hear you clear outside. Now I've sent the child off to find the berry patch.

If you two are going to quarrel, please find a more suitable location."

"We weren't arguing."

"It sounded like an argument." Interest sparkled in her blue eyes. "Do you want to talk about it?"

"No," he said curtly, then instantly regretted his sharp tone. "It doesn't matter, Charlene. Jane just wanted me to get in touch with my feelings, and I did."

Stupid, Jane thought as she pulled the brush through her long hair. Just plain stupid. She'd been stupid to think about coming back to Orchard, stupid to think she and Adam might be able to resolve anything by discussing the past, and stupid to plan to let him know about his daughter.

"Not my finest hour," she muttered, as she dropped the brush, then reached back and began braiding her hair. Her fingers moved efficiently, weaving the long strands into a French braid. The mirror over the dresser reflected her image. She averted her eyes, not wanting to see the guilty flush on her own face. Morning light filtered through the lace curtains and onto the carpeted floor. Like the room Billie slept in, this guest room had been decorated with warm colors and cozy prints. A handmade quilt covered the bed she sat on. The bright yellows and peaches blended in a star-shaped pattern. It should have been soothing. Despite the room, the cool shower and the stern talking-to she'd given herself, her heart still thundered in her chest. Her hands shook from the recent exchange with her former fiancé, and a strand of hair slipped out of her grasp, causing her to release the half-finished braid.

"Stupid." She picked up the brush and began vigorously stroking.

"You're gonna pull it all out," Billie said as she walked into the room.

"What?"

"Your hair. You're brushing too hard. Are you mad at me?"

"No, honey." Jane set the brush on the bed and held open her arms. "Come here." Her daughter stepped into her embrace and they hugged. "I'm not angry at all."

Billie had managed to stay reasonably clean, despite a quick trip to the berry patch. Jane held her at arm's length and studied her. The peach-and-cream floral print sundress brought out the tan on her face and arms. Her hair showed signs of recent contact with a comb. Brown eyes, so much like Adam's that it hurt to look at them, glared back mutinously.

"I'm not wearing that hat," Billie said. "And you can't make me."

"Your grandmother went to a lot of trouble to find one that matched that dress."

"I know, but it's dumb looking." Billie planted her hands on her hips. "I don't think God cares if I wear a dress to church or not."

"We dress nicely to show respect," Jane answered, trying not to smile at the familiar argument.

"Maybe." Her daughter brushed her bangs out of her face. "But I *know* he doesn't need me to wear a hat." She wrinkled her nose. "It's got ribbons and flowers. People will laugh at me."

"You'd look very pretty."

Billie opened her mouth wide and made a gagging noise, showing exactly what she thought of looking pretty.

Jane sighed. Compromise. It was the first rule of parenting. "You don't have to wear the hat."

"Whew. Thanks, Mom." Billie spun in a circle. The hem of her dress flared out exposing the denim shorts she wore underneath. "I'll even leave my softball at home."

"Thank you." Her gaze drifted past her daughter's bare legs down to sneaker-clad feet. "But you have to change your shoes."

"I'm not wearing those patent leather things. Yuk."

"Sandals are fine."

"Okay." Billie dashed from the room.

Jane picked up the brush. She'd given up trying to get Billie not to run in the house. As long as nothing terribly expensive was in danger of being broken, it wasn't worth the fight. Besides, the kid had way too much energy.

She smiled fondly as she remembered her own childhood. Being a tomboy had never been a question, let alone a problem. No, she had been a typical girl. Dolls and books, quiet games with two or three friends and little time outdoors. She hadn't even learned to swim until she was almost twelve.

Her fingers nimbly worked with her hair as her eyes drifted half-closed and she remembered the muggy heat of that summer, when the temperature alone had driven her to the local swimming hole. The big kids—the teenagers—had taken over one side, but the rest belonged to everyone else. Jane had stayed in the shallow part, dangling her feet while she sat on a fallen log. The combination of sun and friends and laughter had wooed her into relaxing. Then she'd seen him.

Goose bumps erupted on her skin as she remembered looking up and seeing a boy—a young man really—poised at the top of a platform one of the fathers had constructed. With the sun in her eyes, she hadn't been able to see his face, but she'd watched him dive cleanly into the water, barely making any splash at all. He'd surfaced close to where she sat.

When he'd gotten out, water streaming off his developed and tanned body, and laughed, she'd found herself giggling with him. Their eyes had met. Adam, she'd thought with some surprise. The boy who lived next door. But he wasn't a boy anymore. He'd shaken himself then, spraying her with water, and had invited her to jump off the platform with him.

She refused. She couldn't swim. Instead of mocking her like the other boys had, he'd held out his hand and led her to a quiet cove. He'd taught her to swim that summer, Jane remembered, finishing the braid and clipping a silk rose at the bottom. Slowly, patiently. He'd been a football player in the fall, a swimmer in the spring at high school. He'd been to the state championships once. A jock. Nothing like her. At eighteen, he'd been a prize catch in a small town like Orchard. She smoothed down her dress and allowed herself a bittersweet smile. He would have been a prize catch anywhere. And despite the other teenage girls ready and willing to spend their days with him, he'd taken the time to teach his twelve-year-old neighbor to swim.

A scholar, an athlete and a gentleman. Her heart never had a chance. He was her first crush. It had been as inevitable as the coastal tide. Her desires had been unfocused, just vague longings that had made her heart beat faster whenever she saw him. It wasn't until high school that she'd recognized the feelings for what they were. Love had quickly followed.

And she'd thrown it all away.

Jane rose from the bed and walked to the doorway of the guest room. The thick carpet muffled her footsteps. It seemed another lifetime ago that she'd been engaged to Adam. They were both so different now. Coming home had been—stupid.

"I just want you to know that I *hate* these," Billie said, joining her in the hall. She flexed one foot and glared at her sandals. "When I'm grown up, I'm never going to wear a dress again."

The shaft of pain caught her unaware and ripped through her heart. Billie was, if nothing else, her father's daughter. Adam had rebelled at dressing up. He'd been active in sports. He'd been—

She drew in a breath. He'd been the one she'd left standing at the altar. Oh, why on earth had she thought returning to Orchard would be a good idea? And if that wasn't bad enough, why had she insisted on pushing him to reveal his feelings about her walking out on him? It accomplished nothing except to bring those awful memories to the surface. If being in the same room with him before had been difficult, now it would be impossible. She'd have to think of an excuse to leave or move or—

"Jane! Billie! It's time to go. What are you two doing up there?" Charlene's voice sailed up the stairs.

"We're coming," Billie called down. "You ready, Mom?"

"Sure," she said, trying not to clench her teeth. If she was uncomfortable now, it was her own fault. Bearding the lion in his own den had been foolish. Maybe Adam would chicken out. Maybe he'd stay home from church. Maybe—

Maybe it was her fate to be punished for the rest of her days. She took Billie's hand and together they descended the stairs. Waiting at the foot stood Charlene in one of her bright voluminous dresses, and Adam. His dark suit emphasized the lean strength of his body. Damp dark brown hair gleamed. The slight waves had been tamed with water and a brush, but soon one or two locks would tumble over his forehead.

She felt heat climb her cheeks and prayed he wouldn't notice. He didn't. He wasn't looking at her, but at some spot over her head and to the left.

"Are you ready?" he asked quietly. Nothing in his voice hinted at the conversation they'd had not two hours before. Only the slightly clenched fists and the stern set of his mouth showed that emotions lurked below the calm facade.

"My tummy hurts," Billie said.

Jane glanced down at her and raised one eyebrow.

The little girl rubbed the top of her right foot against the calf of her left leg. "Okay. It doesn't."

"Billie isn't too fond of church," she explained to Charlene, careful to avoid looking at Adam again.

"I don't mind it too much, but they make you sit still so long." Billie drew in a deep breath and let it go in a sigh. "I like God and everything. The songs are okay. But there's always some old lady telling me to sit still."

"Charm school," Charlene said, taking Billie's other hand, and ushering her toward the front door.

"I don't think that's such a good idea," Jane said. "She's awfully young."

"This is Orchard, dear. We strive to turn girls into ladies, at any age."

"What's charm school?" Billie asked suspiciously.

"You don't want to know," her mother told her, keeping step with them. Adam brought up the rear.

As they walked outside, toward the dark sedan parked in front, she tried not to think about him. It was only for one more night. Her furniture would be arriving sometime tomorrow. If she worked at it, she'd never have to see him again.

Yeah, right, she thought as he held the rear door of the car open. What about her plans for an eventual father-daughter reunion? She still owed them both. Before Jane could make her move, Billie had ducked inside the car, with Charlene quickly on her heels.

"You sit in front," the older woman told her.

Jane swallowed uncomfortably. Adam closed the rear door and opened the front. She murmured her thanks as she slipped in past him. The scent of his body—soap, shaving cream, and some essence of male—taunted her. She wanted to breathe deeply and savor the fragrance. It made her think of sultry Southern nights and velvet-on-silk passion.

The door slamming shut with a bang caused her to jump slightly. In the back seat, Charlene and Billie chatted. Charlene spoke glowingly about charm school, but Jane could tell that her daughter was becoming more and more disenchanted by the second.

"Do I have to?" she asked, leaning over the front seat. "I don't want to learn how to drink tea and dance. And I already know how to walk."

"Not like a lady," Charlene said. "You'll like it."

"I won't!"

Adam slid into his seat. She half expected him to take part in the conversation, but he just started the car and shifted into gear.

"Mo-om!"

Jane drew in a deep breath. "Billie, you don't have to go to charm school if you don't want to. Charlene, she *is* only eight."

"It's never too early to learn how to be a lady."

"I'm going to be a pitcher."

Jane bit back a smile and tried to relax in her seat. The conversation between Billie and Charlene continued as they debated the merits of their positions. She didn't glance to her left, but she was aware of him sitting so close. Except for asking if she were ready, he hadn't said a word. Not that any of this was his fault. It had all been a big mistake and she only had herself to blame.

The drive to church took about six minutes. As they pulled into the parking lot, Jane tensed and waited for the rush of memories to envelop her.

"Did you used to go to this church?" Billie asked.

"Yes, until I—" She cleared her throat.

"Moved away," Adam offered helpfully. She knew she was the only one to hear the sarcasm in his voice. She didn't dare look at him.

"That's right," she said softly. "Until I moved away."

A large crowd mingled on the edge of the lawn. One woman glanced at Adam's car as he parked it. She did a double take and nudged her neighbor. Jane couldn't hear what was being said but she watched as the news rippled through the group. The prodigal daughter had returned.

Oh, no! She'd never given a moment's thought to what it would look like if she arrived at church with Adam and Charlene. And Billie. What would people think? Say? She was doing it again! Acting without thinking and leaving Adam to deal with the consequences.

Darting a quick glance to her left, she waited for him to comment on the interest they'd generated. Instead he opened the car door and stepped out. She fumbled with the handle, anxious to exit before he made his way around to help her. Nervous fingers slipped. He reached her door. When it opened, he held out his hand. Politeness demanded that she accept the gracious gesture. Her fingers brushed his palm. Sparks flew in all directions, landing on her skin and midsection, creating a warmth that threatened to make her tremble. His touch had always affected her. The flash of familiar electricity comforted as it excited. Was there still something between them?

She slowly raised her gaze, past the dark suit jacket, past the white shirt and faintly patterned blue tie. Past the squared jaw and straight lips to his eyes. The anger there, deadly and barely controlled, made her drop her hand and turn away.

While she struggled with her composure, several people came over and said hello. Some of the faces looked familiar, some did not. But they all stared. A few of the people she knew glanced from her to Adam, then back. The speculative look in their eyes made her blush. The rumors would sprout faster than kudzu. This had all the earmarks of turning out to be a crummy day.

Billie bounced beside her. "Oh, look. There's Matt. I met him at the pool. He's a catcher. I'm going to go say hi." She darted off without waiting for permission.

"Charm school," Charlene murmured quietly, before she, too, walked away to greet some friends. Adam also disappeared into the crowd to speak with someone.

Alone, Jane moved toward the front steps of the church. The old-fashioned white building had been recently painted. Green grass stretched out on either side of the path leading from the parking lot to the stairs. Lofty chestnut trees provided shade. They'd grown taller in her absence, she thought, glancing up at them. And the dogwoods had grown wider. Small changes really, not enough to keep her from remembering.

As she climbed the steps, she reminded herself it was all in the past. But it wasn't. As she stepped through the open double doors, time shifted. It bent until that day and this one touched, and she once again stood in the back of the church, her long, white wedding gown dragging at her with each step.

The church had been full, the townspeople eager to see Adam Barrington wed his bride. White roses, always her favorite, filled every urn. Wide ribbons curved along the center aisle, holding small white bouquets at the end of each pew. Even now, the scent of roses swept over her. Someone jostled her gently and she stepped into a corner of the foyer. The shadows blurred, the sounds faded, until all she could hear was her mother telling her it was too late to change her mind.

"You can't back out now," her mother had said, an edge of hysteria in her voice. "The wedding, the reception. It's all planned. What will your father say?"

A familiar theme growing up, Jane recalled. Her father had been the undisputed master of his castle. Her mother the eager subject. It was her mother's willingness to be what her husband demanded that had first given Jane a glimpse of what life with Adam might be like. Adam also made politely worded requests. As she stared at the people waiting to watch her marry, she had wondered if he loved her. Confusion, as real today as it had been nine years ago, filled her. Was she the most convenient bride? Young and easily influenced? Did he want *her* or had she simply fulfilled his list? They were so different. Six years had loomed large between them. He'd been a man.

More than anything, that had frightened her. In those moments when her blood had run cold and her heart had thundered in her throat, she had seen that she wasn't enough. She might love him with all of her being, but she wasn't ready to marry him. It had been her first mature realization. Unfortunately, she had acted like a child. Even as her mother had begged her to reconsider, Jane pulled off the wedding gown and veil. She'd slipped on her jeans and shirt.

"What are you going to tell him?" her mother had asked.

"Nothing."

With that, she had run. Pausing only to peek into the church one more time, stopping long enough to catch Adam's eye and see him smile at her, warmly, trustingly, as any man would smile at the unexpected glimpse of his bride. He hadn't seen she wasn't wearing her gown. In that moment, she'd stopped to question her actions. Had his expression contained affection? Even love?

No, she'd thought as the tears had begun. Not love. Convenience. Suitability. She would never inspire the same kind of soul-stealing emotion that he created in her. Better to find that out now, rather than later. She'd escaped out a side door and had never looked back.

One cowardly, selfish act. Her life had never been the same. She'd lived with that mistake from that moment until this. Adam had been right, Jane thought, pushing away the past and looking around at the church. She hadn't allowed herself to think about the consequences of her actions. Oh, she'd acknowledged that he might be hurt or a little embarrassed, but she'd never considered in detail what he must have gone through.

Her Adam, so strong and proud, handsome. She remembered how her heart had fluttered whenever he'd smiled at her from across a room. She'd publicly humiliated him, had rejected him in the worst way possible. He'd worked hard for all he'd achieved. To think that she might have destroyed that. She shuddered.

She had hoped that by getting him to admit his anger now, she might lessen her own guilt. Another selfish act. She had forced Adam to relive those horrible days. And now, they both felt worse. As she'd said earlier. Stupid.

A soft hand touched her arm. Jane blinked, then tried to smile at Charlene.

"Are you all right?" the older woman asked. In the church the shadows muted the bright color of her hair, but the other woman was still a robin in a flock of sparrows.

"Fine."

Those wise eyes studied her. "There's no way to escape the past, my dear. You must make peace with it."

"Am I that obvious?"

"Only because I care about you."

"I'm just beginning to understand all the trouble I've caused," she said, averting her face from the probing glances of curious neighbors. "It's not flattering."

"You were young, child. You made the best decision you could at the time."

"Everyone paid a high price for that."

"Including yourself."

"I don't care about me. It's Billie that I'm worried about."

"And Adam?"

"Yes," she admitted.

It was as if Charlene's words conjured him out of the morning. He and Billie walked in together, the child's small hand held securely in his. They were speaking about something. Both their heads tilted toward each other.

The best decision possible at the time, Charlene had said. That wasn't true. All she'd accomplished by running was to keep father and daughter apart.

Adam said something and they both laughed. Their smiles were mirror images. How long before everyone guessed the truth? He glanced up at her, then turned away. Inside, a cold lump formed and pressed against her heart.

She'd been hiding, she realized in that moment of rejection. Hiding from the truth. The list of reasons she'd used for coming home—a good job, a small and friendly town in which to raise her daughter—had all been a smoke screen. She hadn't come home for a teaching position, or even for Billie. She'd come home looking for forgiveness and a way to set the past right.

Chapter Five

Despite the board covering the broken window, night noises drifted into Adam's office. He stared at the folders spread open in front of him and struggled to concentrate. The loan committee would meet Monday morning, as it had for decades. He could imagine the looks on his employees' faces if *he* wasn't ready.

Normally he could shut out any distractions. Whether it was neighborhood kids or grunts from Charlene's favorite Sunday night wrestling. But tonight— He closed the top file and sighed. Jane had called Billie in for her bath about fifteen minutes before. The eight-year-old's arguments as to why she didn't need washing had taken the better part of ten minutes. At the end, he'd been grinning broadly at her imagination and inventiveness. What a kid.

But it wasn't Billie's chatter that kept him from working. Nor was it Charlene's television shows or the crickets. It was Jane. He'd gone to church in that same building for the past nine years. Except for an occasional service missed because of illness or vacation, he'd been faithful in his attendance, and his attention. This morning, as now, his mind had wandered. The past, so easily disposed of when there was no reminder, slipped around the walls of his control. It weighed on him, made him lose track of the sermon or his notes on a loan.

When she had left, all those years ago, he'd been able to occupy his mind with the details of picking up the pieces. All the things he'd complained about to Jane that she'd left him to handle had filled his time and his thoughts. The act itself had been pushed aside, first for a few days, then indefinitely, until he'd lost track of it all. Occasionally, something would happen to remind him. He would recall a conversation, a moment, then shove it back where it belonged and get on with his life.

It wasn't going to be so easy this time, he thought as he dropped his pen onto the desk and leaned back in his leather chair. Violent anger had been his persistent companion most of the day. He hated her for making him remember, and himself for being sucked into something that should have ended a long time ago. He'd avoided the family dinner table, instead grabbing a snack in the kitchen and ducking out before Charlene could shanghai him. How long could he avoid Jane?

Damn her for coming back, he thought, staring out into the darkness. And for being the one who still got to him.

After taking a deep breath, he ordered his body to relax. She would be gone in the morning. He wouldn't have to see her again if he didn't want to. There had been weeks, even months between contact with the previous neighbors. Surely Jane was smart enough to want the same thing. If they both took a little time to plan this, they might never have to meet again. Would that be enough to shut her out? Not seeing her, not talking to her? He closed his eyes, but that didn't help.

Memories from years ago filled him. He'd just gotten his Master's degree in Money and Banking and had been putting in a lot of extra hours at the bank to make up for his time gone. Financially it had been touch and go for a couple of years. The town of Orchard had been amazingly tolerant and trusting of a bank president in his twenties. Dani and Ty had needed money for college, not to mention his attention when they were home. And there had been Jane.

Time with her was something he had put on his calendar, scheduled like any appointment. Perhaps, he thought now, he could have wooed her more, but he'd had responsibilities. She'd understood that. All that was to have changed after the wedding. But she'd never given him the chance.

She had been young. Maybe too young, he thought with a flash of insight. She'd wanted him to demonstrate his affection by playing those silly romantic high school games. He hadn't had time to loll around on her porch and sip lemonade while gossiping about the prom. He hadn't had time—

Upstairs, footsteps thumped. Billie, he thought with a slight smile. If things had been different, he and Jane could have been married for nine years. They would have had a child of their own by now. A daughter who looked like—

He sat up straight in his chair. Billie? He started to do some rapid calculations. They were cut short when he realized he didn't know how old Billie was. Even as excitement and expectation flared inside him, he firmly squashed them. Billie couldn't be his. He and Jane hadn't made love often, and when they had, they'd used protection. She'd been embarrassed as hell about the diaphragm, he recalled with a grin. Her mother had refused to discuss any kind of birth control, so he'd been the one to take her to the doctor and wait during her appointment.

His smile faded. Sex. Another place he'd screwed up, he saw now with the twenty-twenty vision of hindsight.

"Adam?"

He glanced up, startled. He hadn't heard her knock, let alone enter. Had his thoughts conjured her from the past? Was the woman standing in front of him real?

He studied her dark hair and the fringe of bangs that ended just above her delicately arched eyebrows. Hazel eyes held his gaze for a second, before flickering nervously toward the floor. One corner of her mouth quivered slightly, as if not sure whether to curve up or down. She still looked too damn young, he thought irritably. But she was real enough. The dress she wore—pale blue and loose fitting with a white blouse underneath—was the same one from this morning. He wouldn't have imagined her in that. In his mind, he liked to think of her teetering on unaccustomed high heels, her upswept hair adding height and attempting to make her look older. Or sitting on his porch, watching the sunset, a sleeveless blouse exposing her tanned arms, while the gauzy full skirt she wore outlined the curvy lines of her legs.

"I'm busy," he said curtly, as much to disconnect himself from his thoughts as to send her away.

"This won't take but a moment."

He made a show of closing the top folder, then glancing impatiently at his watch. "Yes?"

She took a step into the office. The room was large, and he'd taken advantage of the space. Bookcases lined two walls. The big walnut desk that had been his father's was the centerpiece of the room. A comfortable chair with its own table and reading lamp stood in one corner. The couch sat between the desk and door. About five years ago he'd pulled up the heavy rug and had refinished the hardwood floors. It was a comfortable room; a place he could work in.

Her hands fluttered nervously around her waist. She linked her fingers together, as if to still the movement, then rubbed her palms back and forth against each other.

"Sit down and stop fidgeting," he said, pointing to the couch.

"Sorry." Jane walked the three steps, then perched on the edge of the sofa. The black leather provided a perfect backdrop for her delicate features. The harsh color outlined the shape of her head, the curve of her cheek and the graceful sweep of her neck. She wore her hair pulled back.

"A nuisance," she'd said, when, years before, he pulled at the ribbons and freed the silky tresses.

"Beautiful," he'd replied.

Her innocent blush had thrilled him, as he had then taken what no man had seen or touched.

He shook his head impatiently. "What do you want?"

"To apologize."

He raised one eyebrow and waited.

"Not about Billie. She hasn't done anything."

"Yet," he said.

The corner of her mouth raised slightly. "Yet. It is one of the hazards of raising a tomboy."

"But worth the trouble."

She looked surprised. "I wouldn't have thought—"

"I'd never hold your behavior against your child, Jane. If you'd taken the time to know the man you were running from, you would be aware of that."

Hazel eyes flashed anger, as their color darkened to green. "If *I'd* taken the time? You're the one who couldn't bear to be away from your precious bank. I always came tenth on a list of five items. Don't talk to me about—" She stopped, her mouth still open to form more words. She clamped her lips together and sighed. "I didn't come here to fight."

"Why did you?"

"At church this morning... I'm sorry about all that. I should have thought..." She hunched her shoulders as if waiting for him to berate her for not thinking—again. When he didn't, she went on. "Those people, they all stared at us. I'd forgotten what a small town can be like. There will be rumors. I didn't want to cause you any more trouble."

He rose from his desk and walked around it until he stood in front of her. After moving a couple of folders, he perched on the corner nearest her. "I can handle it, if you can."

She nodded. "People will talk, though."

He shrugged. "I've been through it before."

"I know. I'm sorry about that, too."

"Forget it."

"I can't."

"Then it's your problem."

"You dismiss me so easily, Adam, but then you always did. I was too young and foolish. I was never like those other women you dated."

His temper threatened to flare but was put out by her words from the past. "I'm not like those other women." The phrase echoed over and over again. It had been winter. January, maybe, and cold for South Carolina. He'd started a fire and had spread a blanket for the two of them. They'd been kissing for hours, petting. He'd touched her breasts under the wool of her sweater, but when he tried to take off her bra, she'd resisted.

"I'm not like those other women," she said, her hazel eyes wide and afraid. "I've never done this before."

He'd taken her further than she'd wanted to go. He folded his arms over his chest and tried to ignore the flicker of shame. Further and faster. She'd never resisted, or said no, but he'd been aware that Jane would have been happy to keep their physical relationship less physical. Lovemaking had been—he frowned—awkward at best.

The memories made him uncomfortable and he pushed them away. But this time the thoughts refused to return to their small box at the back of his consciousness. They intruded with images that made him wonder if he'd crossed the line from ardent suitor to horny jerk with her. She'd been a young nineteen, he admitted to himself. He looked at her, sitting on the edge of his sofa, her fingers twisting together. She still looked young.

But nine years had passed. She had grown up. She was a teacher and a mother. That reminded him. Billie.

"How old is Billie?" he asked.

Jane swallowed as her stomach flipped over. Why did he want to know? "Eight."

He drew his eyebrows together as if doing the math. "And her father?"

"What?"

"Billie told me she's never met him. You and he want it that way?"

Oh, God forgive her, she didn't have the strength to say it. Not now. Not today. "It seemed like the best decision at the time."

"A kid needs a dad."

"Billie and I are getting by."

"She deserves more than just getting by."

"That's why I brought her home."

"Home?" His mouth curled into a cruel twist. "I'm surprised you'd still think of Orchard as home."

"I grew up here."

"And left."

And left. It always came back to that. "I'm sorry," she said, wondering how many times she would speak those exact words. "I never meant to hurt you. And you were right, this morning. I never did think about what my leaving would mean to the bank. You had all those responsibilities. I should have handled the situation differently."

"Yeah, a note would have been a nice touch. Maybe you could have left it on the church steps, weighed down by your bouquet and the engagement ring."

However well deserved, his sarcasm hurt. She didn't flinch, but had a bad feeling her pain showed in her eyes. She looked away. "I meant that I should have told you about my doubts when they first occurred to me. I should have talked to you. I apologize for that."

"I don't care enough to be angry or enough to forgive you, so seek your absolution elsewhere, little girl."

She stood up and planted her hands on her hips. "I am not a child."

His gaze raked her from the top of her head down to her sandal-clad feet. "You might not look like one, but you're still acting like one. Saying 'I'm sorry' doesn't mean a damn thing to me, Jane. What are you really here for?"

"I'm going to be living next door. We have to—"

"We don't have to do anything."

He straightened and glared down at her. Fire burned in his brown eyes—flames born of pain and suffering and a desire to exact revenge. She wanted to run—it had always been her way of facing problems—but the time for running was long past. She'd returned to Orchard because she needed Adam to forgive her, and because her daughter and her daughter's father deserved to know each other. But to get to that, she and Adam had to lay the past to rest. A high price for a family, she saw now.

"You used to frighten me," she said, fighting the urge to retreat and holding her ground. "But not anymore. Not your temper or your demands or your—" Her gaze dropped to his mouth, then back to his eyes. "You can't tell me what to do."

"Is that what this is about?" he asked, taking a step closer to her.

Back up, her mind screamed. Her muscles tensed to respond to the message, but she stiffened and remained in place. "What do you mean?"

"Don't play games, Jane." His gaze traveled over her face, then stopped at her mouth. "Years ago you wanted pretend passion. A boy, not a man. Is that why you've come home? To see if the woman likes me any better than the girl did?"

"No. I never—"

He reached out and grabbed her arms. Before she could catch her breath, he pulled her up against him. Her breasts flattened against his chest as he clutched her upper arms and trapped her hands between them.

She braced herself for the fury, fully expecting to pay a high price for her defiance. She waited for rage and violence. Instead it was the impact of coming up against her past that caused her to sag against him.

Her sharp intake of air was silenced when his lips touched hers. He kissed her hard, punishing her with the pressure, moving back and forth quickly, without consideration for her pleasure, or even comfort. Before she could protest or even begin to pull away, the kiss softened. Slowly he withdrew, until they barely touched. Familiar, she thought, as his lips brushed hers. Familiar and welcome and wonderful.

The soft contact enticed her. He teased, allowing their lips to join, then withdrawing until only the air whispered against her sensitized mouth. Instead of holding her trapped, his hands began to rub her arms, moving from shoulder to elbow. Against her palm, his heart beat steady, the pace gradually increasing to match the rhythm of her own.

Men had kissed her, she thought as he swept his tongue across her bottom lip, but those memories paled by comparison with the reality of Adam's touch. He had been her first, her only lover. It had been his kisses that had given rise to young passion. But that girl had grown up, she realized as she opened for him. He no longer frightened her that way.

Despite her parted lips, he continued to trace a wet line around her mouth. First the outside, then the inside, teasing, tempting, but never entering. A low moan escaped her. She shifted back far enough to free her hands, then slid them up his arms, across his shoulders and around him until she could hold him close. Her fingers reached the coffee-colored silk of his hair. Sensibly short strands tickled her fingers.

She knew this man. The scent of him. And the feel of him. Those tiny hairs on the back of his neck, the strong line of his jaw, the sensation of a day's worth of stubble rasping against her fingertips. The taste of him. He grew tired of his game and slipped into her mouth.

"Yes," she whispered.

At last. His tongue moved delicately past her teeth to meet and embrace hers. They touched, tip to tip, then circled, rough to smooth. Long strokes imitated the act of love, whirlpool-like plunges dueled. He tasted exactly as she remembered. Sultry sweetness with a hint of the forbidden. His hands dropped from her arms to her waist, then lower and behind to her derriere. He cupped her curves.

Yes, she cried in her mind. She wanted him. He'd aroused her before, but always there had been the fear. Her body wasn't curvy enough. She didn't know how to please a man. She felt embarrassed by his looking and touching her.

She hadn't been taught by anyone but him, and now the fear was gone. She was a woman, ready to be taken by this man. When he pulled her hips close, she felt the length and breadth of his arousal. An answering heat rose between her thighs. He had readied her with a kiss.

"Adam," she breathed against his mouth.

It was as if his name had broken the spell that held him next to her. He stiffened in her embrace; his arms fell to his sides.

Don't, she thought frantically, as the haze of passion lifted and allowed her to recall the difficulty of their situation. He still hated her for what she'd done to him. She continued to withhold the truth of his daughter from him. An impossible circumstance.

She stepped back before he could completely reject her. Her eyes searched his, hoping for a lingering sign of arousal, a hint that his wall of control had been bridged. He stood tall, with his arms at his sides and his hands balled up in fists. There was nothing soft about him. Nothing forgiving. If it were not for the memory of his body next to hers, the sweet taste his tongue had left inside her mouth, she would have wondered if she'd imagined the moment.

Coldness invaded his eyes, stealing away whatever desire might have stayed. He stared directly at her. "That should never have happened."

Of course it should have, Jane thought touching her fingertips to her still-trembling lips. Didn't he get it? She wasn't afraid of him. A liberating thought, heady even. No fear. For months, years after she'd left Orchard, she'd carried around the weight of that fear. Her uncertainty, her knowledge that she wasn't woman enough to please Adam or strong enough to tell him what she was feeling had convinced her that she was so much less than everyone else. As she had survived and raised a child on her own, her confidence had grown, but she'd still shied away from men.

Her gaze dropped to his mouth. They should do it again, she decided, wondering if the passion and fire had been real. Had he felt it? Her stomach and thighs tingled with the memory of him pressing hard against her. He *had* felt something; she'd been touched by the proof of that.

She thought about stepping closer, of trying to tempt him. Even as she took one step toward him, he spun and walked to the window.

"I don't have an explanation," he said, staring out into the darkness. "I don't usually lose control like that. It won't happen again."

He sounded so angry and final. His words battered at her newly discovered passion until she was ashamed. He'd wanted to punish her, make her suffer as he had. The kiss had been about retribution, not affection or desire. The thrill and excitement began to die within her. She tried to hang on to the feelings. The moment had been important to her. Don't let it go, she told herself.

It was too late.

Defeat hunched her shoulders and she folded her arm over her chest. "See that it doesn't," she said, in a flash o self-preservation, then wondered if he knew she lied.

He stood so proudly, she thought as she stared at hi back. Strong and broad. A man. He wore his power easily The athletic prowess from his youth had stayed with him adding grace to his movements. Tonight, however, he stood stiffly. The past weighed on him.

"Once your furniture arrives and you move into your own house, I don't want to see you again."

It hurt, she thought with a flash of surprise. It hurt tha he could dismiss her so easily. Not seeing her wasn't an op tion. Not if he wanted to get to know his daughter. But the Adam didn't know he had a daughter. She'd have to tel him.

Not yet. She again touched her fingers to her lips. The sensitive skin quivered from his kiss. In a few days. Wher she was stronger. When the bridge between them didn't seem so long and dangerous.

"Good night, Adam."

"Good night."

She turned to leave. Before she could open the door to the hallway, he spoke.

"Jane?"

"Yes?" Oh stop, she told herself, hating how hopeful she sounded.

"It won't happen again."

The kiss. Of course not. Why would he have though she'd think otherwise?

"I know." That was the hell of it really. She did know.

Chapter Six

He was as good as his word, Jane thought. He and the moving company.

The large van containing all of her worldly possessions had shown up promptly at ten Monday morning. Adam had disappeared from her life a couple of hours earlier. From the bay window in the guest room, she'd watched him walk out the front door and around the house toward the garage. He hadn't looked up at her or back at the house. Either he hadn't sensed her watching him or he hadn't cared. Probably a little of both.

It was Friday, now. Jane brushed her bangs out of her eyes and stared at the stack of books in front of her. She was alphabetizing them as she placed them on the shelves. She sighed. Okay. She was alone; she could admit the truth to herself, if to no one else. She was lonely.

Returning to Orchard had sounded so noble when she'd lain awake in her bed in San Francisco. She would unite father and daughter, be a wonderful teacher, provide her child with a warm, loving and stable environment. When she'd imagined the scene, there had been a Joan of Arc sort of glow around her head in reward for all her good deeds.

Reality turned out to be very different. She hadn't seen Adam since Sunday, so she wasn't making any progress on that front. School wouldn't start until early September. She'd planned her lessons before she'd left San Francisco. And as for Billie— She smiled. She'd love to take the credit for her daughter fitting in so well, but it was all Billie's doing. Adam had sent, via Charlene, information on the local softball league. By Tuesday Billie had been enrolled in the park's summer-camp program and assigned to a team. She came home every day with new battle scars from her activities and tales of friends made and adventures experienced.

Jane rose to her feet and walked from the den to the kitchen. White tiles gleamed from her thorough scrubbing. Food filled the pantry. Everything had been unpacked and put away.

Maybe she shouldn't have worked so quickly, she thought as she leaned against the counter and stared out the kitchen window into the backyard. But it had been hard not to. She wasn't sleeping well. Only by staying busy could she keep Adam and the kiss they had shared from her mind.

Back in San Francisco, she'd had friends and activities to fill her time. Here she knew people but—she shook her head—they would ask questions she couldn't answer. Not until Adam knew the truth. She could go see Charlene, but the older woman had her own life. She was currently planning a trip to Greece. A movie about an older woman finding if not love then certainly passion in the beautiful islands had inspired her to travel to the Mediterranean. In addition, Billie had mentioned something about Charlene arranging for a few of her trucker friends to stop by before she left. Jane grinned. She wouldn't want to touch that one.

She remembered the time she had casually asked the other woman about her visiting male friends. Charlene's frank lecture of the joys of sex had left her blushing for days. When she'd told Adam about the conversation, he'd laughed for several minutes, then had teased that it was her own fault for inquiring. When she'd protested, he'd pulled her close and offered to illustrate some of Charlene's more interesting points. She'd turned away, embarrassed and scared and he'd—

She groaned. It always came back to Adam. Stop thinking about him, she ordered herself. She forced herself to mentally create a list of other chores she could do to fill her time. There was always the mending. Billie destroyed her clothes on a regular basis. And she could tackle the attic. Her mother had left several boxes up there.

She glanced at the clock. Almost twelve. She should do something about lunch. That would fill a few minutes.

The back door banged open and Billie stormed into the kitchen.

"Mom! I'm home!" she announced as she flew across the room and into her mother's arms.

"So I see." Jane hugged her close. "It's early."

"Friday's only a half day at camp and I don't have a game until tomorrow." Billie looked up at her, her baseball hat pulled down so low, she had to crane her neck to see below it. "Can you make cupcakes for after the game?"

"Sure."

Billie grinned. "Great. I told the guys you would." She stepped back and dug out the ever-present softball from her dirty red shorts pocket. "Sometimes boys are dumb," she said.

Jane chuckled. "Interesting observation. Why do you say that?"

"They tell me I can't do stuff 'cuz I'm a girl."

"So?"

"So I threatened to beat them up." She tossed the softball into the air.

If Jane hadn't been present at Billie's birth, she might have questioned whether or not this child was really hers. "Don't throw that in the house," she warned. "Why not just do what they say you can't and show them up that way?"

"Maybe." She walked to the refrigerator and pulled open the door. "I'm hungry."

"I was just about to make lunch."

Billie peered inside the fridge. "Something good, okay?"

"Are you insulting my cooking?"

"Mo-om. I just thought we could forget about vegetables until dinner. It's Friday."

"So?"

"So, I just thought. You know. For a treat. How come we don't have that center thing in our kitchen like Adam does?"

Jane blinked at the quick change in subject. "Do you mean the island?"

"Yeah." Billie shut the fridge and stared around the room. "It has stools to sit at, like a restaurant counter. I eat there at breakfast."

"What?" Her heart lurched. "I thought you were visiting Charlene in the mornings before camp."

"Nope." Billie smiled, unconcerned. "I went over there Monday, but she said she wasn't a morning person and that I should have breakfast with Adam."

Jane felt faint. "You've been there every day this week?"

"Yup."

She didn't sound too panicky. Billie and Adam eating breakfast together? Every day? It was inconceivable. On Monday Billie had bounced out of bed, her normal cheerful self, and had asked if she could visit Charlene before camp. Jane had known the other woman would have shooed the girl away if she was being a pest—but never would she have imagined Charlene sending her to Adam. Here she'd been worried about him having a chance to get to know Billie and it was already happening right under her nose.

"So, Mom, can we have a center island in our kitchen?"

"We don't have room here, honey."

Jane forced her thoughts away from father and daughter sharing a meal and studied the small room. Counters lined two walls, with a built-in stove in the middle of one and the sink in the middle of the other. Opposite the stove stood the refrigerator; opposite the sink, the old-fashioned Formica table with four matching vinyl chairs. She remembered that set from her childhood. The yellow, green-and-orange abstract shapes had reminded her of Crispy Critters breakfast cereal. Her mother had hated the set, but her father had picked it out, so she'd lived with it. Jane recalled that as she ate her solitary breakfast each morning, she used to make up stories about the imaginary animals running across the Formica tabletop.

"But I like the island." Billie tossed her ball in the air and caught it. "Maybe we could make the kitchen bigger."

Jane pulled off the cap and ruffled her daughter's bangs. "One, don't throw your ball inside. And two, we don't have the money. Besides, it's just the two of us. We don't need more room. We already have three bedrooms."

"I like Adam's house better."

So do I, Jane thought, thinking of the large graceful mansion built before the turn of the century. The inside had been modernized, but each room maintained an elegance that couldn't be manufactured today. By comparison, her house was small and dark. Still, it was home to her. The price was right and when she got a couple of paychecks in the bank, she'd be able to make some changes. Her mother had often talked about remodeling. She'd even made some sketches of the new room layouts and had pinned swatches of carpet and wallpaper to the sheets. Jane's father had vetoed the idea, telling his wife that her foolish plans were just a waste of time and money. Her mother had turned away without a word and the sketches had disappeared, never to be mentioned again.

"It's a nice house," Jane said, pushing away her memories. "And ours will be, too. In time. Now you go play while I make lunch."

"What are we going to do this afternoon?"

"What would you like?"

"The pool." Brown eyes glowed with excitement. "And ice cream."

"I think we can manage that."

"All right!" Billie raised her arm and held her hand open. Jane hit it with her own, then paused for the high-five to be returned. "You're the best."

"Thank you. You're somewhat of an exceptional child yourself."

"I know." Billie grinned, then ran from the room.

Jane pulled out sandwich fixings and the salad she'd been planning on having for herself. After spooning the lettuce and vegetable mixture into two bowls, she used raisins to make eyes, Chinese noodles for hair and a ribbon of honey-mustard dressing for a mouth. If the plate looked interesting enough, Billie often forgot that salad meant vegetables. It wasn't that she didn't like green food, it was more that she felt it was her job to protest eating them. Kids, Jane thought with affection and a flash of longing that she could have had four more just like Billie. It would have been a handful, but more than worth the effort. Her daughter brought her joy and fulfillment. She gave her all the love and— *Crash!*

"Billie?" Jane called as she wiped her hands on a dish towel and walked out of the kitchen. "I told you not to throw your ball inside. What have you broken?"

"Nothing." But the small girl stood beside the living room coffee table and stared at the broken remains of what used to be a glass. "It slipped."

"You didn't throw your ball?"

Billie shuffled her feet. "Not really."

Jane waited.

The girl sighed. "Yeah, Mom, I threw it." Her shoulders slumped in a defeated gesture. "I'm sorry."

"Thank you for apologizing. However, sorry doesn't replace the glass. We've been over this before. No ball throwing in the house."

"I know." The words came out as a whisper. "Here." She held out her ball.

Jane took it.

"Where do you want me?" Billie asked.

"The hallway. Facing the back wall."

Billie shuffled forward slowly, out of the living room, then down the hall until she reached the far wall. She sank to the floor and stared at the blank space. "How long?"

Jane glanced at her watch. "Ten minutes."

Billie leaned her forehead against the wall. "I really didn't mean to do it, Mom."

"A time-out means no talking."

"Sorry."

Parenting was tough, Jane thought as she moved back into the kitchen and set the timer for ten minutes. The punishment hurt her as much as her daughter, but Billie wouldn't believe that for about fifteen or twenty more years. After sweeping up the broken glass, she continued with the lunch. She finished the last sandwich when the timer went off. There was a shuffling noise in the hall.

Billie appeared at the doorway. Tears created two clean streaks down her freckled cheeks. Her lower lip thrust out as she swallowed.

Automatically Jane held out her arms. Billie flung herself against her mother and held on tightly. "I still love you," Jane murmured against her hair. "You'll always be my favorite girl."

"I'm sorry, Mom," Billie said, then hiccuped. "I didn't mean to break anything."

It was the stress of moving, Jane thought as she blinked away her own tears. Usually punishment didn't faze Billie, except that she found the time-outs boring. But sometimes, like today, they affected her deeply. With her bubbly personality and outgoing nature, it was easy to forget that she was still just an eight-year-old little girl.

"Let's forget about it and eat lunch. Okay?"

"Okay." Billie raised herself up on tiptoe and gave her a salty kiss. "I love you, Mommy."

"And I love you."

Jane gave her a last squeeze and pushed her toward the table. Billie looked at the salad and then at her. A tentative smile tugged one corner of her mouth. "I'm not fooled by the clown face."

"But you'll eat it."

Billie stuck a raisin in her mouth. "Maybe."

Jane poured lemonade for both of them and chuckled. Despite the mishaps, parenting was worth it. She felt sorry for people who couldn't have children in their lives. The ones who were infertile or never married or—

The pitcher slipped from her grasp and she barely caught it. What about the people who didn't know they had children? Guilt swept over her; the strong wave threatened to pull her under.

Adam. He had a child he didn't know about. Apparently Billie had already taken it upon herself to get better acquainted with her own father. Oh, please God, what was she supposed to do about the mess she'd made of everything? She had to tell him. And soon. But how? What would he say? What would Billie say? She preached that honesty was the best policy, but she'd told the biggest lie of all. What was she going to do now?

Billie glanced at her. "Aren't you eating?"

"What?" Jane stared down at her full plate. "Of course." She took a bite of her sandwich.

"What are we going to do until we can go swimming?" Billie asked.

"What do you mean?"

"You know, we can't go in the water until our food has digested. We'll get cramps and drown." She made gagging noises and clutched her throat. "I'm drowning. Save me, save me. Ahhhgg!"

"We could walk around town."

"Can we visit Charlene?"

"Not today." Jane thought about those truckers due to arrive at any time. "Maybe we could—"

The idea popped into her mind fully formed. She couldn't. She shouldn't. She bit into her sandwich and chewed. It was wrong. No, not wrong. In fact she had every right to be there. It was, after all, a business.

"We need to go to the bank," she said.

"Bor-ring."

"I have to open a new checking account and we need to move your college fund out here."

Billie sat up straight. "I have money?"

"For college."

"Oh. But maybe I could—"

"No."

"But you didn't let me—"

"No."

"What if I don't want to go to college?"

Jane smiled sweetly. "Baseball scouts go to college games."

Billie nibbled on a Chinese noodle. "I'm going."

"I knew you'd say that."

"Do I have to come with you to the bank?"

"Yes."

"Where's the bank?"

"In town."

"Which one is it?"

"There's only one. Barrington First National."

Billie frowned. "That's Adam's name."

"It's his bank."

"Here are the changes you requested, Mr. Barrington."

Adam stared blankly at the folder.

"From the loan committee meeting on Monday," his secretary reminded him patiently.

"Of course, Edna." He took the offered pages and smiled. "I'll look at them this afternoon."

She raised her penciled eyebrows until they disappeared under the sprayed fringe of hair that curled to precisely the midpoint of her forehead. "When else?" she asked.

"What? Oh, the reports. Yes, I always read them on Friday afternoon. You're right." He glanced at his watch. "On time, as usual. Thank you."

Edna's narrow lips pursed together. Her heavy makeup and the fitted long narrow dresses and jackets she wore made her look like a time traveler from 1940. She'd been with him since he'd taken over the bank and with his father for who knows how many years before that.

"Are you feeling all right, Mr. Barrington?" she asked.

Despite the fact she'd known him since his diaper days, she always addressed him formally. After fifteen years, he'd given up trying to break through to her softer side. He'd begun to suspect she didn't have one.

"I am a little scattered," he admitted.

She nodded as if to agree. "You don't want to talk about it, do you?" She asked the question because it was polite, but her folded arms and the fact that she was inching toward his office door told him that she really didn't want his confidences.

"No, Edna, I don't."

"Well, I'm here." She smiled quickly and let it fade. "I'll be at my desk, Mr. Barrington. If you're sure you're all right?"

"I'm fine."

"Good."

She ducked out before he could begin his confession. Adam grinned and turned in his chair to stare out the big window behind his desk. Green grass stretched out on this side of the building. The bank sat on a corner and backed up on the town square. Pecan trees, the oblong fruit just beginning to turn brown, provided shade. Several employees sat in the early afternoon sun, taking their lunch break outdoors.

Orchard was a long way from New York or Los Angeles or Chicago, the places where his university friends had gone after Harvard. At one time he'd thought about leaving for the big city. But his parents had died at the end of his freshman year while he was at Harvard. He'd been the oldest son, and the Barrington heir. With two young siblings to care for, a bank to keep in business and an eccentric aunt who needed as much supervision as she provided, there had been no room for dreams about moving somewhere else. He didn't mind that his fate had been set when he was born, and sealed by the premature death of his parents. But sometimes he thought about what it would have been like if he'd been able to grow up at his own pace. The parties and social events of his freshman year had given way to extra classes and study. He'd graduated a semester early so that he could return home and take over the bank.

Turning back toward his desk, he picked up the report Edna had left him. He knew he was driving his staff crazy. In the last few days he'd wandered around in a fog, upsetting a routine they'd all grown used to. He knew the cause— as much as he hated to admit the fact that he couldn't drive her from his mind as easily as he'd driven her from his house.

Jane.

He stared at a portrait of his father hanging on the opposite wall. "Did Mom ever give you this much trouble?" he asked quietly. Not that Jane was troubling him, he amended quickly. He barely thought about her at all. And when he did, it was with completely justified anger and indignation. He hadn't forgiven her for her childish behavior and the damage she'd done all those years ago. In fact . . .

Adam shook his head. He was a lousy liar. Always had been. It was his damn Southern upbringing. Too much talk about being a gentleman and the dance lessons they'd made him attend between football practices. He grinned as he remembered Charlene's discussion with Billie about charm school. The girl had been adamant in her refusal, and her mother had backed her up. He wondered if Billie would stay a tomboy long or if the pressure of society would force her to conform. Just this morning, she'd regaled him with stories about her quest for the perfect curve ball. He'd informed her that he hoped she found one that didn't destroy windows.

She'd wrinkled her nose at him. The quick gesture, a mirror of what Jane had done when he'd teased her, had made his resolve to forget falter. Billie had slipped past his guard too easily as well, he thought. With a little help.

On Monday, the morning after— He refused to think about kissing Jane, he told himself firmly. It hadn't meant anything. It had been a flash of temper or an attempt to prove to her that she couldn't affect him. He hadn't kissed her because he'd wanted to. After what she'd done, she was lucky he hadn't run her out of town. Showing up after all this time, with no warning. He didn't care, of course. She meant nothing to him now. He wanted—

Stop thinking about her, he commanded himself. Billie. That was safe. He recalled last Monday morning. He'd been drinking his morning coffee. Charlene had found Billie lurking outside his back door.

"I wanted to say hi to Adam," she'd said. He'd put down his paper, not sure if he welcomed the interruption or not.

"Adam has a very rigid schedule in the morning," Charlene had answered. "He doesn't like to be disturbed." She laughed then and held open the door. "Go right in."

He'd been cursed, he thought, toying with the engraved letter opener that had been his grandfather's. Cursed to endure the women in his life. Charlene. God, someone could write a book about her. And now Billie. A four-foot-nothing bundle of energy who had already wormed her way into his life. She was funny and intriguing as hell. But not as intriguing as Jane.

He pulled out his right-hand drawer and glanced at the brochure lying on top. The neighboring town sponsored a Triple-A baseball team. They were home for the next couple of weeks. Maybe he could get tickets and take Billie. She'd like that. And if her mother wanted to tag along...

Adam slammed the drawer shut. Was he crazy? He didn't want to see Jane. And even if he did, hadn't he learned his lesson? The woman had publicly humiliated him. The only emotion left was anger, and even that didn't matter. He refused to feel anything else. He couldn't. It cost too much.

But the rage, so easily tapped into over the weekend, had faded with the passing week. It became harder and harder to focus on the past and what she had done and not wonder what had drawn her back to Orchard. Why now? Why here? He sensed some secret behind her carefully worded explanations. Had she returned for absolution? A second chance?

He shook his head. Not that. She hadn't cared enough the first time. Why the hell would he think she'd want to try again? And if she did—he picked up the letter opener and stared at the engraving—he wasn't fool enough to get his heart broken a second time. He wasn't interested in Jane Southwick. Not now. Not ever.

Adam rose from his desk and walked to his door. After pulling it open, he stepped into the hallway. To his left were the rest of the offices, the supply cabinet and the lunch room that was only used in the winter. To the right was the bank. A couple of people stood in line. Old man Grayson and his wife hovered by the safety deposit box cage, waiting to get inside. Every couple of weeks or so, they took their box into one of the private cubbyholes and spent a few minutes with their personal treasures. For as long as he could remember, they'd been coming here. He'd give a sizable chunk of his

estate to know exactly what was in the box. As a kid, he and
his friends had speculated about everything from stolen gold
to body parts.

A flash of movement by the front door caught his attention. He turned. And drew in a sharp breath. It was as if his
thoughts had conjured her from thin air.

Jane held the door open for her daughter. Billie skipped
in and looked around. Adam slipped behind one of the old-
fashioned pillars, then cursed himself for being a coward.
This was *his* bank, dammit. He had every right to be here.
But he stayed where he was and watched them.

Like Edna, Jane was a throwback to another time. While
she didn't wear the heavy makeup his secretary favored,
she'd never fully embraced the concept of wearing pants or
shorts. A white T-shirt, with a V front that made him wonder what happened when she bent over, covered her upper
body. A flowing skirt in a feminine print fluttered around
her thighs and fell to mid-calf. The long hair that, years before, had haunted his thoughts until his hands ached to
touch it and his body had throbbed for hers, had been tied
back. No braid this time, but a ponytail that swung with
each step.

She looked young, he thought. Innocent. Incapable of the
deception she had committed. For the first time he allowed
himself to wonder why. Why had she left him? Why
couldn't he forget her? In the nine years she'd been gone,
he'd managed to push her to the back of his mind. She'd
been home less than a week, and she haunted every moment of his day. He must exorcise this ghost from his life,
he told himself grimly. There wasn't room for her anymore.

Chapter Seven

Jane glanced around the bank and sighed with relief. No Adam. Funny how at the house, the decision to go see him had sounded like such a good idea. Yet the reality of coming face-to-face with the person who would least like to see her made her squirm.

She glanced around at the old-fashioned lobby. Not that much had changed. On one side of the building stood the teller windows, on the other, the desks for the various departments. The marble floor had been imported from Italy and would outlast the town. The walls looked like they'd received a recent coat of paint, and the woodwork gleamed from constant care. Everything was exactly as she remembered. Even the old couple waiting by the safety deposit box cage looked as if they'd stepped out of a Norman Rockwell painting. *Going Banking,* she thought, giving the imaginary artwork a title, then giggling nervously. Beside her Billie danced from one foot to the other.

"This place is cool," Billie said, her loud voice drifting up to the arched ceiling and echoing.

"Shh," Jane warned, before her daughter could exercise her vocal cords in a serious way. "People are trying to do business here. No talking."

"You're talking," Billie pointed out.

Jane prayed for patience. Taking a deep breath, she located the desk with the New Accounts plaque and headed that way.

The woman behind the desk looked up and smiled. Then her smile faded, and a faint frown appeared between her eyebrows. Jane struggled to put a name to the semifamiliar face. Oh, no. Old Miss Yarns. She'd taught Jane's fourth-grade Sunday School class and had been stern with her requirements and free with her discipline.

"Jane? Jane Southwick?" Miss Yarns rose to her feet and held out her hand. "It has been several years, has it not?"

"Yes, Miss Yarns." The walls of this old institution would probably crack and fall if Miss Yarns used a contraction, Jane thought. "Nine. Years." She grabbed Billie's hand and drew her closer, as much for protection as to be polite. "My daughter, Belle Charlene."

Billie glared at her mother. "Billie," she said, then smiled. "I bet you can slide real good on this floor, huh?" she said, staring at the marble tiles. "You ever take your shoes off and—"

"No." Miss Yarns blanched and resumed her seat. "I had heard you were back in town, Jane. Do you want to open an account with Barrington First National?"

No, Miss Yarns, I came over to New Accounts because of the stimulating company. "Yes," she said demurely, sitting in one of the cloth-covered chairs in front of the woman's desk and pointing to tell Billie to do the same. "I have an account in San Francisco that I've closed." She slipped her purse off her shoulder and onto her lap, then pulled out a cashier's check.

"Very well." She reached into her desk and withdrew an application form. Miss Yarns didn't believe in rings or bracelets, and she would rather be flogged than wear earrings. Just a plain gold watch and a suit so conservative she'd look at home sitting in on the Supreme Court. "Will this be a joint account?"

"No, it's—" Oh, God. Jane clamped her mouth shut. It was too late. Miss Yarns's perfectly plucked brows rose, and she glanced from Billie, bouncing in her seat, to Jane's bare left hand. Damn small towns, Jane thought. And herself for being fool enough to come back.

"You will be the only person signing on this account." It wasn't a question.

"Yes."

"I see."

They should have gone to the pool right after lunch and taken their chances with drowning. It would have been more fun.

"And the name on the account?"

"Mine."

"I know that, dear. The *last* name."

Jane took a deep breath. In San Francisco, no one had known her well enough to realize Southwick was her maiden name. Everyone assumed she was divorced. Or didn't care. But this wasn't San Francisco. It was her hometown. Maybe Miss Yarns would think she'd gone back to her maiden name because— Yeah, right. It shouldn't matter what this old relic thought of her. In a way it didn't. But rumors got started so easily. And Billie would be the one hurt by them.

"Southwick," she said at last. "Jane Southwick."

Those perfect brows rose a notch higher, as the older woman glanced speculatively at Billie. "I see."

Did she? Jane wondered. What if the town of Orchard figured out the truth before she got the courage to tell Adam?

"Why does that lady keep looking at me?" Billie asked in a stage whisper.

Miss Yarns had the grace to flush slightly and glance away.

"I don't know," Jane lied, knowing she could never explain this to her daughter. Not yet, anyway.

"Need any help here?"

Jane looked up and saw Adam standing beside his employee's desk.

"Adam!" Billie scrambled out of her chair and raced to him. With the trust of a child who knows she will never be allowed to fall, she launched herself upward. He caught her under her arms and swung her around.

"What are you doing here, peanut?"

"Peanut?" Billie wrinkled her nose. "I'm *not* a peanut."

"That's right." He tugged on the bill of her baseball cap. "You're a soon-to-be famous pitcher of our champion Little League."

Jane swallowed against the lump in her throat. It had happened so quickly, she thought. In just five days, they'd become friends. Was it Billie's outgoing nature, Adam's charm or was it genetic? Did they, on some subconscious level, recognize themselves as family? She *had* to tell him, tell them both. Soon. But not yet. There was more at stake than friendship. More than Adam's right to know he was a father. Billie, and how all this would affect her, was Jane's most important consideration.

"You haven't answered my question," Adam said, shifting Billie until she leaned against his chest. Her arms wrapped around his neck and he supported her weight with his left arm. Jane wasn't sure if it was in deference to summer or the fact that it was Friday, but he'd abandoned his suit jacket. His white shirt fit perfectly, the long sleeves showing the ripple of his muscles as he shifted Billie's weight. "What are you doing here?"

"Banking. We're opening an account."

Miss Yarns had watched the greeting and subsequent conversation. Obviously Billie and Adam knew each other well. Her mouth had opened slightly, as her jaw had dropped farther and farther down.

"Billie is a very outgoing child," Jane said, hoping the other woman wouldn't notice the similarities between the man and the little girl.

"I see that." Her face sharpened as lines of disapproval pulled her mouth straight. "Perhaps we could get on with his form. Your place of employment?"

"I'll handle this, Miss Yarns."

The older woman glanced up at her employer. "Mr. Barrington, I assure you I am entirely capable—"

"I know," he said, with an easy grin. "As a favor. Please."

"Well. If you put it like that, I am sure I cannot say no." She rose slowly from her chair and brushed her hands against her skirt. "I will take my lunch now. If it is convenient?"

"Of course."

She walked away as if her back were made of steel. Jane bit the inside of her lip to keep from smiling. No doubt the old biddy was convinced something sinful was going to happen in front of God and everybody, not to mention on *her* desk.

Jane raised her eyes to Adam's face. Their gazes locked for a second, and he winked. The playful moment, stolen between the reality of their mutual past and present, caught her unaware. She smiled back. In that blink of time—before he remembered who she was and what she had done—they connected.

The heat that filled her chest and radiated out along her arms and legs wasn't about sex. It was about the comfortable, the comforting and the familiar. This is the Adam she had adored while growing up. The man with the quick wit

and the ability to laugh at everyone, including himself
These were the flashes of fun, between his days of respon
sibility, that had made her fall in love and want to be every
thing for him. He took care of those around him, so sh
never worried about him not being a good husband or fa
ther. It was that he rarely took time to be anything else. Tha
had frightened her the most. What if he had turned out t
be like her father? She too would have lost her dreams
She'd been too young to even have many dreams, let alon
believe in them.

But he hadn't turned into her father, she realized as h
looked away and whispered something to Billie. The need t
control was still there, as strong as ever, but so was the jo
and the humor. Had she been wrong to not trust him? Wa
she wrong now to want to try?

"All right." Adam set Billie on the corner of the desk
and sat in Miss Yarns's chair. "Let's see if I remember hov
to do this. You're opening a checking account?" He looke
up at Jane.

She nodded.

"I can do that. I think. Address. I know that. Occupa
tion. Teacher. Employer." He filled in most of the card
asking for her social security number and the new phon
number at her house. His thick dark hair showed signs of
recent cut. One stubborn lock slipped down on his fore
head. Billie leaned toward him, her hand casually resting o
his shoulder. They looked right together.

As he wrote the information in his neat script, joked wit
her daughter and tossed her the occasional casual smile
Jane wanted to scream. This was the first time she'd seer
him since the kiss. He was acting as if nothing had hap
pened between them. As if that passionate moment hac
been meaningless. Could he just put it behind him? Did h
kiss so many women that he could easily forget one or two
Or was it Jane he was so quick to forget?

"That seems to be everything. Do you want to look at the check design book?" he asked.

"I'll just take the standard ones."

"Do they have baseball checks?" Billie asked.

"Not yet." Adam smiled at her. "Maybe I'll call the printing company and make that suggestion." He gave the form a once-over, then frowned. "You want the account in your maiden name?"

As unexpectedly as the good humor and friendliness had arrived, they faded. His mouth thinned and the lines of his body stiffened.

"Yes." She looked around the bank, at the tellers watching their exchange, at the interested faces of the people standing in line, to Billie staring intently. This wasn't the time to tell him she'd never been married.

"What's a maiden name?" her daughter asked.

"It's the name a woman has before she gets married," Jane answered, hoping she wasn't about to dig herself a hole. "Southwick is your maiden name."

"How come girls have to take boys' names?"

Jane offered her daughter a shaky smile. "It's a tradition."

"So if you get married, you get a different last name?"

"Yes."

She thought for a moment. "What if I don't like his last name? What if it's dumb?"

"Then you can keep your own."

Adam shot her a questioning glance.

"She can if she wants to."

He raised his hands up as if to show he wasn't armed. "Hey, this is your discussion. I'm not going to say a word. Far be it from me, a mere man, to interfere."

Billie shifted on the seat and looked at her mother. "Why don't you use your married name? Was my dad's last name dumb?"

"No. It was—" She cleared her throat. Not here. Not in the bank during business hours, with half the town of Orchard watching. "I didn't want to—" It was hard to lie to her daughter. Harder, perhaps, to lie to Adam. "We'll discuss this at home."

"But I don't understand," she whined.

Rescue came from an unexpected source. "I've been wondering what's different about you today," Adam said to Billie. "You don't have your softball with you. Did you forget it?"

Billie shot Jane a glare. "I was a reptile."

"A what?" Adam asked.

"Reptile. Reptile behavior. I broke a glass."

Jane sighed in relief. The reprieve gave her time to think. She leaned forward. "I think she means disreputable behavior. Billie isn't supposed to throw her ball in the house. She broke a glass. Part of the punishment is that I keep the softball for the rest of the day."

"Bummer, huh," Billie said with a heavy sigh.

"That's what you get," he said, then made a fist and lightly tapped her chin. "You'll get it back tomorrow, in time for the game."

"You coming? I'm going to pitch."

Adam's gaze found Jane's, as if asking what she thought. Yes, please do, she answered silently to him, then turned to Billie. "Adam might be busy, honey."

"You *always* say that about people. But everybody likes me. They *want* to watch me pitch. Don't you?"

Adam grinned. "Of course."

"See." Billie placed her hands on her hips. "I told you."

"Where do you get this nerve from?" Jane asked. Then she could have slapped herself. Talk about putting her foot in it. But neither Billie nor Adam followed up on her comment.

He passed the form to her to sign, then handed her a stack of temporary checks. Their fingers came close to touching but didn't. She wanted to reach out and stroke the white cuff of his shirt. She wanted to keep him smiling at her. Instead she took the checks he offered.

"That should keep you going until the real ones come from the printer," he said. "Are there other accounts? What about your savings?"

"I don't have one."

He tried not to react, but she read the surprise on his face.

"I've been going to school to get my teaching credential," she said, her voice a little sharper than she'd intended. "And I've been working, as well. There wasn't very much left over each month. There are expenses with a child and—"

"I'm not judging you, Jane."

She leaned back in her chair and shook her head. "Sorry. I'm overreacting. I guess it's because I have this argument with my parents every time I see them."

"Grandma always tries to give Mom money and she always says no. Sometimes they cry."

Thanks for sharing, Billie, Jane thought ruefully, realizing she'd have to be more careful about what she said and did while her daughter was in the room.

"We do have Billie's college fund," she said, to change the subject. She pulled out the forms. "I guess we need to transfer this, or something. I didn't want to close the account and risk the tax status."

He took the papers. "You don't have a savings account, but Billie has a college fund?"

"Yes."

Something flickered in his brown eyes, something warm and genuine. She willed time to freeze, so that he would go on like this forever, but Billie leaned over them, her foot kicking the business card holder onto the floor and sending Miss Yarns's cards scattering in all directions.

"Oops, sorry." Billie slid to the edge of the desk and jumped to the floor. "I'll get them."

Jane watched to make sure she'd landed safely, then glanced back at Adam, but the contact had been broken. He studied the account information.

"It's pretty standard," he said. "We'll put it in her name, with you ATF."

"Fine."

"What's ATF?" Billie shoved the loose cards onto the desk and reached for the holder.

"As trustee for. It means your mom can handle the account for you."

"I want to take care of my own money."

"You can't."

"Why?"

"You're a child."

"It's for *my* college."

"When you're ready for college, then you'll have a say-so. Until then, it is being kept for you."

Billie tilted her chin up. Adam straightened in his chair.

"How do I know the money will be there? What if someone wants to spend my money?"

"No one will do that."

"How do you know?"

"I'm the bank president. It's my job to know."

Billie planted her hands on her hips. "What if *you* spend it?"

"That's against the law."

"Oh."

Identical pairs of brown eyes flashed with identical fire. Billie's cap hid most of her hair, but Jane knew the color was close, too close, to her father's. Matching shoulders squared against the opponent, similar mouths straightened.

How couldn't they know? Why didn't everyone see it? They were two peas in a pod, a matched set, father and daughter. It was as if a fist closed over her heart and began to squeeze. She was playing with two lives. What would the price of honesty be? Would she lose them both?

Billie gave in first. She looked away. "Then I guess it's okay."

"Thank you."

Billie looked at her. "I'm thirsty."

"There's a soda machine in the lunch room," Adam said, before she could respond. "It's at the end of that hallway. Go pick out what you'd like." He shrugged. "If it's all right with your mother."

"Fine. Thank you." Jane reached for her purse.

"No charge," he said. "The bank gives them to the employees."

"Cool." Billie turned to race away.

"No running in here," Jane cautioned.

"Mo-om."

"You heard me."

"Okay."

Billie moved off at a pace too slow for a run, but too fast for a walk. By the end of the teller line, she was skipping, and when she reached the hallway, she whooped loudly and raced down the slick floor.

Jane stared after her. "Sometimes I think I've failed completely with her."

"Billie's her own person."

"She is that."

She looked back at Adam, then wished she hadn't. Someone somewhere had turned a switch. The friendly man from her past had disappeared and in his place sat the cool, controlled stranger. She couldn't see the wall between them, but she felt its thickness. When she offered a tentative smile, he simply stared.

"You must be very busy," she said, clutching her purse to her chest. "I don't want to keep you."

He blinked and looked at the application form in his hands. Was he wondering about her maiden name or the existence of an ex-husband somewhere? Did she flatter herself with the question?

"You're doing a good job," he said.

"What?"

"With Billie. I can imagine how hard it is to raise a child alone."

He surprised her. She set her purse on the floor and folded her hands together on her lap. "I wanted to be self-sufficient. My parents..." She sighed. "The first couple of years, I couldn't have made it without them. Then I began to realize that I was becoming dependent. I started returning the money they sent, got a better paying job and went back to school."

"All this with a baby?"

"By then, Billie was around two." She laughed. "You can imagine what the terrible twos were like with her."

One corner of his firm mouth tilted up slightly. "I would have liked to have seen that."

His words hit her like a blow to the midsection. What would he think when he found out the truth? "Let's just say, I went through a lot of baby-sitters," she said, hoping her voice didn't tremble.

"She's a wonderful girl."

"I know."

"She reminds me of Dani at that age."

"I hadn't thought about that, but you're right." Did she look like his sister at that age, as well? Don't panic, she told herself. He wouldn't figure out the truth on his own. She still had time; just not as much as she'd thought. She collected her purse and stood up. "Thanks for everything, Adam. I appreciate the personal attention."

He rose and walked around the desk. Her foolish heart fluttered slightly. He'd always been too damn good-looking, she thought, wishing it didn't matter. Her lips tingled as if the closer proximity brought to life the remembered sensations of their kiss. Did he think about it, too? Did he lie awake at night and remember their lovemaking, all those years ago? Did he think about how different it would be now that she was grown and willing to take him on her own terms?

"Charlene said that she'd like to invite you and Billie to dinner on Sunday," he said without meeting her eyes. "Four o'clock. Can you make it?"

The invitation surprised her, but not the way he distanced himself from it. "I..." She wasn't sure she'd be ready to face Adam so soon after today. But she didn't have a choice. She had Billie to consider. "We'd love to."

Maybe another meeting with him would give her the courage to tell him the truth.

He nicked himself shaving. Adam stared in disbelief at his reflection in the mirror. Sure enough, a drop of blood formed just to the left of his chin. As he watched, it trickled down and dripped onto the bathroom counter. He hadn't done that in years. Muttering a curse, he tore off a piece of tissue and stuck it on his cut, then finished shaving. He should have gotten out while he had the chance. An old friend had called to invite him to a play in Atlanta. The old friend—a woman—had included dinner and breakfast in her invitation. He'd been tempted for less than a second.

Jane wasn't the reason he'd said no, he told himself for the hundredth time as he pulled on twill trousers and a polo shirt. He didn't give a damn if she was coming over for dinner. It was Charlene's invitation, not his. Just because his aunt entertained all her friends—except for the truckers—in his house didn't change anything. Hell, he didn't even have to show up. He could work in his study, or watch the game on TV.

That's what he'd do, he decided, as he brushed his hair, then straightened the collar on his shirt. He would watch the game. After slipping on his shoes, he started down the stairs. There was a knock.

"I'll get it," he called to Charlene who was already hard at work in the kitchen.

Just as he reached the front door, he remembered to brush the piece of tissue from his face.

"We're here," Billie said, walking in slowly, a pie balanced precariously in her hands. "Mom made fresh blueberry pie. Yum. I could smell it all morning, but she wouldn't let me have none."

"Any." Jane came in behind her daughter and offered him a shy smile.

"Any," Billie repeated. "Or none. It's the same." She thrust the pie at Adam. "Where's Charlene? I want to say hello. Then can we watch the game?"

"Billie! I told you this was a visit. No sports."

"But the Braves are playing San Francisco. That's my team. I'll *die* if I don't watch."

He took the pie. "In the kitchen," he said, jerking his head in that direction. "Then go on into the study. The TV is already on the right channel."

"Cool." She dashed away.

He stared after her. "No softball, and she's wearing a dress. I'm impressed."

"Don't be. She's wearing shorts under the dress and is convinced you have a hardball somewhere she can play with." Hazel eyes met and held his. "If you do, please don't let her get her hands on it. I can't make any promises about breakables."

"I'll keep it hidden. Please, come in."

She stepped past him, into the foyer. Her perfume followed like a soft floral breeze, teasing his senses and making him wonder what the anger had been all about. Again she offered a tentative smile. This time he returned it.

"You look beautiful." He spoke without thinking.

She blushed, but didn't look away. "Thank you."

A green-and-white dress hugged her curves from shoulder to hips, then flared out around her thighs. The off-the-shoulder sleeves left her neck bare. But it was her hair that captured his attention. For once, she'd left it long. Soft curls cascaded down her back. A small spray of tiny white flowers had been pinned over her right ear. Light makeup made her hazel eyes darken to green and her lips look full and kissable.

The kiss. He couldn't forget it, wouldn't repeat it. His gaze centered on her mouth. She'd tasted sweet, willing. Not the shy timid girl he'd remembered. He would have thought he'd miss that, when he'd kissed her. He'd been wrong. There was something to be said for experience, and a woman who wasn't afraid of what she wanted.

"Adam!" Billie called from the back of the house. "The game's already started. And *my* team just scored a run."

"I'd better go help Charlene," Jane said, reaching out and taking the pie from his hands. Their fingers brushed.

Funny thing about the past, he thought, resisting the urge to touch her face. What they had shared years before made it so easy to forget the distance they'd traveled. He'd thought he'd have to fight hating her. Perhaps he still did. But he'd never imagined he'd have to fight wanting her.

"And I should check on your daughter before she destroys something valuable."

Her tongue swept across her lower lip. His body vibrated with need.

"Charlene is waiting," she said, swaying toward him.

"Adam!" came the call.

"So is Billie."

"I guess I'll see you later."

"Yeah, later."

He stood in the foyer until she walked away, then moved toward the family room.

"Have you broken anything?" he asked as he turned into the room. Large pieces of furniture filled the L-shaped space. One end contained a pool table and wet bar. The other, a huge sectional sofa, large-screen TV and enough audio-visual equipment to stock a small store.

Billie sipped on a can of soda and shook her head. "Not yet. Pretty good, huh?"

"The best." He sat next to her on the long sofa and pulled on the bill of her cap. "That hat doesn't go with the dress."

"I'm wearing shorts." Billie pulled up her skirt to show him. "Mom can be tough about clothes, especially on Sunday. This is our compress."

Compress? "Do you mean compromise?"

"Whatever." She pointed at the screen. "Bottom of the second. Atlanta's up, but the Giants have already scored."

"There's still several innings, peanut. Don't get your hopes up."

She stuck out her tongue. He grinned. When the next batter popped a fly into left field, providing the third out, Billie crowed her pleasure.

"Told you, told you."

With that, she scooted over until she was next to him, then snuggled close to his chest. Adam sat there stiffly, not sure what to do with his arm. Finally he rested it against her slight back. She smiled up at him and sighed with contentment. Such a powerhouse, he thought with amazement, yet still a little girl. Her body felt warm against him. Small and in need of protection, although he could never tell her or her mother that.

"Am I going to talk funny?" Billie asked.

"Funny?"

"You know. 'I declare, chile, you are simply too charmin',' " she said in a fair imitation of a Southern drawl.

He chuckled, then stretched out his legs and rested his feet on the coffee table. "Probably."

"Why?"

"This is Orchard, Billie. You're going to hear people speak with accents all the time. You can't help imitating."

"My mom doesn't talk too funny, and neither do you."

"Your mother has been away for nine years. It'll come back to her. And I've never had much of an accent."

"I'm not going to, either."

"It's too late, peanut." He shook his head when she offered him a drink out of her can of soda. "Accept the fact that you'll soon be a Southern belle."

"Well, I'm *not* going to charm school."

He didn't answer. She snuggled closer and they watched the game. At the next commercial break, she pulled away and tucked her feet under her. "Adam?"

She looked serious. "What's wrong?" he asked.

"Do you remember at the bank, we talked about maiden names and dads?"

He nodded, sure he wasn't going to like what was coming.

She stared down at her drink, then up at him. Tears pooled in her dark brown eyes. She was close enough that he could hear her shallow breathing and count the freckles across her nose. The pattern reminded him of something but before he could figure out what, she sniffed.

"Billie?" He rested one hand on her shoulder. "It's all right, peanut."

"I made my mom cry."

"How?"

"I asked about my dad. I knew I shouldn't. It always makes her cry. But sometimes, I just want to know. Where is he? Doesn't he love us anymore?"

As he pulled Billie into his arms, a soft sound came from the hallway. He looked up and saw Jane standing in the doorway. The expression on her face—pure pain—stabbed at him. Before he could say anything, she turned and fled.

He continued to hold her daughter, murmuring words of comfort, but his mind raced. Obviously Jane had heard what Billie said. Obviously her ex-husband had hurt her very deeply. Obviously she still cared for the man.

Chapter Eight

"Are you all right, child?" Charlene asked as Jane hurried into the kitchen.

"What?" She stared at her friend, then tried to smile. "Oh, I'm fine."

"You look like you've seen a ghost. Now don't go getting any ideas. The Carolina Barringtons have always been too well-bred to allow ghosts in the house."

Jane moved through the kitchen and picked up the plates for dinner. "I'm a little tired. That's all."

"Mmm." Those shrewd blue eyes saw more than they were supposed to. Still Jane knew that she was safe. Despite the truckers that visited from time to time and her rather flamboyant wardrobe and ways, Charlene was too much of a lady to pry. "I thought you were going to ask Billie to set the table."

"She's...ah...Adam, that is, they're watching the ball game. I didn't want to disturb them."

"Well then, you'll need to get out the good silver. It's in the middle drawer of the hutch."

Jane nodded, then escaped from the kitchen to the quiet of the formal dining room. Lace-covered windows let in the soft, afternoon light. Underfoot, an antique Oriental carpet provided the color in the elegant room. The beautiful carved table could seat twenty, with all the leaves. Even at its smallest, it was too big for four, but Charlene liked to use the good pieces on Sunday and that meant eating in the dining room. Jane didn't mind; the formal setting, remembering which forks went where, would occupy her mind. If she tried hard, maybe she could forget Billie's conversation with Adam.

It was futile, she admitted, as she smoothed the pressed linen cloth over the table. Her daughter's pain had ignited her own. "Where is my daddy? Doesn't he love us anymore?" Her words echoed over and over again.

"I never meant to hurt you, Billie," she murmured softly, as she folded the napkins. She had hurt her though, and Adam, too. All in all, she'd botched the whole thing. Now what? Should she tell him today? Could she?

"You have to tell him soon. That's what this is all about, isn't it?"

She hadn't heard Charlene enter the room. "Yes," she said, as she continued to fold the napkins.

"You have to tell him," Charlene repeated.

"I know."

"He's going to guess, and if he doesn't, people in town will. She has too much of the Barringtons in her."

"But she doesn't really *look* like him," Jane said, hopefully, as if convincing Charlene would mean putting off the deed for another day.

"You're right. She looks like Dani."

"You think so?"

"Of course. All she needs is to be blond. She's even got the freckles."

"I never thought of that."

"Start thinking." Charlene placed a silver trivet on the table. "Sophia Yarns called me yesterday."

Jane opened the center door of the hutch and picked up a handful of flatware. "She was at the New Accounts desk at the bank."

"She wanted to know if *I* knew you were unmarried and had a child."

"She's just an old busybody."

"She's an influential member of this town. And no dummy. You think you can keep your secret after she spends an hour or two with Billie and Adam?"

"I'll make sure that doesn't happen." She placed the forks at all four places, then went back to collect the knives.

Charlene stepped next to her and laid a restraining hand on her arm. "You can't run forever."

"I know." Jane wanted to crawl away and hide, but she forced herself to look up at Charlene.

The older woman patted her gently. "He'll hate you for keeping Billie from him."

Her throat grew tight. "Yes," she whispered.

"But he *will* eventually understand."

"I hope you're right."

Charlene hugged her close. Jane leaned into the embrace. The scent of gardenias, the womanly figure, the clinking of the bracelets brought her comfort with their familiarity.

"I am right," the older woman said. "He'll forgive you. What I'm worried about is whether or not you can forgive yourself."

They had dessert on the front porch. The sounds of summer, birds, children playing, a soft breeze rustling through the leaves, lent themselves to another time when everything had been easier. If this had been the 1800s, her life would have been different, Jane thought taking a bite of blueberry pie. Back then, despite her concerns about Adam and their pending marriage, she wouldn't have run. Society and circumstances would have forced her to stay and fight for her man. Now, with the vision of hindsight, the lack of opportunity sounded heavenly. If she couldn't risk, she didn't fail. But even as the simpler time tempted her, she acknowledged that the past nine years had made her a stronger person. However much she regretted the pain she'd caused and was still going to cause, she'd arrived in the present as a mature human being. A difficult price to pay, she thought as she glanced up and met Adam's gaze.

He offered her a quick, sympathetic smile. He'd been nice ever since he'd seen her in the doorway, listening to Billie talk about her "missing" father. No doubt he had a few theories of his own as to why she'd bolted. At this moment he probably felt badly, maybe even let himself like her. All that would change as soon as she worked up the courage to tell him the truth.

"This is delightful," Charlene said, picking up her last blueberry in her fingers and popping it into her mouth. "You always did magical things with a crust."

"It's my mother's recipe. I'll pass along the compliment."

"Do that. And give her my best. I should probably call her before I leave for Greece. I've just been so busy what with my various—"

"Charlene—"

"Don't say anything—"

Adam and Jane spoke together. His aunt drew herself up straighter in her wicker chair and frowned. "Why do you always assume I'm going to say something inappropriate?"

"Because you usually do," Adam said wryly.

Billie looked up from her dessert. She'd perched herself on the steps leading up to the porch, while the adults sat around a glass and wicker table. "What's inappropriate?" she asked.

"It means—" Jane paused. "Something that's not appropriate."

"Now that's a clear definition," Adam teased.

"You think you're so clever, you try," she shot back.

"Yes, Adam," Charlene said, putting her plate on the table in front of her. "Go ahead."

"Inappropriate means something that isn't polite."

Charlene shook her head. "I was going to be very polite." She glared pointedly at Jane. "And appropriate."

"All right." Adam took another bite of pie and chewed thoughtfully. "Inappropriate."

"Yes." Billie waited patiently. "Should I go get the dictionary?"

Jane chuckled.

"Absolutely not," Adam said. "I won't be defeated by a word. It means—"

"It means that your mother and Adam think I was about to say something you're too young to hear." Charlene rose to her feet. "And they were wrong. But my feelings are already hurt, so I'm leaving." She held out her hand. "You can come with me, Billie, and help with the dishes."

"Aw, do I have to?"

"Yes. Because I found out that someone here broke one of my prize roses. And I have a feeling it was you. Not—" She glared at Jane, then at Adam. "I repeat, *not* that anyone had the good manners to tell me. I had to find out on my own. The poor thing is crushed beyond repair."

Jane stared intently at her plate and struggled not to laugh. "Charlene, I know how much you care about your roses. I meant to say something earlier. It slipped my mind."

Billie hung her head. "I'm sorry. I'm always breaking stuff."

Charlene squeezed her hand. "I forgive you. Children are supposed to break things."

"I'll be happy to reimburse you," Jane offered.

"No, thank you. But this is a good time to remind you that charm school would take care of many of her problems."

Billie rolled her eyes. "I don't want to go to charm school. It's dumb, girl stuff."

Adam leaned back in his chair and folded his arms across his chest. "Explain that to me, Charlene. You are the least conventional woman I know, yet since you've met Billie, you've been trying to turn her into the Southern ideal of a lady."

Charlene shook her head. Tendrils from the upswept style bounced off her cheeks and her long silver earrings jingled. "Power, Adam. It's all about power." She gave Billie the plates and urged her toward the door. "First you have to learn the rules, then you can break them. That's always been our strength. What was that movie? *Steel Magnolias*. Look at Jane here. Nine years ago she was a child with no direction, confused. Afraid. Now she's grown into a beautiful woman capable of taking care of herself. We're strong. We just don't want everyone to know right off."

Billie balanced the plates in her arms. "I don't understand."

"You will," Charlene said, patting her head. "Learn to be a lady and control the world."

"I'd rather learn a curve ball." Billie thrust out her lower lip. "Do I have to help with the dishes?"

Charlene nodded. "Think of it as repaying me for that rose you killed." She followed Billie inside, then turned back. "You two just sit here and talk. We'll take care of everything else."

"What do you think of Charlene's theory?" Adam asked.

"I think she's right about the rules. I tell my students that in my English classes. You have to know how to construct a sentence before you can start switching things around. As for the power—" She shrugged, then laughed. "I've never felt especially powerful. Maybe that's saved for the true Southern belles.''

He leaned forward and rested his forearms on the round glass-covered table. They sat across from each other. If she leaned forward and rested *her* forearms on the table, their hands would touch. The thought tempted her. Tonight, while Adam was warm and friendly, she found herself needing to play a dangerous game. She wanted to push a little, perhaps find out if he wanted to kiss her as much as she wanted to be kissed. His compassion made him approachable. The night made her bold. That and the knowledge that his friendliness would be gone as soon as he found out the truth.

"Why don't you see yourself as a Southern belle?" he asked. "You grew up here. And if I remember correctly, you went to charm school."

"And dance classes. Yes, everything appropriate."

He grinned at her word choice. Those dark eyes flashed amusement and something else that might have been caring. Lies, she thought. This fragile peace was built on lies. Just tonight, she swore, sending a promise out into the cosmos. Just this one evening when the cold stranger had disappeared and in his place sat the handsome lover she had always adored.

"And?" he prompted.

She placed her hands on the table and held on to the curved edge. Rubbing her thumb against the wicker, she stared at the glass surface. And what? "You have to be pretty to be a Southern belle," she blurted out, then died a little inside.

She didn't dare look up.

"You were always pretty," he said quietly, from the other side of the table. "Sweet and soft-spoken."

"Adam, don't. There's no need to make up things just to make me feel better. I lived my life. I know how much I did, or rather didn't, date in high school. Until you asked me out—'' She shrugged again. "Let's just say I wasn't Miss Popularity."

"Boys can be stupid, going after the obvious and common, instead of what's rare and precious."

She raised her head and looked at him. Rare and precious? Her? She half expected to see a teasing light in his brown eyes. Instead he radiated sincerity. The handsome lines of his face, familiar and strong, made her heart beat faster. One corner of his mouth tilted up.

"Why are you looking at me like that?" he asked.

"Like what?"

"As if you've never seen me before. Did you think I would have asked you out if I thought you were unattractive?"

"No. It's just..." She folded her arms on the table. "That's the nicest thing you've ever said to me."

"I'm not a complete jerk."

"That's not what I meant." The night closed around them, making her feel that it was safe to expose bits of her soul. "I never understood why you did ask me out. I always felt so inadequate."

"Inadequate? In God's name why?"

His genuine surprise made her laugh. "Thank you for that."

"For what?"

"Acting shocked."

"I am shocked." He leaned back in his chair. "I knew you felt young and inexperienced, but I had no idea you felt..." He paused, searching for the right word.

"How about completely out of my element?"

One dark brow raised slightly. "I can't believe that."

"Think about it, Adam. You were the heir to all the Barrington wealth. Too damn good-looking, charming, funny. You always knew what to say and do. Everyone liked and admired you. I was nobody."

He gave her a slow smile that sent heat coursing all the way to her feet. Her toes curled inside her white pumps.

"I had no idea I was looked upon so favorably."

"Oh, stop. You knew it then and you still know it. You were the catch of the decade. How could I not feel inadequate? I kept waiting for you to figure out I was just some gawky teenager who'd had a crush on you since she was twelve."

As soon as the words came out, she wanted to call them back. In all the time they'd dated, even after they'd become lovers, even after he'd proposed, she'd never confessed that to him. A heated blush climbed up her chest and throat, then flared across her cheeks. She started to stand up, but he shot his hands out and grabbed hers, holding her in place.

"Oh, no you don't," he said. "Not after that bombshell. You had a crush? On me?"

"Don't sound so surprised," she said, daring only to stare at their joined hands. His, broad and tanned, next to her paler skin. He turned his wrists so that her fingers rested on his palms. He brushed against the sensitive skin on the inside of her wrists. Electric sparks flew between them. She half expected to see little flashes of light bouncing over the table.

"I *am* surprised. I never knew. You didn't say a word."

She risked glancing up at him. "Why would I have gone out with you if I hadn't liked you?"

"I knew you liked me, but a crush is different. From the time you were twelve." He drew his eyebrows together in concentration. "Did something special happen, or did you just wake up one morning and realize you lived next door to someone wonderful?"

"Stop!" She pulled one of her hands free and hit him on the forearm. Before she could retreat, he grabbed her hand back. His thumbs began to trace slow circles on her palms. "You taught me to swim that summer."

"I remember. You were always so serious. All legs and eyes."

She grimaced. "Skinny and flat-chested."

"You were only twelve."

"Some things never change."

The slow movement of his thumb continued. Jane found herself thinking more and more about his touch and less about what was being said. It felt good to have a man hold her hands. This man, especially. It felt good to be in his company, talking about each other and the past.

"You're not skinny anymore," he said.

"Thanks."

"And I've never understood the importance you placed on breast size. Yours are perfect."

"Mmm." She continued to stare at his hands cradling hers. The circling of his thumb hypnotized her until all she could think about was— She snapped her head up and stared at him. "What did you say?"

Humor flashed in his eyes. "I said that there is nothing wrong with your breasts. In fact I've always—"

"Never mind." She jerked her hands free and crossed her arms over her chest. "I get the gist of it. Thanks for the share."

"You want to change the subject," he said kindly, his gaze never once flickering below her face. Still she kept her arms in place.

"How'd you guess?"

"Body language."

"Oh." She glanced at her arms. "Pretty obvious."

"Would you feel better if we talked about your crush?"

"No."

"So it was my teaching you how to swim. My sculptured body. The devil-may-care gleam in my eyes."

He was laughing at her, but she didn't care. "Actually, you took the time to be nice."

Now it was his turn to look uncomfortable. He leaned back in his chair and shrugged. "I was just being neighborly."

"I know, but it meant a lot to me. You always had time to smile and say hello. That goes a long way with a twelve-year-old girl." She bit her lower lip. Could she ask him the same sort of questions? Did it matter anymore? A slight breeze whispered against her bare arms, bringing with it the scent of night-blooming jasmine and rich earth. "When did you first notice me?"

"When you were about six months old and screaming loud enough to wake me up at four in the morning."

"Adam! You know what I meant."

"Yeah, I know." He raised his arms and laced his fingers behind his head. The lights from the house highlighted the right side of his face and outlined his profile. "Charlene gave me a party for my twenty-first birthday. She went all out, hiring a band and a caterer. There must have been a couple hundred people here."

"I remember." It had been her first grown-up event. The first time her mother had taken her into Atlanta to buy a formal dress. The white confection of ribbons and lace had made her feel special.

"You danced with Ty," he said. "I watched my brother lead you around the floor, but you couldn't dance in your shoes."

"Oh, God." She buried her face in her hands. "It's not fair that all my embarrassing memories are public knowledge. I'll never live them down. I must have looked like a geek."

"It was very charming."

She shook her head. "Geek."

"I found you out by the garden, walking barefoot, like a nymph from a storybook."

She straightened, smiling at the memory. "You told me I looked pretty."

"You did."

"And that was it?" she asked, surprised that one of her favorite memories might have influenced him.

"You were a little young, but yes, that was it. I kept my eye on you until you were old enough for me to date."

"I fell in love with you that night," she said, daring to look at him. "Out there, under the stars. It was terribly romantic and I was quite young, but I fell all the same."

"So we were heading in the same direction." His features hardened slightly, as if he remembered something more. Like the fact that she left him at the altar.

"I did love you," she insisted, as if her words could keep reality at bay.

"It wasn't enough."

"Adam—"

"No." He rose and walked over to the porch railing. The shadows swallowed him until only a vague outline remained visible. "It's true. You were too young. I see that now. The blame—" He drew in a breath and released it. "You weren't ready."

"No, I wasn't."

"And I pushed you."

"I wanted to be pushed. Sort of." It was so complicated, she thought, standing up as well and walking toward him. "So many things confused me. I wanted to believe that you cared about me, but I was never sure I measured up. You were so perfect, and I was just this dumb kid."

"Hardly that." He shifted until he sat on the railing and looked out into the yard.

When she reached him, she leaned against one of the pillars supporting the covering. They were nearly at eye-level. The darkness made it easier to confess almost everything.

"I wanted to please you," she said. "More than anything, I wanted to be everything *you* wanted. But there was so much that scared me."

"Like me?" He asked the question bitterly.

"Yes," she whispered.

"You could have told me."

"I was afraid of what you'd think and say. I was afrai
you'd finally figure out that I wasn't enough."

He looked at her then, regret tightening his mouth. "
wanted to marry you, Jane. No one else. You were exactl
right for me."

"We were compatible?" she asked.

"I thought so."

"The perfect banker's wife?"

"You could have been."

Convenience, she thought. While she spoke of love an
need, he remembered that she was malleable. Had he love
her? She wanted to ask the question. Had he cared?

"I always thought—" He offered her a quick smile. "
had plans for us. Changes in the house. Trips. A future.
supposed I could have talked more about that. Times wer
hard for me then. What with the bank, and Dani and T
needing things." He turned back to face the yard. "I kno
that I could have been there more for you. We were so sui
able, I assumed that you'd know all that. I should have r
alized your youth would be a problem as well as an asset.'

It was as close to a confession of responsibility as she wa
going to get. Suitable. He thought they were suitable. Wha
about passion? she wanted to cry out. Tell me that you use
to lie awake nights and dream about making love with m
Tell me that you ached for my touch. Explain to me how w
would grow old together, loving each other more and mo
each day.

He did none of those. And she didn't ask him to. It didn
matter anymore.

"I'm sorry, too, Adam," she said at last, because the
was nothing else to say. It was as she'd suspected. She'
loved with her whole being, while he'd followed a logic
course of action. Running had been wrong; not marryir
Adam had, however, been the correct decision.

He looked at her. "I feel as if this is a significant moment. A truce of sorts. Maybe we should commemorate it."

"In case it doesn't last?"

She meant the question as a joke but he didn't smile. Instead, he stood up and took the single step that separated them. Before she could move away, he trapped her between the pillar, the railing and himself.

"Adam?"

He reached up and cupped her cheek, then drew his hand to the side, slipping his fingers through her curls. "I never expected to get over the anger. I never expected not to hate you." He gave her a slight smile. "I never expected to see you again."

He took her breath away. His gentleness, the scent of his body, his warmth surrounding her. Except where he wove his fingers through her hair, they didn't touch. She wanted him with a fierceness that threatened to overwhelm her. This was more than a woman's need for man. This was a lethal combination of past and present. She hated that it didn't matter that he'd never loved her. She hated herself for being so weak where he was concerned. But she understood the phenomenon. He was her first love, her only love. He could, with just a look, tap into a lifetime of memories. How could she resist him?

He placed his other hand on her shoulder. His skin felt warm against hers. His pinky slipped under the strap of her dress, his thumb traced a line from her jaw to the hollow of her throat. Slowly, he twisted his fingers in her hair, until she was forced to lean her head back, exposing more of herself to him.

Anger, disappointment, regret, guilt all faded under his sensual assault. She swayed toward him. Tomorrow, she thought vaguely. She'd tell him tomorrow. Please, God, let her have tonight with the man she had once loved with her entire being. Just one perfect night to remember.

The screen door slammed. "We've finished the dishes. Hey, where are you guys?"

Billie!

Adam instantly stepped back. Jane cleared her throat and turned to look out at the yard.

Billie walked over to them. "What are you guys doing over here?"

"Looking at stars," Jane said, hoping her voice sounded normal.

"Why?"

"It's fun. Can you find the Big Dipper?"

Billie came up to the rail and leaned out to look at the sky. "It's there." She pointed.

"Very good."

Billie turned to Adam. "I'm very smart for my age."

"So it would appear." As always, she had the power to make him laugh and forget what was ailing him, Adam thought. This particular time, it was a case of misplaced passion. Jane wasn't a woman for him to fool around with. She'd already wounded him big-time. Giving her a second chance to screw up his life would be idiotic. Telling himself it was strictly physical might sound good, but he knew better. The heart was a very physical organ and had a nasty habit of getting in the way. He didn't want to risk that kind of involvement again. Caring meant losing. Jane was proof of that. So why had he almost kissed her again, and why was he frantically thinking up an excuse to see her? Wasn't he the one who had convinced them both that if they really made an effort, their paths didn't have to cross?

"It's late," Jane said. "We should get this one home. She's got a big day tomorrow."

"Mo-om, it's barely dark. My bedtime's not for a couple of hours."

"Your mother's right," he said, suddenly needing to be away from Jane before he said or did something he would regret. The control he'd prided himself on for so long seemed to be failing on a regular basis.

"Thank you, Adam." She shifted her weight from one foot to the other, as if not sure what to do with herself. "We had a lovely time. Tell Charlene thank you as well."

"I will."

Billie held out her arms, and he obligingly picked her up and gave her a kiss on the cheek. "You're the best," she said as she leaned forward and rubbed her nose against his. "Too bad Atlanta lost."

"Yeah, we'll get you next time." He squeezed her tight, then set her on the porch. "Oh, I almost forgot." He hesitated, telling himself not to ask. Damn. "The triple-A team is going to be opening a home stand. Would you like to go next Saturday?"

"Sure!" Billie spun in a circle. "Can I, Mom? Can I?"

"Calm down." Jane brushed her daughter's hair out of her eyes. "Certainly, if Adam doesn't mind."

Billie rolled her eyes. "He *asked,* didn't he? Why would he mind?"

"You're welcome to join us," he said, then wondered why the hell he was playing this game. Did he want to see what else Jane could do to him? What exactly was his problem?

"I'm sure you'd rather spend the time alone with Billie."

Billie jabbed him in the stomach. "She's just saying that. She wants you to *really* ask her."

"Billie!"

Her daughter hunched her shoulders. "Sorry. I'm going to go to the house and wait for you, Mom. Maybe I'll start my bath water."

"You do that," Jane said.

Billie scurried between the hedge dividing the two properties, then stomped into the smaller house.

"She can be a trial," Jane said, not meeting his eyes.

"But you love her."

"Of course. She's my daughter." She bit her lip, then stared at the ground. "I should go, too. Thanks for dinner."

She reached up and gave him a quick kiss on his cheek. Her perfume whispered around him, like a sensual ghost.

"You're welcome."

She walked down the steps and toward the hedge. "Oh, Adam, I'd love to go with you to the game. If you're sure?"

He wasn't. About anything. "Of course."

"See you Saturday, then."

"Saturday." He watched her disappear into the night.

Rain fell from the sky. Sheets pounded into the earth as if a permanent rift had been created somewhere in the atmosphere.

"I can't believe you went to all this trouble," Jane said as she studied the contents of the refrigerator. Hot dogs and salads sat on the top two shelves. An assortment of sodas filled the door. A bottle of white wine rested on its side on the bottom.

"I'd promised the two of you a baseball game," Adam said, pulling out the wine and closing the refrigerator door. "What else was I supposed to do?"

"But a barbecue in the rain? We could have rescheduled."

"The porch is wide enough to handle the grill. Besides, did you *want* to have Billie to yourself all day? She strikes me as the type of kid to go stir-crazy in this kind of weather."

"She is a little trying. I was thinking about driving into town to catch a movie with her. It was that or lock her in a closet."

He smiled. "We still can. The movie part. After we eat."

"Sure. Unless you've made other plans for tonight?" She sounded to herself as sophisticated as the twelve-year-old who'd first fallen for him. Get a grip, she told herself.

"Not at all."

When she'd woken up to a gray wet day, Jane had been convinced that Adam would excuse himself from seeing her and Billie today. Disappointment had flared, her distress much stronger than it had a right to be. It had been almost a week since she'd seen him. Every day she'd strolled in her yard after he got home from work and had hoped he might come outside, too. He hadn't, and she'd gone inside each night feeling foolish and lonely. It was worse than being a teenager again. Back then she hadn't known what she was missing.

Billie had been almost as crushed as she was. Adam's phone call had rescued them both from a case of the blues.

In concession to the muggy heat, he wore shorts and a T-shirt. She tried not to stare, but his long lean legs, tanned from his morning jogs, stretched endlessly down to deck shoes. The T-shirt wasn't any safer to study, she thought, taking in the broad expanse of chest and rippling muscles. The man was a walking cliché. Tall, dark, handsome. How had she ever found the strength to walk away?

Upstairs, in the far reaches of the house, something thudded to the floor. Adam looked up. "Should we go investigate?"

"No. Knowing Billie, she's found something to throw, or hit."

"I must admit, I didn't think she'd want to play dress up."

Charlene had sent the girl up into the attic with the promise of chests of old clothes and secret treasure.

"She will. Only don't expect her to come down dressed as a princess or movie star. She'd rather be a pirate. Maybe she'll find the secret Barrington treasure lost during the Civil War."

Adam opened a drawer in the center island of the kitchen and removed a corkscrew. "You've been gone too long."

"Why?"

"It's the War of Northern Aggression."

"Sorry."

"Besides, there isn't any secret Barrington treasure." He opened the wine and poured them each a glass.

"How do you know if it hasn't been found?"

"You have a point." He raised his drink toward her. "To friends?"

It was a peace offering, she realized with a sinking feeling in her stomach. A token that, after their intimate conversation last weekend, left certain doors opened. She was a coward and a liar.

"To friends," she answered, tightening her grip on the stem so that he couldn't see her tremble.

He rested his hand on the small of her back and pressed lightly, urging her toward the front parlor. The thick clouds made the late afternoon seem more like evening. Shadows filled the corners of the rooms. The steady drip-drip onto the porch railing should have soothed her, but the sound of rain only seemed to repeat the same refrain. "Tell him, tell him, tell him." She would. Now.

He seated her on one end of the floral print sofa, then sat next to her. He'd left enough space between them so that they weren't touching, but he hadn't sat on the far end, either. Brown eyes regarded her thoughtfully. What would have happened if Billie hadn't interrupted them? she wondered. How far would his caresses have gone? Would he have hated her more or less when he found out the truth? There was only one way to find out.

"Adam, I—"

"I've been—"

They spoke at the same time.

"You first," he offered.

"No. Go ahead."

He took a sip, then set his glass on the table in front of them. Half-opened shutters allowed in the dusky light. A single lamp in the corner illuminated the area by the hall way door. He turned toward her and rested his arm along the back of the couch, his fingers inches from her shoulder.

"I've been thinking about our last conversation," he said.

That look. She knew it. Sultry brown eyes caressed her face, then dipped lower. The filmy gauze of her tank top provided little protection against what he sought. Her small breasts swelled as her nipples hardened inside her bra.

"Me, too," she confessed.

"Everything between us is different," he went on. "I didn't expect—" He shrugged, as if not sure how to put his feelings into words.

"I know." His long fingers brushed her bare shoulder. She leaned forward. "But first, Adam, I have to tell you some—"

Something heavy thumped down the stairs, followed by clattering footsteps.

"Look what I found!" Billie called. "Hey, where are you guys?"

"In here," Jane said. Timing, she thought grimly. Just when she'd been about to spill the beans. Maybe locking Billie in a closet wasn't such a bad idea. She shook her head. She'd just have to wait until her daughter went to bed. Then she and Adam could be alone and she'd tell him the truth.

"There's a bunch of sports equipment and uniforms. I found this softball and bat. Can I have this jersey, Adam? And where'd you get the wig?"

At last Billie stepped into the doorway. The light from the lamp highlighted her appearance, including the blue and white numbered jersey that hung down to her knees and the long blond wig perched on her head. In one hand she held a softball, in the other a mitt.

Jane felt her breath catch in her throat. That wasn't her daughter standing there smiling proudly. It was another girl. Funny how with dark hair, Billie didn't look much like Adam's sister at all. But with the long wig, and her old high school team uniform, she was the spitting image of Dani Barrington.

"Well?" Billie asked. "What do you guys think?"

It was like in the movies, when everything suddenly happened in slow motion. Billie's question sounded as if she were a hundred miles away. Jane felt her muscles clench as panic chilled her blood.

He knew.

She didn't have to look at him to confirm her suspicions. She could feel it in the way he sat so quietly and stared at her daughter. *His* daughter.

Without saying a word, he rose to his feet and walked over to Billie. He crouched in front of her and touched her face.

"What?" she asked, puzzled. "Why are you looking at me like that?"

"Billie." His voice sounded hoarse. He kissed her cheek, then took her hand.

"Where are we going?"

"To see Aunt Charlene. You're going to visit with her for a few minutes while your mother and I have a talk."

Chapter Nine

"When were you going to tell me?" Adam asked.

The shock had sustained him for the time it had taken him to walk Billie over to Charlene's. The older woman had taken one look at the girl's outfit and blond wig and had gasped. The look in her eyes had been compassion for him, but not surprise. She'd known, as well. Looks as though he was the only one kept in the dark around here. He'd left Billie with his aunt. He would deal with Charlene and her betrayal another time. Right now all he cared about was Jane.

He leaned against the doorframe and stared into the dimly lit parlor. As the shock faded, cold deadly rage took its place. She'd made him angry when she'd first arrived and pushed him to get in touch with his feelings. Then he'd lost his cool, but nothing like what was about to happen. Images formed in his mind—disconnected pictures of Billie laughing at him, smiling, burrowing in his arms. No wonder they'd gotten along so well.

A sharp pain jabbed his heart. A daughter. He had a daughter. His gaze narrowed as Jane rose from the sofa and walked toward the shuttered window.

"I asked you a question," he said, struggling to keep his voice low and even. "When were you going to tell me?"

She laughed sharply and without humor. "You wouldn't believe me if I told you."

"That's not an answer."

"It's the best I have."

"Come on, Jane. You can do better than that." He folded his arms over his chest. "What the hell kind of game have you been playing? I don't even know where to begin."

"It's not what you think."

"Oh? Billie *isn't* my daughter? You haven't kept her from me for over eight years?"

"I . . ." She touched the shutter and swung it open. Dim light crept into the room and illuminated her profile. "Yes. Billie is yours."

Her simple answer opened the floodgates. "That's it?" he asked, stepping into the room. "That's the whole confession? After all this time, you calmly announce she's mine? Where do you get off, lady? You stole my kid. You ran away and had *my* child and didn't tell me. How dare you play with my life, with Billie's life?"

"I'm her mother." She glanced up at him, her eyes flashing with temper.

"So?" he asked, taking another step closer to her. "Does that give you the right to lie to her? To me?"

"Dammit, Adam, I made the best decision I could at the time."

"You think I care about you? After what you've done?" He clenched his hands into fists. "You had no right to steal my child from me. You had no right to keep her a secret. How long, Jane? How many years would have gone by until you told me?" He shook his head. "If we hadn't been interrupted, you would have come to my bed last weekend. You would have made love with that lie between us.''

Her gaze faltered until she dropped her head toward her chest. ''There's nothing you can say that I haven't already told myself.''

''So what's your excuse? What reason do you have for cheating me out of Billie? Who gave you the right to make that decision?''

She snapped her head up and glared at him. ''You did, Mr. High and Mighty.'' She pointed her finger toward his chest. ''The day you coerced me into your bed.''

''Don't give me that. I never did anything you didn't want.''

''Now who's lying? I wasn't ready. You scared me. I would never have told you no, and you took advantage of that.''

A small measure of guilt joined his rage. ''What are you saying? Are you accusing me of something?''

She held his gaze. ''No. I'm telling you we both made choices we've come to regret.''

''You regret Billie?''

''Never.''

''Then what?''

The sound of rain filled the room, the steady drumming from the roof, the drip-drip off the porch covering. In the distance, he heard the rumble of thunder.

''I should have said no. Even though we were engaged, I wasn't ready to be your lover. I should have told you.'' She turned away and gripped the windowsill. ''Aren't you curious, Adam, about how I came to be pregnant? After all, you're the one who decided it was time for us to go all the way, so you took me to the doctor and waited while I was fitted for a diaphragm. You're the one who drove me to the next town, because I was too shy to get the prescription filled here in Orchard.''

He didn't like the way the conversation had shifted. Thi was supposed to be about what *she'd* done. She's the on who'd lied. Who'd had Billie. He had to focus on that. In stead the past intruded.

"I don't care about any of this," he said.

"I didn't use it." She spoke quietly.

"What?"

"The diaphragm. I couldn't."

"That's the most ridiculous—"

"I was embarrassed."

He turned away and swore.

"That doesn't change anything, Adam."

"Why didn't you tell me?"

She shook her head. "I couldn't talk to you about any thing."

"Then what the hell were you doing marrying me?"

"I didn't, did I?"

That one hit below the belt. He struggled to regroup hi thoughts. "I'm not the villain in this piece. You're the on who kept the secrets."

"Only one."

"Oh, yeah, just the fact that you were having my child Is that why you ran? Because you found out you were preg nant?"

"No."

He raked one hand through his hair. He couldn't dea with this. Too much information in too short a time. He fel like exploding or lashing out or— "When?" he asked "When did you figure it out?"

"When I got to San Francisco." She continued to stare a the windowsill. Lightning ripped across the sky. The brie flash lit up the room. Three seconds later, a boom shook th house.

"Why didn't you come home then? I would have—"

"Would have what? Married me? After I ran out on you' What was there to come home to? This town, where every one would know I was a pregnant teenager? You didn't want a baby, Adam. Why else would you have gone to all that trouble with the birth control? We'd never talked about kids."

"Of course I wanted children. Maybe not right away, but that doesn't give you the right to choose for me. Do you think I would have abandoned you?"

She leaned her forehead against the windowsill. "No."

He hadn't expected that to be her answer. He glanced at her, then began to pace the length of the parlor. The marble floors gleamed as he strode across them. He reached the fireplace and turned to face her.

"I don't understand. If you didn't think I'd abandon you, then what was the problem?"

"I couldn't come back with Billie. My pride wouldn't let me. I'd run out on the wedding. What sort of person would I be if I'd then come back because I was pregnant? Yes, you would have taken me in, but what was between us had already been determined. We would have had nothing but obligation."

"That's a tidy rationalization of your actions."

She sighed. "I deserve everything you're saying and I'm willing to listen if it makes you feel better. But don't let your anger hide the truth. Telling you about the baby would have meant you'd be there, but only because you had to be." She looked out the window and into the storm. "You didn't care about the relationship anymore. If you'd really wanted me, you would have come after me. You never did."

If you'd really wanted me, you wouldn't have left, he thought, surprised that her leaving still had the power to hurt him. He should be grateful that he'd learned the lesson so early. Given a chance, people you love will leave you.

"I would have been the perfect banker's wife," she said. With one finger, she traced the trail of a raindrop against the glass. Another clap of thunder shook the house. "Young, easily trained. I wasn't important enough to you. I realized that before the wedding. That's why I ran. And when I found out I was pregnant, I couldn't bear the thought of being an obligation for the rest of my life."

"You selfish bitch."

She jerked her head around to stare at him. Surprise widened her hazel eyes. Her long braid trailed over one shoulder, but for once the thick silken length didn't catch his attention.

"I realized—I couldn't bear—" He mocked her in a falsetto voice. "It's all about you, isn't it? Did you ever once think about what *I* might want? That I might care about my daughter, want to see her born, watch her take her first step, hear her first word? You've taken a piece of my life away. You've stolen time that I can't recover. Worse than what I might regret, you have stolen your daughter's birthright. Made her suffer when her life might have been easier. There were advantages I could have—"

"Money isn't everything."

He dismissed her with a wave of his hand. "I'm not talking about money. I'm talking about people, a culture. A place to grow up knowing that generations before have walked the same path, lived in the same house. Your decision, blamed on me and circumstance, has destroyed two lives."

"I'm sorry," she whispered. A flash of lightning showed the trail of tears on her cheeks. "You're right."

He turned and hit the fireplace mantel. "That doesn't make me feel better."

"I know."

"Why? Why did you come back? Why are you doing this?"

"I wanted Billie—" Her voice cracked. "I wanted the two of you to meet."

"Was it all a sick game? We met. Big deal. Did you think I wouldn't guess eventually? Who else aside from Charlene knows?"

"No one."

"Your parents?"

"Yes."

He cursed.

"I couldn't tell you." She took a step toward him as if to beseech him to listen. When he glared, she moved back. "When I first arrived, I wasn't sure you'd want Billie in your life. She seems tough, but she's still a little girl. If I'd told you about her right away, you would have been angry and might have said or done something that would have scarred her."

He spun and walked over to stand next to her. "And you haven't? You dare to judge me, when you're the one telling all the lies?"

"I'm sorry."

"So you've said. I don't care about you, or your apologies." He raised one hand to rub his temple and she flinched. He didn't care that she thought him capable of hitting her. "That's right, Jane. Be afraid. You can't manipulate me anymore. You've taken something precious from me and by God, you'll pay."

By ten-thirty that night the storm had passed, leaving behind wet earth and clean damp air. A few stars braved the clouds, peeking out and winking. Now what? Jane asked herself for the thousandth time. Did she leave, or did she stay? A soft breeze cooled her heated skin. She shivered at the slight contact and pulled her knees up closer to her chest. Unlike Adam's yard, hers didn't contain as many trees. From her seat on the front porch steps, she could see out to the street. There wasn't any traffic this late on a tiny street in Orchard. A few houses glowed with lights from within, but most of her neighbors had already retired for the evening. Her porch light didn't chase away enough shadows to allow her to forget.

She felt as broken and battered as a board washed ashore from a shipwreck. She supposed it was possible to have handled the situation worse than she had, but she couldn't figure out how. After Adam had threatened her, she'd fled the room. Charlene had agreed to keep a bewildered Billie for the night. That left Jane free to deal with her emotions and the tears that refused to be halted. Every time she thought she couldn't possibly cry anymore, she would start again.

Her life lay crumpled around her. She had no one to blame but herself. Adam was right—so many of her choices had been wrong ones. She had deprived him and Billie of each other. Had she been a bad mother as well? She closed her eyes and rested her forehead on her bent knees. She recalled the months she'd struggled to make ends meet, to pay the rent and provide food and utilities for their tiny apartment. Billie's face flashed before her, the four-year-old's tantrums when her mother had left for work. Had she damaged Billie? Had she chosen incorrectly? She was willing to admit to some of the blame, but all of it? She groaned softly. She just didn't know.

Was Adam right? Should she have come home? Was living in a big house better, even if that house didn't have any love to fill it? Could he have learned to care about her and his child? Could she have lived with the knowledge that she was little more than an obligation?

She'd only ever wanted Adam to love her. That's all. Not want her because she was appropriate, or easily trained, or because he'd felt obligated. She'd wanted to be loved. For herself. Was that wrong? Selfish? Wrapping her arms around her legs, she wished she could disappear.

From her left came the soft crunch of footsteps on the path between the two houses. Jane sat perfectly still, as if her lack of motion would make her invisible.

Adam. She sensed it was him even before he sat next to her and she could smell his after-shave and the unique male essence of his body.

"Go away," she murmured, refusing to look up.

"I had dinner with Billie," he said without warning.

Oh, God. Her heart froze in her chest. Had he—

"I didn't tell her."

Thank you, she prayed.

"I wanted to," he said, anger still apparent in his voice. "I was going to blurt it out over the salad. I even thought about kidnapping her and running until you couldn't find us."

She turned her head so she could see him. He sat next to her on the steps of her front porch. Two feet separated them. He mimicked her pose—he'd drawn his legs up close to his chest and rested his arms on his knees.

"I couldn't." He looked at her then. She saw that she'd been wrong about hearing anger in his voice. It wasn't rage—it was pain. The loss he'd suffered deepened the lines around his eyes and the hollows in his cheeks. "I don't give a damn about you, but I couldn't hurt her."

"Thank you."

He looked straight ahead. "Where do we go from here?"

"I don't know."

"You don't have any ideas?"

"No."

"You never planned to tell me."

"Oh, Adam, I can't convince you of it, but for what it's worth, yes, I did want to tell you about Billie. Today, believe it or not. Telling you is one of the reasons I came home. I wanted her to grow up here with a family, like she'd always wanted. But I didn't know how to say it without risking it all. I was afraid you'd use Billie to get back at me. That you'd hate me so much that you'd punish her. The longer I was gone, the more time passed, the harder it got."

"I do hate you."

She forced herself not to cry out. Of course he did. But telling herself that he would and hearing the words were two very different things. He still got to her. She'd been foolish to think she'd escaped that.

"How dare you," he said. "How dare you assume would punish an innocent child."

She stared at her lap. He sounded cold and angry. Worse he sounded like a stranger. "You have every right to be furious with me," she said. "I *should* have known you'd never do anything like that."

"Why do you keep agreeing with me?"

"You're telling the truth."

"But it makes it damn hard to hold on to the rage."

"Good."

He turned toward her. The anger and the bravado were gone. "Damn it, Jane, you hurt me."

She bowed her head. The tears flowed fast and hot trickling down her arms and dampening a spot on her skirt.

"Say something," he demanded.

"I . . . I can't."

He swore. She heard him slide on the step, then felt his hands on her arms, pulling her close. He angled their bodies so that her head rested on his shoulder. Their legs touched from hip to knee. She clutched at his T-shirt, bunching the soft fabric in her hands. The tears continued, replenished by the aching in her heart.

"I'm s-sorry," she said, her voice cracking with a sob "So sorry, Adam. I l—loved you so much. I never wanted to hurt you. Or B-Billie. I was afraid for her, I swear."

"I know. Hush." He enfolded her in his strength, rocking back and forth while she cried. The minutes passed. She struggled for control. Finally the tears subsided.

She sniffed and forced herself to straighten. Unshed tears darkened his brown eyes. His words earlier in the day—his speech about stolen time and memories missed—had made her feel bad, but she hadn't had the chance to really think about what he was saying. Now, seeing him emotionally exposed for the first time in her life, she felt what he felt and knew that her crime was far greater than she'd imagined. It hadn't been a speech. He *had* lost all those times she'd taken for granted. And even meeting Billie now couldn't make up for that. She'd cheated them both. It didn't matter if he couldn't forgive her; she'd never forgive herself.

He cupped her face and brushed away her tears with his thumbs. "Where do we go from here?" he asked, repeating his earlier question.

"I wish I knew."

His touch comforted her. She didn't deserve it, but couldn't bring herself to pull away. Still, when Adam straightened, she forced herself to smile slightly and wipe her face.

"I guess we should tell Billie," she said, shifting on the step.

"What is she going to say?"

"I don't know." Jane thought for a moment. "She'll be happy about getting a dad. She's wanted one since she figured out most kids have two parents. But she'll be angry that I lied to her."

"She'll get over it."

She smoothed her skirt over her knees. "That depends on you. Are you going to say things?"

"What are you talking about?"

"Are you going to tell her that I'm the worst mother since the invention of the institution, that I've deprived her of her birthright and family?" She closed her eyes and waited.

"You must think I'm a real bastard."

Now it was her turn to be surprised. "No. Why would you think that?"

He shook his head. "You don't have a very high opinion of me."

"You're still angry and I thought you might—"

"I don't plan to bad-mouth you to Billie. She's the innocent one in all this. She might be pleased to take my side at first, but in the end it would only confuse her."

"Thank you."

"I'm not doing it for you."

Right. She couldn't allow herself to forget that.

"What about her name?" he asked.

"You don't like Billie?"

"Her *last* name. You didn't give her mine."

"I didn't want you to know. It would have been pretty obvious if I'd named her Belle Charlene Barrington."

He sprang to his feet. "You named her Belle Charlene? After Aunt Charlene?"

"Yes. Is that okay?"

He jammed his hands into his pockets. "I don't even know my kid's name."

Jane wanted to bite off her tongue. She'd already hurt him enough—couldn't she stop saying things without thinking? "Adam, I—"

"Don't," he said. "Don't say anything. We'll deal with the name thing later. What about custody? We live next door, so it shouldn't be a problem. Am I listed as a father on the birth certificate?"

He was moving too fast. All this talk about living arrangements and legalities. "Yes, but we need to deal with this later."

"Why? Are you going to disappear again?"

"I didn't come all the way back just to leave. I had planned to have a life here with my daughter."

"My daughter."

"Our daughter." What was going on with him? Why did he have to—

Control. He was trying to control an uncontrollable situation. Of course. What else would Adam do?

She rose to her feet and moved next to him. When he didn't step back, she risked putting a hand on his arm. His

kin felt warm to the touch. Alive. The black hairs tickled
er palm. Stubble outlined the strong line of his square jaw.
'he young woman who'd left him would have been al-
owed to touch that skin and stubble, but she wouldn't have
ppreciated the contrast of smooth and rough, warm and
ool. She wouldn't have noticed the shape of his mouth, or
hat his muscles coiled when he was tense. She hadn't
earned that losing, even if by choice, was hard to get over.

It had been nine years and Jane still hadn't gotten over
Adam.

"Billie is our first priority," she said. "We have to tell her
hat you're her father."

He stiffened. "Father. How am I going to be her father?
don't know how."

"You'll be fine." She was about to go on with the logis-
ics of where and when to tell Billie, when he cut her off.

"What if I say something wrong? What if she decides she
oesn't want me for her dad?"

She stared at him. Adam Barrington, *the* Adam Barring-
on, expressing doubt?

He shrugged out of her touch. "Why are you looking at
e like that?"

"I'm surprised you're worried."

"Why wouldn't I be? I don't know Billie that well and she
oesn't know me. What if she doesn't like me?"

"She adores you."

"Maybe."

She shook her head.

"What?" he asked.

"I was just thinking I wish you'd been like this nine years
go."

"Like what?"

"Insecure. Scared."

His eyes met hers and for the second time that night she
aw into his soul. "You scared the hell out of me, Jane."

The confession came nine years too late.

"Hell of a day," she said, blinking frantically and ordering herself not to cry.

"You're telling me." He sighed. "Tomorrow, over breakfast?"

"Okay."

"What do you want to say?"

"I haven't a clue." She forced herself to smile. "Maybe we should wing it."

He nodded. "Nine. My kitchen."

"I'll be there."

She stood in front of her house until he walked through the hedges that separated their properties. Her mind raced. Thoughts of Billie and what her daughter would say competed with those eight simple words. "You scared the hell out of me, Jane."

Had he been frightened of losing her? Had he cared? Had she destroyed three lives to get away from a demon that didn't even exist?

Adam stepped quickly through the dark night. He'd grown up on this land, he knew every inch of the path from his house to Charlene's. Even without the moon to guide him, he made his way through the trees and up the brick lined walkway to her back door. He knocked softly and waited. She'd still be up. They had a lot to talk about.

"Come in," she called.

He opened the door and stepped into her kitchen. Charlene stood at the stove stirring a pot. Long red hair tumbled around her shoulders. Her full-length burgundy robe clashed with her hair color. Usually he teased her about the combination. Not tonight.

"Is Billie asleep?" he asked.

"Yes."

She didn't turn around to look at him. The silence between them lengthened. "You knew," he said at last.

"Yes."

"She told you?"

"I guessed."

"When?"

With a sigh she tapped the spoon on the edge of the pot, then placed it on the counter. Turning slowly, she raised her chin and looked up at him. "The day she arrived."

He cursed. All the emotion of the past few hours had left him feeling drained, as if someone had pulled the plug on his energy. He didn't have enough in him to sustain anger. He could only feel disappointment and hurt.

Charlene continued to watch him. Her blue eyes, less vivid without any makeup to accentuate the color, didn't show remorse. "I didn't tell you," she said as she leaned against the counter. "Because that wasn't my decision to make. I warned Jane she didn't have much time. If she didn't say something you'd figure it out."

God, he was tired. "You betrayed me."

"How?"

"You're my aunt. You should have been looking out for me. How dare you keep Billie a secret?"

"Adam, I understand your pain. Believe me, this was not an easy thing to keep quiet about. Yes, you're family. But by virtue of having Billie, so is Jane. It wasn't my secret to share or not. It was hers." She picked up the spoon and began stirring the pot again. "Do you want some cocoa?"

"You can't fix this problem that easily," he said, moving into the kitchen and pulling out one of the chairs in front of the window. "I'm not a kid anymore."

"You haven't been for much too long. But cocoa can still make you feel better. Trust me."

He looked at her.

"Adam, I love you. I also love Jane and Billie. Please don't trap me in the middle."

He wanted to hate her, but he couldn't. There was too much at stake. "I don't know what to do."

"About Billie?"

"About all of it. What am I supposed to say when she finds out I'm her father?"

"When are you going to tell her?"

"Tomorrow. At breakfast."

Charlene took down two cups, then measured out cocoa and sugar. "You'll think of something. Billie is a bright girl. She'll handle this better than you imagine."

"I hope so."

She poured the steaming milk into the mugs and stirred. After handing him one, she took the other and sat opposite him at the round oak table. "You'll be a fine father."

"How do you know?"

"Because I know the kind of man you are, Adam Barrington. Have a little faith in yourself." She picked up her cup. "To fatherhood and one more generation of Barringtons."

They tapped mugs. In the corner of her kitchen, the CB unit squawked. "Breaker, breaker, I'm lookin' for my redheaded Southern belle. Charlene, you listenin' to me, darlin'?"

Adam raised one eyebrow.

Charlene tossed her head as she rose to her feet. "I'm just keeping busy."

Chapter Ten

Adam laid out the dozen cinnamon rolls Charlene had brought over, then set the plate in the center of the kitchen island. He moved them slightly to the left. Next he put out place mats, some fruit and napkins. He was about to check the front window to see if Billie and Jane were coming over yet when he remembered that he had to start the coffee.

He hadn't been this nervous since he— He shook his head. He'd never been this nervous. It wasn't every day a man was introduced to his child. Usually it happened in the hospital while the kid was an infant and too little to make judgments about liking and not liking. Billie was eight and very opinionated. What if she decided she didn't want him for her father? He couldn't force himself onto her. It hadn't taken a hell of a lot of soul-searching to realize how very much he wanted to be part of her life.

He gave the kitchen a quick once-over, realized he'd forgotten plates, then set them on the place mats. As he straightened the napkins, he heard a knock on the back door.

Billie didn't bother to wait for him to answer. She barreled into the room and grinned. "I *told* her we didn't have to knock. We have breakfast together almost every day. I said you were 'specting me."

"*Ex*pecting," he answered, before bending over and giving her a hug.

"Whatever," Billie said as she hugged him back, then wiggled out of his embrace and climbed up onto a stool at the center island. "All right! Cinnamon rolls. My favorite." She picked one up and began licking the icing.

"Good morning, Adam," Jane said as she hovered in the doorway. The shadows under her eyes told him she, too, had had a sleepless night.

The nervousness, anticipation and concern swirling in his stomach didn't leave any room for other emotions like anger or resentment. He and Jane were in this together. The first order of business was to tell Billie the truth. Once that was taken care of, he and Jane would have plenty of time to work through everything else. He knew he'd have to come to terms with what Jane had done. He couldn't continue to hate the mother of his child; not without hurting Billie. And she was his main priority.

"Morning." He waved toward the chairs. "Have a seat."

"Thank you."

She sounded as awkward as he felt. As she walked by him, the hem of her floral-print skirt brushed his bare leg. The cotton tickled. He'd thought about dressing up for their talk with Billie, but had decided shorts and a polo shirt would look less as though he was interviewing for the job of father.

"I made coffee. It's almost ready," he said. "Would you like some juice?"

"That would be nice." She seated herself next to Billie, leaving the chair at right angles to the girl for him.

He poured one glass. "Billie?" he asked, holding up the pitcher.

"Sure." She grinned. "And milk, please."

Icing coated her face from her nose to her chin. Crumbs collected at the corner of her mouth. The ever-present baseball cap had been abandoned on the counter and her bangs stuck up along her forehead. She looked adorable.

Her hair— He stared at it for a second, then glanced at Jane. They didn't have the same color. Jane's was darker, a true brown with no hint of blond or red. Billie's hair was lighter. He finished pouring the juice and gave them each a glass. She had *his* hair color. He peered closer. And his eyes. His heart clenched in his chest, as if a giant fist squeezed it tight. It was real. He couldn't believe he'd never noticed.

"Why are you looking at me like that?" Billie asked.

Adam shrugged an apology, but couldn't take his eyes from the girl. The freckles on her nose looked just like Dani's. Her mouth—he glanced at Jane, then back at Billie—belonged to her mother.

Billie leaned across the counter until their faces were inches apart. "You're still staring at me."

He kissed her forehead. "I'm done."

"Good." She grabbed a piece of watermelon and bit into it. Juice ran down her chin. She caught it with the back of her hand.

"Billie, we have to talk," Jane said.

Instantly Billie set the fruit down. Her smile faded and she looked at Adam.

"Am I in trouble?"

"No." He took the seat on the other side of her. He sat on the end of the island, at a right angle to her. He could see Jane over her head. Their eyes met for a brief moment. He saw Jane's uncertainty. He wanted to promise her that it was going to be okay, but he didn't know *how* the situation would end up.

Jane angled herself toward her daughter and rested one
arm on the counter. "Adam and I—"

"I slid down the banister," Billie said, staring at her plate.

"What?" he asked.

"Last week, when you got that phone call from the bank,
I sneaked out of the kitchen and slid down the banister."

Adam frowned. "I told you not to do that. It's very high
and you could get hurt."

She thrust out her lower lip. "I didn't fall."

"That's not the point. The point is—"

"Adam." Jane shook her head. "Billie, you know better, but that's not what we want to talk about."

She nodded and pushed her half-eaten piece of watermelon across her plate. "I know. I didn't *mean* to. It just
happened. I was going to say something." She looked up at
Jane. "Honest." She turned back to Adam. "You weren't
home, so I couldn't tell you. Then when I came to breakfast, I didn't want you to get mad at me. I'm sorry."

He stared horrified as a fat tear trickled down her cheek.
"What the hell are you talking about?" he said loudly.

Billie jumped.

"Adam, don't swear," Jane said.

"Mom, he said a bad word." Billie sniffed. "Adam, you
shouldn't say *hell*."

He'd lost control, he thought as he struggled to stay sane.
He wasn't sure he'd ever had it, but it was gone now. He slid
off the stool and grabbed the coffeepot. After filling two
mugs, he handed one to Jane, then resumed his seat. "Okay,
let's try this again. Billie, you're right. I shouldn't say—"

Jane raised her eyebrows.

"I shouldn't swear. I apologize. What were you talking
about before? The thing you didn't want to tell me."

Another tear rolled down her cheek. "I broke a window
in the shed."

"You what?"

"There's no need to raise your voice," Jane said, putting an arm around her daughter. His daughter.

"I'm not raising my voice." He spoke through clenched teeth. "I'm calmly asking Billie to tell me what happened with the shed."

She sighed and sat up straight. Jane kept her arm around the girl's shoulders. "I was playing ball in the back. It was kinda windy, you know?"

"Go on." He sipped his coffee.

"Well, I was working on my curve ball and—"

"This isn't important," Jane said, staring intently at him. "This isn't what we wanted to talk about."

"But I want to know about the window."

"Fine. If you think that's more important, be my guest."

Billie looked from one to the other, her eyes getting wider and wider. "Are you guys fighting?"

"No," he said grimly.

"Yes," Jane answered, picking up her napkin and snapping it open. "Adam is easily distracted. Do you want to talk about the window or should we discuss something more relevant?"

"You're right," he said, wondering how he'd been moved off the subject at hand. "Billie, we'll deal with the shed another time." He took her hand. The short blunt nails needed cleaning. She had a cut at the base of her thumb. A child's hand, small and full of promise. His child's hand. "Billie—"

"Yes?" She looked up. "Do you have tickets to the Triple A game?"

He smiled. "No, honey, I don't."

"Can I have another roll?"

He pushed the plate toward her. She pulled her hand free and grabbed for the sweet.

"I can't," he said, leaning back in his seat. "I don't know what to say, or how to handle this situation." He looked at Jane. "Any suggestions?"

"I'll try," she said. "I've had longer to think about this than you."

"Think about what?" Billie asked, her mouth full.

"Honey, I've got a secret."

Billie looked up at her mother. "A good one?"

"Yes." Jane smiled weakly and brushed her daughter's bangs out of her eyes. "You've always asked me about a father. Where yours was. Why he couldn't be with us."

Adam swallowed. Here it comes. What would Billie say?

Billie set her roll on the plate and licked her fingers. "You know where my dad is?"

"Adam is your father, Billie. Your real father. I—" Jane cleared her throat. "He didn't know until yesterday. We wanted to tell you together."

Billie glanced at him, her eyes as big as the softball she carried in her shorts pocket. When he offered her what he hoped was a reassuring smile, she dropped her chin to her chest and stared at her lap. "Did you know?"

Jane nodded. "Yes," she said, her voice thick with unshed tears. "I knew Adam was your father."

Billie looked up at him. He tried to read her expression, but couldn't. "Do you want to be my father?"

"More than anything."

She pushed her plate away. "It's okay, I guess."

"Good." He started to lean forward to hug her, but she slipped off the seat and picked up her baseball cap.

"I'm going to go play ball." She stopped by the back door. "Okay, Mom?"

"Fine."

"What about church?"

"We'll try to go tonight."

She ran out without looking back.

He breathed a sigh of relief. The conversation had been anticlimactic at best, but had gone better that he'd hoped.

"She handled that very well," he said.

"I don't think so." Jane stared after her daughter. Her makeup couldn't hide her sudden lack of color or the stricken expression in her eyes.

What had he missed? Panic threatened. "Why do you say that?"

"Billie is bright and inquisitive. At the very least I thought she'd ask how I knew you were her father. Which would lead to . . . well, you know. But she hardly said a word."

"Would you have preferred her to get upset?"

Jane moved her cup along the edge of the tiles. "I think so. She doesn't understand what we told her. Not really. That will come later. I hope—" she sighed "—I hope she can forgive me."

"For what?"

"You were right last night. I lied to her, for her whole life. I wouldn't talk about her father. It would have been one thing if I hadn't known where he was, but I knew you were here. She's going to figure that out."

He felt vaguely uncomfortable. He didn't want to hear Jane's side of the story; he only wanted to be angry at her. Besides, if the truth were told, he didn't mind if Billie was irritated with her mother for a couple of days. "Maybe you should have thought about that when you chose to stay away all those years. You only have yourself to blame."

The long morning got longer. Jane glanced out the kitchen window and saw Billie sitting under their chestnut tree. The girl had been there for almost an hour. The only time Billie stayed still voluntarily was when she was sick. Even asleep she tossed and turned like a puppy having a dream.

Jane pushed opened the back door and walked down the steps. When she reached the shade, she knelt on the grass and laced her fingers together on her lap.

"How you doing?" she asked.

"Okay." Billie turned her softball over and over in her hand. The bill of her cap hid most of her face.

"You want to play catch?"

"I don't think so. I'll just sit here."

"Do you have any questions?"

"Uh-uh."

Now what? Jane wondered. "We gave you a lot to think about."

Billie nodded. "Is Adam really my dad?"

"Yes."

"Are you divorced from him?"

Jane grimaced. She hadn't seen that one coming. "No, honey. Adam and I didn't get married."

Billie looked up. Her mouth twisted as she wrinkled her nose. It was her I-can't-solve-this-problem expression. "Don't you have to be married to have a baby?"

"Not always. Adam and I were going to get married. But then we decided we shouldn't." It wasn't exactly a lie, she told herself. Besides, the truth was difficult for *her* to understand, let alone an eight-year-old.

Billie rolled her ball along the ground. It stopped in front of Jane and she rolled it back. "You didn't marry Adam, but you had me, anyway?"

"Yes."

"Why?"

"I wanted you."

Billie picked up the ball. "And Adam didn't?"

"Adam didn't know about you, honey."

"Why?"

"I didn't know when I left."

"But you knew later?"

"Yes."

Billie stood up and stuffed her ball into her pocket. "Every Sunday when we went to church, I always asked God for a dad. He gave me one. I guess I'm happy."

"I know it's a lot to get used to."

Billie nodded. "I'm going for a walk, Mom."

"Lunch is in an hour."

Billie shuffled off deeper into the backyard. Jane watched her go. This quiet sedate child wasn't hers. Had telling Billie been a mistake? Was the damage permanent? She wanted to run after her and hug her and love her until all the questions and fears disappeared. It didn't work that way. Billie had to figure this thing out on her own. Nothing would be the same again.

Jane made her way back to the house. Should she invite Adam over for lunch? How were they going to handle that now? Coming home and reuniting father and daughter had seemed like such a good idea in San Francisco. But she'd never thought through all the logistical problems. Where did they go from here?

It was almost two o'clock when Jane burst into Adam's study. "She's not here, is she?"

He looked up from his work and frowned. "Billie? I haven't seen her since this morning. I was going to call you later and see if you thought we could all have dinner."

She turned toward Charlene who was standing behind her. "She's not here. That's it, then. She's run away."

"Who's run away?"

"Your daughter." Jane rubbed her temples. "I last saw her about three hours ago in the backyard. We had a talk about, well, you know. I told her lunch was in an hour. When I went out to get her, I couldn't find her."

Billie? Gone? He glanced at his watch. "And you're just now coming to find me?"

"I wanted to check the yard and then the house. Charlene looked around here while I went to the park."

"And?" he asked, already knowing the answer.

"No one's seen her."

He'd been a parent less than twenty-four hours and it had been one crisis after another. His first inclination was to tear out of the room and begin a search of his own. "Let's keep calm," he said, as much to himself as to them.

"Calm?" Jane shrieked. "Calm? My daughter is out there. Alone. And you want to stay calm?"

"Jane, please, dear. This isn't helping." Charlene took her arm and ushered her into the room. "Have a seat and we'll all think this through. She can't have gone that far."

"You don't know Billie. She's very resourceful."

"She's also a little girl. And that is what she's going to act like. Now, think. Where would Billie go?"

Jane crumpled into the chair in front of his desk. She shook her head. "I don't know. I *can't* think. Oh, God, she's lost and it's all my fault."

Charlene looked at him. "Adam?"

He came around the desk and crouched in front of Jane. Taking her hands in his, he squeezed them reassuringly. Her skin felt icy to the touch. "This isn't helping Billie. Please, Jane. You must get a grip on yourself. Where would Billie go?"

"I don't know." Her hazel eyes, wide and unfocused, swept the room frantically, as if her child might be concealed in some corner. A shiver racked her body. "She's never done this before."

"She probably wants time to think. Where does she go when that happens?"

Jane jerked her hands free and tried to stand up. "Get out of my way. We need to call the police."

"Not yet." A memory walked along the edge of his consciousness. It stayed tantalizingly out of reach, but there was something familiar. A sense of having been through this before. Dani had disappeared after his parents' funeral. He'd searched for hours until—

"Did you try the old tree house?" he asked.

"What?" Jane stared at him. "Is it still there?"

"Pieces. I think Billie mentioned something about it the day you arrived. You'd told her stories. Maybe she's there."

Hope brightened her pale face. "You think so?"

"There's one way to find out. Come on."

He grabbed her hand and led her out of the study. Charlene followed on their heels. Most of the two-acre backyard had been landscaped, but a patch of woods still existed in the southwest corner. Adam went first along the overgrown trail. Billie had spent part of her days exploring his yard; it wasn't unreasonable to assume she'd found the tree house.

He kept repeating the thought over and over as if thinking it enough would make it true. The real truth was that he was as anxious as Jane. But after years of dealing with crises at home and at the bank, he was better at hiding his feelings. Be all right, Billie, he repeated like a prayer.

As they neared the tree house, he motioned for them to move more quietly. He wanted to get close enough to see her before she spotted them. He didn't want to give her the chance to run. Jane held on to his hand as if it were her lifeline. He returned her pressure and glanced over his shoulder to give her a reassuring smile.

They rounded a curve in the path. The old cottonwood stood like a battle-scarred warrior among the newer saplings and willows. A ladder hugged the trunk of the eighty-foot tree. Stout branches fanned out. The thickest, about fifteen feet off the ground, supported the remains of a tree house.

At first he didn't see anything. Then the sun caught a flash of red among the leaves. He closed his eyes and pictured her at breakfast that morning. Red T-shirt, denim shorts.

"She's there."

Jane sagged against him.

"Do you want to go talk to her?" he asked.

"We should go together." Jane glanced back at Charlene, as if to confirm her opinion.

"I agree. I'll wait here."

Adam stepped along the path. When they were almost at the tall tree, he stepped on a fallen branch. It snapped. Billie stuck her head over the side of the tree house.

She wasn't crying, but she didn't smile at them, either. "I'm in trouble, huh?"

"You bet," he said, finally realizing the extent of his worry as relief flooded his body. "You're not allowed to go off without telling someone."

She frowned. "How'd you know that?"

"It makes sense."

She nodded and looked past him to her mother. "Am I going to get a whippin'?"

Jane tried to laugh. It came out sounding a little shaky. "I've never hit you."

"I was just checking." Billie adjusted her baseball cap. "You probably want me to come down."

Adam released Jane's hand. "I'll come up."

"Be careful," Jane said, touching his arm.

"I will. I've been climbing this tree since I was younger than Billie."

"When was the last time?"

He hoisted himself onto the first step and looked back. "About nine years ago. Are you saying I'm too old?"

"I'm saying be careful."

He climbed the rungs leading up to the tree house. As he pivoted and lowered himself onto the floor of the open platform, he gave Billie a smile. "Nice view."

"Yeah." She took her ball out of her pocket and studied it.

"With the walls gone, it's not safe up here for you. If you'd like, I'll put the walls back."

She shook her head. "I won't be allowed up here. My mom won't like it."

"How do you know?"

She shrugged. "She just won't."

"Maybe I can talk to her about it."

"Really?" She eyed him suspiciously. "Is that a dad thing?"

Was it? Now he shrugged. "I used to play up here when I was your age. I had a lot of fun. I'd like the same for you."

She offered her first smile since she'd heard the news. "Sometimes famous pitchers need a place to play."

"I bet. I'll talk with your mother in a couple of days. Right now, though, I'd like you to come down with me. Can I give you a piggyback ride to the bottom?"

"Okay."

She walked over to him and leaned against his back. After stuffing her ball back into her pocket, she wrapped her arms around his neck and her legs around his waist.

So small, he thought, fighting the sudden tightness in his throat. So young and fragile. His daughter. His child.

"All set?"

"Uh-huh."

He stepped back onto the ladder and quickly brought them to the ground. Jane met them at the bottom. She pulled Billie off Adam and hugged her close.

"I was so frightened," she said, burying her cheek against her daughter's hair. "Don't scare me like that again."

"I'm sorry, Mom. I'm in trouble, huh?"

Jane continued to hold her tight. "No. You're not in trouble."

Adam expected several reactions, but not for Billie to start crying. The tears fell fast and furious down her face, but she made almost no noise.

"Mommy," she said. She squirmed to get closer. Her hat fell to the ground.

"Hush, Billie. You're safe now. You'll always be safe. I won't let anything happen to you."

"I love you, Mommy."

"I love you, too, baby."

The sobs continued, as if the child's most precious possession had been torn from her. Adam stood helplessly beside the two of them and watched as Billie suffered a pain he couldn't begin to understand. He thought about offering comfort, but to whom? And for what?

Charlene walked over and touched his arm. "We'd better head back."

He shook off her hand. "I don't want to."

"Adam!"

He glanced at her.

"Let Jane handle this."

"She's my daughter, too."

"In name only. Right now Billie needs her mother."

Jane looked up and nodded. "Please, just a couple of hours. Come by around five and we'll talk over dinner."

It was Billie who made the decision for him. He reached over to pat her back, but she shrank out of reach and clung tighter to her mother. It hurt, he acknowledged, allowing Charlene to lead him back to the house. Telling himself Billie was a child and simply reacting to the situation didn't help.

When he reached the curve in the path, he turned and stared at Jane and Billie. The woman who should have been his wife, holding the child that belonged to him. In a moment of passion, he and Jane had made that precious girl. He didn't understand all the ramifications of being a parent, but he would die for that child. As Jane's gaze met his, then slid away, he realized something else. The risk he took. He couldn't stop Billie from finding a place in his heart. It was too late for that; the process had already begun. He had to find a way to keep her from disappearing from his life. He knew the rule; if you love something, it leaves you. He couldn't let that happen now.

Chapter Eleven

She was as nervous as the day she'd arrived. Jane wiped her palms against her skirt and paced the small living room. It was silly, she told herself. Adam was the same man he'd been yesterday, before he'd known. He would be the same tomorrow. He might be angry and hurt and confused, but he was still Adam.

That's what scared her. In the brief time they'd spent together, she'd come to see that the young man she'd run from was not the person he'd become. She'd run from phantoms. Vague fears of a young woman too inexperienced to understand what frightened her and too cowardly to speak about those fears. She freely admitted running had been wrong. But what about not marrying Adam? Had she made the right choice there?

"Mom, I'm hungry." Billie stood in the doorway of the living room. The ever-present softball bulged at the pocket of her denim shorts.

"We'll be having dinner in less than an hour. Adam is due here any minute."

"Is he going to eat with us all the time now?"

"I don't know."

"Maybe we can use his kitchen instead. You know, eat at the island?" Billie smiled hopefully. "I'll be real careful not to spill anything."

"I'll be sure to let him know."

"I'm still hungry."

Jane sighed. "There are a couple of apple slices on the plate in the fridge. But that's all."

"Thanks." Billie stifled a yawn.

"Early to bed for you, young lady."

"Mo-om!"

She followed her daughter into the kitchen. "Don't 'Mo-om' me. I have a feeling Charlene kept you up well past your regular bedtime."

Billie grabbed a slice of apple and slammed the fridge door shut. "Maybe, you know, a couple of minutes."

Jane bit back a smile and leaned against the counter. "And what did the two of you do?"

"Well, we, huh, you know, talked."

"About?"

Billie hunched her shoulders. "Baseball."

"Did you play cards?"

"Cards?" Billie took a bite of her apple. "Can't talk with my mouth full," she mumbled.

"How convenient."

There was a knock at the screen door. "What's convenient?" Adam asked as he let himself in and paused just inside the kitchen.

Jane straightened and told herself not to stare. It didn't help. He'd showered recently. Dampness darkened his short brown hair, and he looked as if he'd just shaved. The smoothness of his jaw made her wonder what it would feel like against her hand. The crisp cotton short-sleeved shirt stretched across his broad shoulders and chest. The open V allowed a few hairs to peek out. She recalled touching that chest, so many years ago. A light dusting of hair, broad at the shoulders then narrowing toward his waist, had teased her fingers. Even now, her fingers curled into her palms at the memory of how he'd sucked in his breath when she'd accidently brushed her fingers across his flat nipples. It had been a moment of triumph for her, she remembered. A brief time when she'd been able to ignore her fears and reduce this strong man to hungry passion.

His chinos hugged slim hips and outlined the lean muscles in his thighs. Her gaze dropped farther down to the casual loafers, then began to move back up. His carefully constructed wall of control didn't seem to be working tonight, she thought in surprise. She could see his discomfort in the way he shoved his hands into his pockets, then removed them. She studied his face. The square jaw, the firm mouth that had claimed hers so recently, the eyes that he'd passed on to Billie.

Pain flickered in the brown depths. And confusion. And something that might have been longing. For the time lost? For the fact that he'd missed those years with Billie? Or for her? No, she thought. She couldn't allow herself to think like that. It cost too much.

"I'm glad you could make it," she said softly.

"Thanks for inviting me." He gave her a quick smile, then looked at Billie. "How are you feeling?"

"Okay." Billie finished the last of her apple and began to lick her fingers. She yawned suddenly.

"She's a little tired," Jane said. "I think Charlene kept her up last night. Can I get you something to drink?"

"Thanks. Whatever's easiest."

"Beer?"

He raised his eyebrows.

She shrugged. "We went to the market."

"Yeah," Billie said. "She bought this bread. The long kind." She held out her hands to show him the length. "We're going to make garlic toast. I know how."

"Maybe I could help you."

Billie tugged on the bill of her cap. Jane held her breath. It had been a gesture of friendship by Adam. She hadn't forgotten the look on his face when he'd watched her with Billie that afternoon. The need in his eyes, the obvious disappointment at being shut out. Go on, she urged her daughter silently. He's not so bad.

"Okay," Billie said. "I have trouble stirring the butter sometimes. You can do that."

"Great." Adam tugged off her hat.

"Gimme!"

He held it out of reach. She jumped up and tried to grab the cap. When that didn't work, she grinned. "Please."

"Why should I?"

"'Cause it's mine."

He chuckled and pulled the hat over her head.

"Here." Jane handed him a glass of beer.

Adam leaned against the counter and took a sip. His gaze flickered over her, and she was glad she'd taken the time to shower and change her clothes. The sleeveless sundress with its rows of tiny buttons up the bodice made her feel pretty. And right now she could use all the confidence she could get.

Billie yawned again. Adam frowned. "What time did you go to bed?"

"I don't know."

"Was it past your bedtime?"

Billie's smiled faded. "I don't have a watch."

He glanced at Jane. "I don't like the sound of that."

"Charlene wouldn't have done anything really horrible."

He raised his eyebrows.

"Oh, dear. I guess she would. Billie, did you and Charlene play cards?" Billie pulled out her softball and studied the seams. Jane knew that look. "Just tell me."

"A couple of games."

"Poker?"

"No." Billie shook her head. "We did a counting game. She gave me cards and I had to count them. Whoever got closest to twenty-one won. We played for cookies."

She moaned. "I told her not to teach you card games."

"It's hopeless," Adam said. "She's always been that way. I guess I shouldn't be surprised. She taught me to play poker when I was around Billie's age. It never bothered me much before."

"It makes a difference when it's your kid."

Their eyes met. For a second she regretted her statement. But Adam didn't lash out at her. There was a flash of understanding between them. Something warm and shared that made her long for all the moments they'd missed as a family. Had he been right? Had she deprived Billie of two parents? And what about the things she'd deprived herself of? Sharing the responsibilities made the load seem lighter.

"I see that," he said. He took another drink. "Early to bed for you tonight, Billie. And no more card games."

Her good humor vanished. "You can't tell me what to do."

"I certainly can."

Jane moved next to him. "Adam, I don't think—"

"We've established that point."

Her temper flared. "This is neither the time nor the place to bring that up."

"Don't yell at Adam," Billie interrupted, using her own brand of logic. Jane stared at her. Just seconds before *she'd* been the one saying he couldn't tell her what to do.

"Don't talk to your mother that way," Adam said, setting his glass on the counter. "You may not like what she's saying, but you will listen and respect her. Do you understand?''

Both women stared at him. Jane recovered first. "I think we've had our first fight as a family."

Adam folded his arms over his chest. For a second she thought he was going to stay mad. Then he grinned. "Was it good for you?"

"Yeah, it was."

Billie stared at both of them. "You guys are weird. I'm going outside to play ball."

"Dinner's in an hour. Don't run away this time."

Billie rolled her eyes. "I won't. Geez, Mom. Give me a break." With that, she ran out the back door.

Without her the kitchen seemed smaller. That didn't make sense, Jane told herself, but the feeling persisted. Perhaps it was the way Adam studied her. She walked over to the refrigerator and began pulling vegetables out of the bin at the bottom. "I thought we'd have pasta. I hope that's all right."

"It's fine."

She picked up the broccoli and stared at it. "Thanks for telling her to listen to me. You didn't have to take my side."

"I did it instinctively. The parents against the kids, I guess."

"A united front is best, especially now."

"There's so much I don't know."

She set the broccoli on the counter and looked at him. He shrugged. She saw the worry in the frown lines on his forehead.

"You just have to feel your way," she said. "At first I didn't know what to do, either. A lot of the time, I still don't. I just try and be fair and consistent. I also try not to sweat the small stuff. There are enough big things to worry about."

"Such as?"

When she least expected it, the pain caught her off guard. He stood there, so tall and handsome. In control. A perfect catch. If only he'd loved her. She shook her head. If she had a dollar for every *if only* in her life, she'd own the Barrington mansion and he'd be living next door.

"Oh, nothing I can think of offhand."

Before she could turn away, he reached out his hand and cupped her face. The touch, gentle, concerned, broke through her resolve and her pride. She started to look down, but he moved his index finger along her cheek and jaw until it rested under her chin and she was forced to stare up at him.

"Don't shut me out," he said. "What do you worry about?"

If he'd stopped touching her, she might have been able to lie. But he continued to hold her face, occasionally stroking her cheek with his thumb. The warm caress, more comforting than anything else, wore her down.

"Not Billie," she admitted. "Somehow she got the best of both of our families. I know in my heart she'll be fine."

"Then what?"

They stood alone in her kitchen. It wasn't the least bit romantic, what with raw vegetables scattered around on the counter and the sound of their daughter playing in the backyard. Yet she felt in tune with Adam. Perhaps he *would* understand.

"It's not my finest hour," she said tentatively, waiting to gauge his reaction.

"Are you waiting for a promise that I won't judge you?" She nodded.

His brown eyes searched her face. He struggled with her request. She saw the battle rage in his eyes. Then she saw victory. Her victory, and it tasted sweeter than she would have imagined.

"I give you my word."

How ironic. She'd given hers once, and it'd had no value. Yet she would risk her life on the strength of Adam's word.

"I'm afraid of losing Billie."

"But you said you thought she'd be fine."

"Not to anything bad. To you."

He frowned. "I don't understand."

She started to step away, but he tightened his hold on her face just enough to let her know he wanted her to stay. She relaxed. He eased her forward, slipping his hand around her neck and under her braid, until she rested against his side. His arm came around to hold her close.

"I've always been first in her life. The only constant in a changing world. That's all about to change. She likes you already, Adam. She can't help but grow to love you."

"You're assuming I'll do well."

"You will."

"I wish I could be as sure." He took a deep breath, then released it. "If you knew this was going to happen, why did you bother..." Now he was the one who stiffened slightly.

She wrapped her arm around his waist and held on. "Don't, Adam. Why did I bother coming back, if I knew the risk I was taking? Is that the question?"

"Yes."

It was easier this way, she thought, closing her eyes and resting her head against his chest. His cotton shirt felt warm and smooth against her cheek. She inhaled the scent of him. Better not to see the emotions in his eyes. Or worse, to see the shutters closing her out.

"I came back because it was time I stopped thinking only of myself. I took the risk because Billie deserves a father in her life and you deserve your daughter. I love her. She loves me. I have to trust that love to last through this. And if it doesn't..." She didn't allow herself to visualize that scenario. "I can't make her care if she doesn't want to."

"Sounds dangerous to me."

She could see why he would think that. After all, his parents had died when he'd been quite young. The next big relationship in his life had ended when she'd run off. No wonder Adam had his doubts about the strength of love.

"You're going to have to trust me on this one," she said.

"That's a big order," he said quietly.

She squeezed her eyes shut against the pain. She deserved the comment, but it still hurt.

"I didn't mean that the way it came out," he said.

"Yes, you did."

He stepped away from her and walked to the other side of the kitchen. The physical rejection hurt almost as much as his words had, but she forced herself to stand upright and not let it show. The hard part was that she felt as raw and exposed as an open wound. The broken promises, fears and lies from their past might never be overcome. And then what?

From the window, he could see out into her backyard. "Look at her," he said.

Jane walked over to stand next to him. She glanced out. Billie had a bucketful of softballs on the ground next to her and was pitching them through an old tire he'd hung in the yard. Her running commentary was barely audible through the glass.

"What are we going to do about all of this?" he asked, as if he could read her mind. "Where do we go from here?"

"I haven't a clue."

"Mom said she'd rather bake something, but there wasn't time, so we're having store-bought dessert." Billie leaned closer to Adam and lowered her voice. "I love my mom's cookies and stuff, but sometimes it's fun to have it from the store. They have that thick icing she doesn't like me to have."

No doubt about it, Adam thought as he returned her grin, Belle Charlene Barrington was a charmer.

"Did she let you pick it out?"

"Uh-huh. German chocolate cake." She licked her lips. "I took a taste of the icing before. It's great."

"I'm sure." He rose to his feet and collected their plates.

Dinner had gone better than he'd hoped. Despite the awkwardness between him and Jane, conversation had been lively at the table. With Billie around, there wasn't much fear of silence. So far she seemed to have accepted him with few reservations, although she did stick close to her mother. Charlene had told him it was perfectly natural in a child her age. He had to bow to her superior wisdom in this area. Funny, Jane was worried about losing Billie, while he was concerned about not being accepted. They were both afraid.

Billie picked up the empty bowl that had contained the pasta.

"Have you got that?" he asked. "Is it too heavy?"

She rolled her eyes. "I'm not a kid."

"Oh? What are you?"

She wrinkled her nose. "Okay, *maybe* I'm a kid, but I'm not a little one."

"Point taken." He held open the swinging door to the kitchen, and she ducked under his arm.

"Are you going to live with us?" Billie asked.

Even though he'd been worried about her handling the heavy glass bowl, he was the one who almost dropped the dishes he carried. He stepped into the kitchen and sought Jane's gaze. She looked about as startled as he felt.

"Live with you?" he repeated.

"You know, in the same house? Families do that. Are we a family?"

Jane took the bowl from her daughter's hands. "Yes, Billie, we're a family. As for living together, there are a lot of details to be worked out."

"What about the houses? We shouldn't have two. Can we live with Adam? I promise I won't slide down the banister."

Jane smiled at the girl. Adam wondered if Billie saw how her mouth quivered at the corner and the panic in her eyes. "I've told you about not making promises you can't keep."

Billie sighed heavily. "I'll *try* not to slide down the banister too often."

"That's better."

"So can we?"

Jane looked at him and silently pleaded for help. He set the plates on the counter and crouched in front of Billie. Without her baseball cap, she looked smaller and more feminine. He tapped her nose. "Your mother and I have to work out the details of this arrangement. As soon as we've come to some sort of agreement, we'll let you know. Agreed?"

"Agreed." Billie peered at him. "Are you my dad forever?"

The lump appeared in his throat without warning. "Yes. Forever."

"You won't go away?"

"What do you mean?"

"Sometimes dads leave. There were two girls in my class last year whose dads left. One of them had to move."

He didn't dare look at Jane. "Sometimes parents do things their children don't understand. But no, I won't ever leave you. Not after I've just found you." He rose to his feet. She held out her arms and he swung her up into his embrace.

"What does a dad do?" she asked.

"I'm not sure. We'll find out together."

"Do you buy me presents on my birthday?"

"Yes."

"And Christmas?"

"And Christmas."

"Like a bike?"

"Billie!" Jane shook her head.

Billie leaned closer to him and whispered, "In case you wanted to, you know, ask what I'd like for Christmas, I'd like a bike."

"I'd never have guessed," he said, holding back a smile.

"Enough," Jane said, planting her hands on her hips. "Billie, finish clearing the table. Adam, do you want cake?"

He lowered Billie to the floor and watched her scurry out of the room. Then he turned back to Jane. Several strands of hair had escaped from her braid and now drifted around her face. She wasn't wearing much makeup, just something to make her lashes longer and her eyes look mysterious. Any lipstick had long since worn away. But that didn't stop him from staring at her mouth.

If he concentrated, he could almost taste her sweet passion. It hadn't been that many days ago that he'd kissed her in anger. Despite the rage he'd felt and his need to punish her, she'd more than met him halfway. It had been a joining of equals, not of teacher and student. A blush stained her cheeks, but he didn't stop staring. His gaze drifted down to her chest and the row of impossibly small buttons marching from the top of the scooped neck down to the dropped waist of the dress. Her loose clothing hid her shape. Nine years ago she'd felt self-conscious about her small breasts. Had another man taught her that it was the soul of the woman that drove a man wild; that her body was simply packaging? Had other hands taught her that size didn't matter, that smaller might be more sensitive, that skin as smooth as hers could only ever be perfect? How many lovers had completed what he had begun? How many had made up for his boorishness?

"Adam?" She spoke his name softly, responding more to his look than asking a question.

He took a step toward her. Billie burst into the room carrying three glasses and a serving plate balanced precariously on top. He leapt toward her to rescue the china. The plate teetered. He caught it as it fell.

"Oops," she said.

"*Oops* is right, kid."

Billie set the glasses on the counter and turned to her mother. "When are we having dessert?"

"Right now."

Jane opened a bakery box and pulled out the cake inside. Billie grabbed forks and grinned. "My favorite part of the meal."

"Mine, too," he said, trying to ignore the panic building up inside. It was all happening too quickly and too easily. Billie liked him; Jane— He drew in a breath. Something was happening there all right. Hormones or memories or both. And it scared the hell out of him. He was risking too much. This whole thing could explode in his face, leaving him worse off than before.

"But I want *both* of you to put me to bed," Billie whined when Jane told her it was time to take her bath.

Jane shook her head and glanced at Adam. "There's still time to back out."

He sat on the sofa with Billie curled up next to him. With a lazy flick of his hand, he sent her baseball cap sailing. She chuckled and ducked after it, then climbed onto his lap.

"I'll take my chances," he said, holding Billie in his arms as he rose to his feet. "How about if I give you a piggyback ride to the bathroom, then *after* your bath, I'll help tuck you in?"

"Okay. But I want a *long* ride. The tub's real big and takes a long time to fill."

Jane watched Adam gallop down the hall, with Billie clinging to his back and urging him to go faster. He ducked to avoid bumping her against the hall light fixture. As they passed under the glow, the hair on their heads gleamed. Identical shades of brown reflected in the light. She forced herself to stand and walk up the stairs to the bathroom.

The raw feeling hadn't gone away, she thought, as she adjusted the water temperature. She needed some serious comforting. As she added bubble bath to the tub, she realized that an hour-long soak and a good book wasn't exactly what she was thinking of. She wanted to be held. By

Adam. The trouble with that scenario was that he was part of the problem. A big part. No doubt he was feeling a little on edge himself. Who would he go to for comfort? Was there someone special in Orchard, or maybe the next town, that he could call?

The thought of Adam with another woman fired up her temper, but she told herself she had no right to care. She'd given away that right the day she'd run out on him. She was lucky he wasn't married with a dozen kids of his own. At least Billie would have him all to herself while they got acquainted. Charlene had warned her that Adam hadn't spent the last nine years waiting for her. She would do well to remember that advice.

While the tub filled, Jane went into Billie's room and pulled a clean pair of pajamas out of a dresser drawer. After clicking on the lamp, she drew back the bright red spread and smoothed the sheets. The worn old teddy bear, with one ear missing and most of the fur rubbed off, was the only vaguely feminine thing in a room full of baseball posters and sports equipment. She picked up a couple of dirty T-shirts and dropped them into the basket, then walked to the doorway and surveyed the room. Where would they live when the dust settled on this new situation? The three of them? Here? She shook her head. Adam would never give up his family home; nor did she want him to. He belonged to the Barrington estate; it was as much a part of him as his eyes. Would they continue to live next door to each other? There didn't seem to be much option. She wouldn't move into that big house. She had no right.

Thundering footsteps on the stairs drew her attention away from her thoughts. She stepped into the bathroom and turned off the water, then returned to the hall and watched Adam carrying Billie up the stairs. They were both laughing at something. Billie tugged on his shirt collar as if it were the reins. Her pulling had unfastened two buttons exposing nore of his broad chest. Jane felt herself flush and looked away.

"One child delivered for bathing," he said, turning his back on her and grabbing Billie's arm to help her slide down.

"Just in time," Jane answered. "The bath is ready."

"Aw, Mom."

Jane laughed. "We have this conversation every night and 've never changed my mind about your bath. Why do you keep trying?"

Billie grinned. "You might say I don't have to."

"Hope springs eternal." She pulled off her daughter's aseball cap. "In." She pointed to the bathtub. "Now."

Billie glanced up at Adam. "Will you help tuck me in?"

Jane told herself not to look, but she couldn't help it. She glanced at his face. The shutters opened to reveal a longing o intense, it took her breath away. He reached out and apped Billie's nose. "Yeah. I'll be there."

"Cool." She ducked into the bathroom. "I'm not really dirty, Mom, so this shouldn't take long."

Jane rolled her eyes. "We go through this every night."

Adam smiled. "I can imagine. Call me when she's done."

She watched him retreat down the stairs. He moved with a powerful grace that made her long for a second chance.

"I'm in the tub," Billie called. "I'm splashing."

"I'm coming."

"Now Adam kisses me good-night," Billie demanded royally.

He leaned forward and obliged.

"Enough," Jane said. "No more kissing or conversation. Go to sleep. You're exhausted."

Billie yawned suddenly, then rolled onto her side. "Okay. G'night."

Adam hovered by the bed, as if he didn't want to leave her just yet. Jane waited by the door. Billie sighed, then her eyes fluttered closed. He leaned over and kissed her again, then joined Jane. They shut the door behind them and walked toward the stairs.

"All that energy," he said. "It's hard to believe she's actually going to sleep."

"I know. But as tired as she is, she'll be out in about twenty seconds."

They reached the hallway and stopped. Jane bit her lower lip. She should send Adam on his way. That was the sensible thing to do. They were both emotionally at the end of their ropes and needed the time to regroup. But to be honest—and selfish—she didn't want to be alone. Not yet.

"Would you like some coffee?" she asked, not daring to look at him.

He didn't answer at first. Slowly she raised her gaze to his. Confusion, acceptance and pain swirled in the brown depths. "You have anything stronger?" he asked.

"Brandy?"

"Perfect."

"I'll meet you in the parlor."

Chapter Twelve

Jane found the box of brandy her parents had given her last Christmas and opened the package. After collecting glasses, she turned off the kitchen lights and made her way to the front of the house.

The storm from the previous evening had passed, leaving clear skies and slightly lower temperatures. Even so, the South Carolina summer night swirled around her, bringing with it the scents and sounds that were uniquely home. Night jasmine, her mother's favorite, filled the air with its sweetly sensual fragrance. As she entered the parlor, she saw Adam standing by the front window. As at his house, shutters protected them from prying eyes. He'd pulled them back and opened the windows, but hadn't turned on any lights. A streetlamp provided slight illumination, as did the light in the downstairs hall. Enough to see the size and shape of him, but not his expression when he turned to look at her.

"Can you open this for me?" she asked, her voice a little softer than normal.

He took the bottle. "Are you sure you want to? Are you saving it for a special occasion?"

"I can't imagine anything more special than you finding out about Billie."

Even though he would be as unable to see her face as she was to see his, she turned away, embarrassed at exposing herself to him. She couldn't let herself forget that he was still angry and had the potential to wound.

But all he said was "Thank you." He tore off the protective covering and opened the bottle. She held out the glasses and he poured them each a half inch of the dark liquid.

"To Billie," she said, raising her glass.

"To Billie," he answered. But instead of drinking, he stared at her. She would have sold her soul for the courage to turn on a light and see the look in his eyes.

Uneasily she took a sip of the brandy, wincing as it burned a path down to her stomach. But in a few seconds the fiery heat became pleasant and she felt her tension begin to ease.

"Would you like to sit down?" she asked.

Without answering, he walked to the long sofa opposite the window and sat. Not on the edge, but not in the middle, either. She chose the opposite spot on the same couch. They didn't touch, but they could. If they wanted to.

Don't! she ordered herself. It was the night that made her foolish. Or the man. But it wasn't anything real.

The furniture loomed large in the semidarkness. She picked out the shape of the armoire she had carted with her across the country because of all the memories it contained. Two wingback chairs sat under the big window. In front of the sofa stood a coffee table. She leaned forward and set down her drink.

"Not a brandy drinker?" Adam asked.

"No."

"Me, neither. But it sounded good." He placed his glass next to hers. "Some of this old furniture sure brings back memories. I recognize that." He pointed to the armoire.

"I helped my mother refinish it. I guess I was a little older than Billie." She sighed. "I'm sorry, Adam."

"Don't be. It's been a lot for both of us to deal with. Let's worry about the apologies another time."

It would be easy to accept his kind offer, she thought. Easy to push her shame away and go on with her life. But that was the coward's way, and she'd been doing that for too long.

"No, I *am* sorry. About everything." She shifted on the sofa, turning until she faced him. She tucked one leg under her and spread out the full skirt of her sundress. "I'm sorry for the way I left you."

"But not for leaving?" He sounded bitter.

"I don't know."

"At least you're being honest."

For a change. He didn't say the words, but she heard them, anyway. "I'm trying," she said.

In the darkness she saw his right shoulder rise, then lower. But she couldn't see his face or the secrets in his eyes. She pulled her braid over her shoulder and began to toy with the end.

"My mother went to art school," she said, not looking at him. "She was very talented. There are some pictures of hers in the attic. I keep meaning to go get them down, but I can't. Not yet."

"Why?"

"I'm afraid of what I'll see in her paintings. She loved my father, but he didn't understand her desire to be more than his wife and my mother. He didn't like her painting or changing the house." She pointed at the armoire. "He was furious about that. He liked everything to stay the same. Including her. She wasn't allowed to grow or be her own person."

"I'm not your father."

"I know. But..."

He leaned forward and rested one arm on the back of the couch. "Don't blame me for his behavior. I had nothing to do with that. I would never have prevented you from changing. If you remember, I'm the one who encouraged you to plan on continuing with college after we were married."

"It's not that easy, Adam." She plucked at the ribbon at the end of her braid. When the cloth loosened, she pulled it free, then removed the rubber band. "You wouldn't have *said* anything, but I would have known just the same."

"What the hell are you talking about?" he snapped.

"Expectation. You were looking for the perfect banker's wife. I couldn't be that."

"You said that before. I didn't understand it then and I still don't. There is no 'perfect banker's wife.' I wasn't looking for a job applicant, I wanted a partner."

He sounded hurt. She wanted to go to him and offer comfort, but she didn't have the words and he wouldn't accept the gesture. Not from her. It was the darkness that made her brave, she realized. That and the fact that she was already so exposed to him. There wasn't much more he could do or say to hurt her. What was there to lose by speaking the truth?

"I wanted to be that partner," she said, loosening the braid. "I wanted to be everything. But I was so afraid."

"Of what?" He jerked up one hand in an impatient gesture. "What was so damn frightening about me?"

"Everything."

"That's a big help." He turned his head and she caught the flash of white as he smiled.

"You, Adam. You're what's frightening. You're so damn perfect."

"Perfect? Come on, Jane. That doesn't wash."

"You knew what you wanted and you went after it. I didn't know anything, except how I felt about you. Your direction and intensity scared me. I thought I'd get lost inside of you and never find my way out." She sighed. "That sounds silly."

"No, it doesn't."

She nodded. "Thank you for that. There was so little of me that I'd discovered. I felt that if I became a part of you, there would be nothing left. You wanted so much. What if I couldn't do it?"

She raised her hands and continued loosening the braid. With a shake of her head, she tossed the freed strands over her shoulders. Part of her hair swept across the back of the sofa. He twisted one curl around his finger.

"I wish you'd told me." His voice sounded husky.

"I was wrong not to."

"I'll admit that I could have spent more time with you," he said slowly. "There were difficulties at the bank and with Dani and Ty, but I should have made the time. You were important to me. I never meant to scare you away."

Perhaps it was her admission that freed him to confess his own secrets. She still couldn't see his face or read his eyes, but suddenly that didn't seem to matter.

"I know," she said softly. "I was too young for you. I didn't know at the time. It's only now, looking back, that I see I was—"

"What?" he asked urgently. "Tell me."

"A girl. A fool. You needed a woman, but I couldn't be that." It hurt to confess her shortcomings, she thought, surprised that after all this time it still mattered.

He swore. "You were all I ever wanted. Why can't you believe that?"

"I was too afraid."

"Of me?"

"Of the sex."

He bowed his head. "Now I'm the one who's sorry. Jane
I had no right to—"

Without thinking, she scooted forward and pressed he
hand against his mouth. "Don't," she whispered. "I wante
to please you. What I said the other day, about pushing m
further than I'd wanted to go...." She shrugged. "I wante
you, too. Maybe not in the same way, but I needed th
closeness and to feel you holding me. The rest of it, I'll ad
mit, didn't thrill me . . . but never believe that you coerced m
or hurt me. I came to your bed willingly, Adam Barring
ton. I loved you. There wasn't any other choice." When sh
finished her speech, she realized she still held her han
against his mouth. His firm lips moved slightly against he
palm. She dropped her hand. "Sorry. I got carried away."

But before she could pull back, he twisted his hand in he
hair. "I like it when you get carried away."

"Adam?"

"It's the night," he said softly, staring at her intently. "/
time for secrets. Here's mine. You drove me wild. So swee
and funny, so eager to please."

She ducked her head. "You make me sound like
puppy."

"No, just innocent. And beautiful. You stared at me a
if I were the most—"

"Perfect man," she whispered. "My fantasy come t
life."

Whatever had smoldered between them since her arriva
burst into life. Her body leaned toward the flames, absor
ing the heat that started another fire deep inside her. Th
wasn't the time. They were dealing with problems tha
would only be complicated by a physical relationship be
tween them. But she had to know. She had to find out if th
time they had been apart had changed anything. She had t
know if being a woman in heart and mind made it diffe
ent.

"Never perfect," he murmured, lowering his head closer to hers. "I had my share of flaws."

"No. I won't—"

He silenced her with his kiss. She'd wanted this, she thought, as his firm mouth pressed against hers. She'd wanted to be with him, just the two of them, in the dark, with no secrets between them. He continued to hold her hair, as if he were afraid she would try to leave. It was the farthest thing from her mind. Her hands crept up his arms and around his neck. She rubbed the hard strength of him, felt the ripple of his muscles as she kneaded his shoulders. Yes, she thought, letting her eyes drift shut. This is what he'd waited for.

He angled his head so their mouths met more fully. Lips pressed. She leaned forward, encouraging him to take more. His free hand rested on her bare shoulder. His thumb stroked in slow circles, singeing her skin with his heated touch. But still their kiss remained chaste.

She pulled back so that she could look at him. The darkness that had been so kind and allowed them to share their secrets now kept her from reading his expression. Did he want her? Was she looking for something that didn't exist?

"Adam?"

"After you left, I tried to figure out what it had been that had drawn me to you. Was it your hair?" He cupped her face with both hands, then drew his fingers through the strands at her temples and fanned them over her shoulders. He felt the curls as they were drawn across her skin.

"Like silk," he said quietly. "Or was it your smile?" His thumb swept across her lips. "Was it the shape of your mouth or the size or the way the edges curve up even when you're not smiling?" He touched each corner with his index finger. "Was it your body? The gawky picture you made in high heels?"

She didn't move as he ran his hands up her thighs to her hips. Heat flared wherever he touched, and turned her blood to fire.

"Did I want you because you had no idea about what you were doing to me?" he asked. "Was it the innocence?"

His hands moved up to her waist. She caught her breath but he didn't reach farther to soothe the ache. Her already hard nipples strained against her lacy bra. Her breasts throbbed in time with her rapid heartbeat.

"Or was it here?" He returned his hands to her face. "Inside. Was it your mind? Why were you the one?"

The control slipped away. She felt it flow out of him and disappear into the night. They were lost, she realized. Lost in a cauldron of emotion. Past and present blurred. The grayness of time overlapped until what had been and what was now had no distinction. The flames continued to race through her, but with them came the pain. As the fire burned away layers of facades, she was left with the sharp edges of her soul.

"Hold me," she whispered, feeling her eyes fill with tears. "Hold me tight."

He wrapped his arms around her and pulled her next to him. His heartbeat thundered in her ear. His breath fanned the hair that rested on her cheek. Without breaking their contact, he shifted on the sofa, sliding lower against the back corner, then easing her down until she nestled on top of him.

This felt right, she thought, loving the feel of his body against hers. His hard lines a contrast to her curves. No even the sensation of his arousal pressing against her hip disturbed her. This was as it was supposed to have been.

"I don't want to deal with the past anymore," she said "But I can't seem to let it go."

"Neither can I."

She raised her head to look at him. "Help me. Let's try to forget together."

He stiffened. "Like this?"

"Yes."

"I don't think that—"

"Don't." She shook her head. "Don't think about it anymore. Please. You want me." She rocked her hips and felt him strain against her.

"Tough to deny the obvious."

"Then what is it?"

He stared at her. "How much of that girl remains? Are you doing this for me or for yourself?"

He wanted to know if she was still afraid, she realized. The stigma of what had happened nine years before stood between them, an almost uncrossable barrier of guilt and conscience.

She sat up and tossed her hair over her shoulder. When he moved his head to follow the movement, she did it again. Without saying a word, she rose and crossed to the parlor door, then closed it. The clicking of the lock sounded loud in the still room. Only their breathing filled the continuing silence.

She reached for the small floor lamp in the corner and flipped on the switch. The sudden light made her blink. The look on Adam's face made her heart stop. Etched in the lines of his handsome face, desire and guilt battled for control. Everything else faded as the primal emotions raged inside him. She walked back to stand in front of the coffee table. He sat up straight on the sofa. She could tell him not to feel guilty about the past. He wouldn't listen. Better to show him the truth. There had been a time when he *had* frightened her. With her naïveté, she hadn't thought she could ask him to go slower. She wasn't that child anymore. She was a woman, with a woman's need. She slipped her hands up through her hair and fanned it over her shoulders. Slowly, so that he couldn't mistake her meaning, she reached for the first button of her dress. She never made it to the second.

He crossed the few feet between them and gathered he
into his arms. His mouth slanted across hers, pressing
seeking, probing as if she were his only lifeline. She parte
her lips to admit him and he pushed his tongue inside.

Her hands clutched at his shoulders and back. His hand
pulled her closer. Their tongues mated, slipping togethe
circling, brushing back and forth, drawing sustenance fro
the contact. She slipped her fingers through his hair. Th
short strands teased the pads of her fingers. His hands sli
down to her derriere and gently squeezed her curves. Fi
licked through her. She strained to get closer, but he hel
their hips apart. She punished him by forming an O aroun
his tongue and sucking gently. She felt more than heard th
moan in his throat and instantly he ground his pelvis int
hers.

The hard ridge of his desire pressed against her stomach
She raised on tiptoes to move it toward her needy center. H
tore his lips away and took her ear lobe in his mouth. Eve
as he bent his knees to oblige her wish, he nibbled the sen
sitive skin.

The combination of sensations—his mouth trailing dow
her neck, his hands rubbing her derriere, his need rotatin
against the apex of her thighs—made her feel like scream
ing.

She spoke his name over and over again, as if the soun
would save her from the coming storm. He raised his hea
and looked at her. She saw the question hovering in his eyes

"Yes," she said.

He straightened and reached for the front of her dress
His knuckles bumped her breasts as he worked the smal
buttons.

"Stupid design," he muttered.

She reached under his hands and easily opened the fron
of his shirt. "You're right."

He stopped long enough to step out of his shoes and socks and pull the shirt free of his pants. She kicked off her sandals.

When he freed the last button, he drew the sundress off her shoulders. Jane felt a flash of concern. She'd grown up in the last nine years, but not out. Still, he'd known that before they got started here. She squared her shoulders and shrugged out of the dress. It paused at her hips. She gave a slight wiggle and it fell to the floor. Adam's shirt joined her dress. But instead of looking at her body, he stared into her eyes.

"You still doubt yourself," he said, tracing the line of her jaw from her ear to her chin. "Hasn't anyone taught you that you are exactly right?"

She shook her head.

"Then they were fools."

This was probably the time to tell him that there hadn't been a lot of men to do the teaching. She'd dated some, in the nine years they'd been apart. Some of those dates had included heavy petting. But none of them had progressed to lovemaking. At the time she'd blamed it on lack of chemistry or dealing with a toddler or being busy with school. Now she wondered if it was because none of them was Adam.

He moved behind her. When she started to turn to face him again, he held her in place.

"Trust me," he said.

He moved her hair off one shoulder. From the sweet spot behind her ear, down to her bra strap, he kissed her heated flesh. Shivers racked her body, and her skin puckered. He licked her shoulder, then moved back to gently bite her neck. Her breasts swelled. Her nipples, already hard and eager for his touch, jutted out even more. Her hands fluttered in front of her. She didn't know where to put them. She started to reach behind her, but he pushed her away.

"Not yet," he murmured. "Trust me."

Did she have a choice?

He drew his hands around her waist, then up. She held her breath in anticipation. With one finger and his thumb, he released the front hook of her bra. The white lace drew back, only to catch on her nipples. The friction made her inhale sharply. He pulled at the straps until the garment slid down her arms and fell. Then he wrapped his arms around her waist and drew her back.

"Lean on me."

"Why?"

"Because I'm going to make your legs tremble and your body weak."

That statement practically did the job for him, she thought as she sagged against him. His bare chest felt warm against her back. She rested her hands on his forearms and closed her eyes.

"Watch me," he said, his mouth breathing the words into her ear. "Watch me touch you."

She lowered her head to look.

His hands moved up and engulfed her breasts. His palms moved in slow circles, completely covering her. At last, she thought as pleasure shot through her body. It was as if each individual cell had screamed out at his touch. Her head lolled back on his shoulder.

He raised his hands until just his fingers touched her. They circled around and around moving closer to her nipples. Her eyes fluttered.

"Watch!" he commanded.

She did. Her nipples strained forward, eager for their own pleasure. Moisture surged between her legs. Her muscles trembled, as he had promised.

At last he brushed his fingertips across the tips of her breasts. She felt the lightning all the way down to her toes. Her grip on his forearms tightened, and she moaned. Again and again he caressed the puckered skin, making it harder and tighter. Her hips began to rotate in a dance of their own.

Her knees threatened to buckle. Her hands longed to touch more of him. But she didn't want him to stop.

"Adam," she said breathily.

Moving quickly, so she didn't have time to register exactly what he was doing, he turned her, then lowered her to the carpet. His shirt and her dress provided a barrier to the rug. Barely pausing to settle her, he continued to touch her breasts. The magic his fingers created made her strain toward him. Pressure built inside. No one had ever taken the time, she realized, to show her how sensitive her body could be.

He lowered his mouth to hers. Wanting to pleasure him, as she was being pleasured, she wrapped her arms around him and went on the attack. When his tongue would have found hers, she sought his out and battled him within his mouth. She traced the edges of his teeth, nipped the inner smoothness of his lips, then sucked on his tongue until he drew back to gasp for air.

And still his hands played with her breasts. At last, when he wondered how long she could endure the glory, he trailed his mouth down her chin and neck and across her chest. She drew in a breath and rose toward him. He pulled away his hands and looked at her.

"Perfect," he said.

She blushed.

"Still the innocent?" he teased.

She didn't answer. If only he knew.

He continued to moisten her skin as he moved closer to her breasts. At last, his mouth closed over one throbbing nipple. The damp heat caused her to jerk and her pelvis to rise toward his. Her hands clutched at him. He suckled her, then circled the beaded tip. Her other breast swelled in anticipation. He didn't disappoint. As his hand continued the same his mouth had begun, he laved the other side with equal attention.

When she had no breath left, he lifted his head and smiled. She touched his face, the smooth-shaved cheeks, the straight nose, the firm mouth, still wet from his loving her. The rightness of their mating made her fearful of the future, but she pushed away the concerns. They were for later. This was her only point of sanity in a world gone mad.

"You make me tremble," she said.

"As you do me."

He drew her panties from her hips and peeled them off her legs. He had done this before, she remembered. Touched her there, before claiming her. It had been mildly pleasant. She was about to tell him he didn't have to bother, when his finger slipped between her damp curls. He touched some secret spot and she jumped.

He grinned. "I guess that means you're ready."

"For what?"

He started to laugh, then saw she wasn't kidding. His smile faded. "You've never had an orgasm."

It wasn't a question. They were adults. She was already naked. It shouldn't have embarrassed her. It did. The heated flush began somewhere around her toes and climbed all the way to the top of her head.

"I can't," she whispered, turning her head away.

He lay down beside her on the rug and touched her hair. "Who told you that?"

"No one, but I know."

"Have you tried?"

She closed her eyes. "I never did with you."

"Thanks."

His wry tone made her turn back to him. "It's not your fault. I was—"

"Yeah, well, could we *not* talk about my lack of performance and get on with the rest of it?"

"I don't want you to think it was your fault."

His self-deprecating smile eased her embarrassment. "It was only the two of us, Jane. And you were the virgin. Whose fault was it?"

"Oh."

"Yeah. Oh. What about the other men?"

She pulled her hair over her shoulder and studied the ends. "I've done a few things but I never—"

"Had an orgasm?"

"Went all the way."

"What?"

She swallowed. "I didn't feel the need."

"It's been nine years."

"I can count, too."

"Jane?" He sounded confused.

"Don't read more into it than it is. It just never felt right."

"Does it feel right now?" He touched her breast. She gasped and arched her head back.

"Oh, yes."

"Good."

She wanted to wipe that self-satisfied male smirk off his face, but he continued to tease her breasts and it became more and more difficult to remember why.

He moved his head to her chest and trailed his fingers down her stomach. This time she was prepared for the jolt when he brushed that secret spot. She wasn't prepared, however, for him to keep touching it. The contact created an aching pressure inside. She shifted her legs as if that would help her ease her need.

"Adam?" she asked, confused by what was happening inside. She needed him to stop. No, that wasn't right. She needed him to never stop.

"Hush. Trust me. Just feel it. I won't hurt you. And I won't let you fall."

Fall? She was lying on the floor. Where was there to fall to? Then he began to move faster and she didn't have the presence of mind to ask questions. Her world shrank down to his mouth and his hand. She vaguely felt his erection pressing into her leg. She should let him satisfy himself, she thought as her hips began to rotate in time with his fingers. Not just yet, she told herself as the pressure built.

Her breathing came in short gasps. His fingers danced around and around working their magic until she couldn't move, couldn't breathe, couldn't do anything but feel.

Falling. He was right. She could fall because he took her so high. Her muscles tightened until she thought she'd snap. He moved faster. She was going to fall. It was the only thing that would save her. But she was afraid. She didn't understand this or know what to do. Her hands clenched into fists at her sides. Adam.

She drew in her last breath and exhaled his name. He sucked deeper on her breast and the ground shifted. Her muscles rippled as she sailed out into nothing and began her free-fall back to the world. Pleasure surrounded, supported, carried her forward. Adam caught her as she neared the bottom of her descent. He held her close and promised she'd be safe forever. She'd known that, she saw in a moment of clearness. That's why she'd come home.

"Be in me," she whispered, parting her legs in invitation. "Feel this with me."

He quickly shed his trousers and briefs, then positioned himself between her thighs. Their gazes locked. Need and desire and pleasure at her release lit his dark irises. She wondered if she looked as satisfied as she felt. His hardness probed. She lifted herself toward him. He withdrew and frowned.

"What's wrong?" she asked.

"I don't have any protection with me. This wasn't planned."

"Don't worry." She smiled shyly. "I'm okay."

"Good. Because I didn't know how I was going to stop."

He plunged inside her, filling her with his arousal. This wasn't the uncomfortable pressure she remembered. Her body shivered as a last wave of her pleasure rippled through her. Adam groaned.

"You could feel that?" she asked.

He lowered himself until they could kiss. "Every quivering muscle. It's heaven. You're heaven." His mouth claimed hers.

He continued to thrust into her, the long slow strokes causing her to tighten around him. Every time he moaned his satisfaction, she felt her insides tremble. She drew back her knees and closed her eyes. The ascent began.

This time she knew what to expect from the journey. She reached forward, grasping his buttocks and pulling him closer. His thrusts grew faster, deeper.

"More," she gasped out, her lungs barely able to draw in enough air. She met him stroke for stroke. In her mind's eye, she saw the frightened girl she'd been, lying limply beneath Adam's hungry body. She remembered the ineptness and feeling of failure that had swept over her as he'd groaned his release. She'd been afraid and confused and too much in love to risk voicing her concerns and displeasing him. She'd grown up, she thought as she surged forward to meet him. His body grew harder, thicker inside her. His hips bucked under her hands.

She opened her eyes. His face, a tight mask of tension and raw desire, made her own need increase tenfold. She was his equal now.

He looked at her. The shutters fell away as if they'd never been in place. He smiled slightly, then held her hips and pressed in farther. She was so close. Too close. He reached one hand between their bodies and touched her. His thrusts stopped suddenly as his fingers circled her secret core. Then he moved faster, deeper and she sailed out into the ecstasy. The ripples within her milked his hardness. He cried out her name.

They held each other as they fell.

Even the crickets were silent. Adam pulled the sheet up over Jane's shoulder and watched her sleep. It was hours past midnight. Sometime after they'd first made love, they'd climbed to her bedroom. There, against the soft cushion of the mattress, she'd shown him that she was a quick study. Even now, his body hummed with the pleasure of her touch.

He was weary. Pleasantly so from their lovemaking. And emotionally from all that had happened. In less than thirty-six hours, he'd found out he was a father, been accepted by Billie and made love with Jane. The latter, he acknowledged, was a reaction to the former. They were both too near the edge to not succumb to the temptation. It didn't mean anything.

He rose to his feet and pulled on his clothes. Better for him not to be discovered in her bed. They discussed it, but she had protested she wasn't ready to let him go. So he'd waited until she'd fallen asleep.

He leaned over and kissed her cheek. Then, taking his shoes in his hand, he crept down the hall and opened Billie's bedroom door.

The girl—his daughter—slept on her back. An old teddy bear rested against her chest. Moonlight drifted across her cheek and made her look as sweet and innocent as an angel. He chuckled softly. Billie was a lot of things, but angelic wasn't one of them. Still—

He closed the door and stepped back. He could feel himself sinking in deeper. What was he going to do? Not caring didn't seem to be an option anymore. If he couldn't turn away from them, he'd have to find a way of keeping them with him. If he wasn't careful, they'd leave. Love meant losing. Jane had already proved she could leave him. This time he might not survive.

No matter what the cost, he had to find some way to get control and keep them here. If he didn't, he would lose them forever.

Chapter Thirteen

Jane looked over the stack of boxes in the attic.

"There's a ton of stuff here," Billie said, "but Charlene has lots more. Are there any clothes for me to play dress up?"

Jane shook her head. Not that again. Look at the trouble it had created the last time. Then she smiled. No more secrets, she thought. There was nothing to hide, nothing to fear. "I don't think my mother kept anything like that, honey. Grandpa didn't want her to save old clothes."

It was late afternoon. The sun had slipped behind a large tree in the yard, putting the attic in shade. A couple of bare light bulbs hung from the rafters and provided light, as did a window at the front of the room. Dust motes floated in the air. They'd left a trail of footprints from the door to the boxes where they stood now.

Billie knelt next to the small window at the front of the attic. "You can see Adam's house from here. The whole thing. It's big, huh?"

"Yes. It's big." Without meaning to, she joined her daughter and stared out at the Barrington mansion. The wings stretched well past where her own house ended. Windows gleamed from constant care. It was a lovely home, she acknowledged. At one time it was to have been hers. With a sigh she shifted until she was sitting on the dusty floor and staring up at the underside of the roof. She hadn't seen Adam since Sunday. She smiled. Okay, technically Monday morning. When sleep had finally claimed her, he'd crept out of the house.

Yesterday a crisis had kept him tied up at the bank. He'd called to explain and sent a huge bouquet of roses. But she hadn't really talked to him since they'd made love.

Had it been a mistake? Was it about the past or the present? Were they going to repeat the experience?

Just the thought of his hands and mouth touching her was enough to make her heart pound and her body flush. She'd spent most of yesterday wondering how she could have missed out on the wonder of it all for so long; and she'd spent most of today fearing that her feelings weren't so much about sex as they were about Adam.

"Whatcha thinking about?" Billie asked, rolling over to sit next to her.

"Your father."

"I like Adam."

"I'm glad. I like Adam, too."

Billie pulled the softball out of her shorts pocket. "Are we going to be a real family?"

"We're going to try. And don't throw that in the house."

Billie's sigh was long-suffering. She stuffed the ball away in her pocket. "If Adam's my father, how come I don't have his last name? Didn't you say that kids get the boy's name?"

The questions were inevitable, Jane told herself. So far she'd gotten off pretty light. But Billie was a verbal child and very bright. She couldn't walk around the truth forever. "Usually. But Adam and I didn't get married, so I didn't take his name. I gave you mine so that we would have the same name and people would know we belonged together.''

"How are people gonna know I belong to Adam?''

Interesting question. "We'll work something out. Come on.'' She rose to her feet. "Let's get to work on these boxes.''

"What are we looking for?'' Billie scrambled up next to her.

"Paintings. Your grandmother took several art classes. She's very talented. I know she did a couple of seascapes and a few watercolors of the area. I'd like to find them and hang them in the house.''

Billie frowned. "I've never seen Grandma paint. She won't even do finger paints with me.''

"I know.'' Jane opened the first box and peered inside. Old tax records. She closed the box and reached for another. "She had a dream, but she had to give it up.''

"Why?''

Oh, that was hard. "Sometimes we want to do something, but we know it will hurt someone else, so we don't do it.''

"Like throwing my ball in the house.''

Jane smiled. "Something like that. Grandma wanted to paint, but it made your grandfather unhappy.''

"Why? If the pictures are pretty wouldn't he want her to make them?''

"You'd think so. Grandpa is a different kind of person than Grandma.'' She pulled off a cover and peered inside. "Oh, look. Here's a couple.'' She carefully drew out several flat canvases. The first watercolor painting showed a garden in full bloom. Luscious colors blended harmoniously. Small, sure brushstrokes added depth to the plants and a gazebo in the corner.

"I like this one,'' Billie said, leaning against her arm. "What are the others like?''

Jane showed her, one by one.

"That one is like the roses Adam sent you."

She was right. Pale peach-and-cream flowers floated in a glass bowl. She had a dozen of the same roses downstairs in the parlor. She'd placed them deliberately so that when she looked at them, she saw the patch of carpet where they'd first made love.

"Are we going to hang these up?"

"Yes."

Billie touched the corner of the painting. "I don't understand why Grandpa wouldn't want her to do this. It's nice. Can I have one in my room?"

"Sure." Jane placed the watercolors on the floor by the door of the attic. "I think there might be some more pictures. Let's look for them for a little longer, then I'll go start dinner."

"Is Adam coming over tonight?"

"I hope so."

She needed to see him and reassure herself that what had happened between them had been as perfect and right for him as it had been for her. She wanted to see him and touch him and—

"Should I call Adam 'Dad'?" Billie asked. She wiped her hand down her face and left a trail of dust.

The question shouldn't have been unexpected, but it was. So many changes. Still, she'd done this for Billie. And Adam. "If you want to."

Billie shrugged. "I guess. I'm glad I have a father now. I wanted one for a long time. But when I think about him in my mind, he's Adam. I'm afraid I'll say it wrong."

"It's up to you." Jane smiled at her daughter and ignored the small tug at her heart. It was going to be hard to learn how to share the affection of this eight-year-old. She'd been the only one for so long. "You could practice for a while. Soon you'll start thinking of him as Dad instead of Adam and that will make it easier to say."

"Okay. Dad." She tried out the word. "Dad, Dad, Dad." She twirled in the room, bumping into boxes and chanting the word like a song. She stopped and stared at her. "Did you love Ad—Dad?"

Where had that come from? It would be easy to make up a story, but she was so tired of the lies. "Yes, Billie, I loved your father with all my heart."

"Then why did you leave?"

That was tougher. She wasn't so sure anymore. At one time the answer to the question would have made a lot more sense. "I didn't think I was ready to be married. Adam was all grown up, but I wasn't. Relationships between men and women require that both people are ready."

"Did he want you to go?"

She thought of all that he had told her. The bald way he talked about having to pick up the pieces of his life, the details of the failed wedding, the anger when he spoke of her betrayal. "No, Billie, he didn't. I hurt him very badly."

"Are you sorry?"

"Yes."

"Did you 'pologize?"

She smiled. "Yes, I did."

"Then it's okay. You always told me 'pologizing helps make it right."

Jane held open her arms. Billie rushed into her embrace. She hugged her daughter close. "You're a smart girl."

"I know. This is going to be great. You and me are going to have Adam now. He loves us and we love him."

Jane released Billie and walked to the window. Did she? She thought about her decision to come home from San Francisco. She recalled the way she'd pushed to have a confrontation with Adam, how she'd resisted telling him the truth because she didn't want to face what she'd done. So many of her concerns had been about keeping Billie safe. Had those genuine fears allowed her to hide another truth? She thought about how easy it had been to make love with

m. And it had been making love, she thought with a sure-
ss that surprised her. It had been more than sex, because
dam was more than just a man from her past. She hadn't
veloped a relationship with anyone else, because she'd
en waiting and growing up. When she was finally ready,
e'd returned, willing to pay any price to set the past right.
She loved him.

It didn't matter that he might not want her now. It didn't
atter that he wouldn't easily let go of his need to control.
didn't matter that she had nine years to make up for. She
ved him. That's why she'd come back to Orchard. She'd
me home to Adam.

"Something smells good."

Jane turned at the sound of Adam's voice. He stood in
e doorway of her kitchen. She hadn't heard him knock,
t Billie had been playing out front and had probably told
m to go in.

It was a little after four. He'd obviously come straight
om the office. He'd removed his jacket and rolled up his
irtsleeves, but had left on his tie. Stubble darkened his jaw
d highlighted the firm lines of his mouth. She wanted to
n to him and kiss him and tell him how much she'd been
inking of him. She wanted to have him whisper those
ords back to her.

Instead, paralyzed by a sudden burst of shyness, she hung
ck. "I'm trying a new recipe. It uses chicken and—"

He crossed the room in three long strides. "I wasn't talk-
g about the food." With that he gathered her close.

Her arms went around his neck. She raised her head and
brushed her lips with his.

"I missed you," he said, then kissed her again.

"Me, too."

"You're all I've thought of."

"Me, too."

"I thought this day would never end."

"Me, too."

He grinned. "Is that all you can say?"

Now that he was here, holding her, the shyness fle
chased away by desire. "No. I can ask why you feel the nee
to talk so much."

With that she held his face still and raised herself up c
tiptoe. She brushed her tongue across his lips. He tasted w
and warm and wonderful . . . like Adam, she thought, clo
ing her eyes and leaning closer. His hands moved fro
around her waist up, until he cupped her breasts. Instantl
her nipples hardened and he teased them.

She broke away. "Billie's outside."

"I know." He planted one last quick kiss on her mout
then stepped back. "How about something to cool m
down?"

"There's still beer in the fridge."

"Thanks." He walked across the room. "I'm sorry
couldn't get over here yesterday. It was one crisis after a
other. I didn't want you to think it was because Sunda
night didn't mean anything to me."

"You explained this on the phone as well as with th
roses. They're beautiful."

He twisted the top off the bottle and shut the refriger
tor. After taking a swallow, he looked at her. "I wanted
make sure you understood."

He was so damned decent, she thought, feeling her lov
for him swell inside of her. For a moment she toyed with th
idea of telling him what she'd realized that afternoon in th
attic. But it was too soon. There was still so much to wor
out. Besides, she wasn't sure that Adam was interested in h
love. He hadn't had time to come to grips with all the su
den changes. Neither of them had. And he had a lot mo
forgiving to do than she did.

"I understand. Do you want to stay for dinner?"

"I'd love to."

"Should I invite Charlene?"

"She's busy with her packing tonight. I don't know that e'll have time."

"I'll call and ask. When does she leave?"

"In the morning."

Jane smiled. "I admire her. Going to Greece. Alone. At r age."

"I'm not so sure she's going alone."

She turned back to the counter and continued dicing the getables she'd been working on when he arrived. "Then ith whom?"

"I haven't a clue. Maybe one of her trucker friends. I was inking about Billie," he said, approaching her from be- nd and resting his hands on her shoulder.

"She's been thinking about you, too," she said. She tilted r head and rested her cheek on his hand.

"And?"

"She wanted to know about calling you Dad." She smiled at him. "I hope you don't mind that I encouraged her."

He swallowed. "I'd like that."

"She said that it would take a little getting used to, but I n't think it will be all that long."

He picked up the beer bottle and took a drink. "Speak- g of Billie, I thought I'd better bone up on this whole renting thing."

"What does that mean?"

"I'll show you." He walked into the hallway and re- rned with a bag from a local bookstore. "I picked up a w books on raising children. Just to give me a frame of ference."

He spread them out on the counter. She scanned the ti- s, then wiped her hands on a nearby dish towel and picked the top one. "*Assertive Discipline For Children.* Don't t Billie see this one."

"She's going to need a firm hand."

Jane shook her head. She didn't like the sound of that. Billie is her own person."

"She'll be a teenager in a few years."

"She's only eight."

"I've done a little reading. It's important to control—'

"Stop." She held up her hand. "I know *control* is yo
favorite word, but it's not mine. I want you to be a part o
Billie's life, but that means we'll be working togethe
Adam."

"I've been thinking about that, too."

"And?"

"What about her last name? Shouldn't it be mine?"

First Billie and now him. Did they have some sort of ps
chic communication she didn't know about? "I don't thir
that's important."

"It will be." He stared down at her. The warm lover wh
had greeted her with a kiss was disappearing and in his pla
stood the cold stranger she'd come to fear. "School starts
a few weeks."

"I'm aware of that. I have a planning meeting ne
week."

"My point is Billie isn't going to keep quiet about me.'

"So?"

"Orchard is a very small town. As soon as word gets ou
people are going to talk."

She covered her face with her hands. "I know. I didr
want to think about that, but you're right."

He touched her arms and lowered them to her sides. "I'
not trying to be difficult, Jane, but these are things we hav
to talk about."

"But do we have to deal with them now?"

"Why not?"

Because I've just realized that I never stopped loving yo
she thought. Because I want you to hold me and love me ar
promise me this time we can make it. Because I need to he
that I'm not too late. "I just thought—" She shrugged.

"What about her birth certificate?"

"What about it?"

"Am I listed as her father?"

"We went over this already. Of course."

"Good. Then we won't have to deal with the formalities in adoption."

"Adoption! What on earth are you talking about?"

He folded his arms over his chest and leaned against the inter. "I want to legally recognize Billie as my daughter. meeting with my lawyer and changing my will. Every- ig will be left to her—in a trust of course. There are cer- family heirlooms that will go to Dani and Ty, but the k of the estate—"

"Stop!"

he walked out of the kitchen and down the hall. He fol- ed. When she reached the front parlor, she instantly re- tted leaving the safety of the other room. The scent of es filled the parlor. The soft light from the lamp caught ir peachy color and made the individual petals look as if y glowed.

"You're going too fast," she said, without turning und. "We have to handle this situation one crisis at a e. The first item is dealing with the three of us as a fam-

"But I want Billie to be taken care of."

"I've done that." She spun to face him. "She's been en care of just fine. By me. I've been responsible all these rs and we've managed to survive without you."

"That isn't necessary anymore."

he saw by the stubborn set of his jaw that she wasn't ing through to him. "We don't need your money."

"Don't let your pride interfere with what's best for the d. There's medical insurance, contributions to her col- funds. I want to take care of the details. You shouldn't e to do it on your own. Billie is my daughter, too."

Vhere had he gone? she wondered as she looked search- ly at his eyes. The deep brown gave nothing away. But ietime between the last time she'd seen him and this,

she'd lost her ability to find his vulnerable side. The need
control had returned in full force.

"You want too much, too soon," she said, rubbing h
hands up and down her arms. Despite the muggy heat, sl
felt cold.

He leaned against the doorframe. "I'd also like to go wi
you when you meet with her teachers."

"Dammit, Adam, are you listening to me?"

"Of course."

"Adam, I'm not a child anymore. You can't push n
around."

He frowned. "I don't understand why you can't be re
sonable."

"Reasonable?" It hurt so much, she thought as the tea
formed. She blinked them back. "You can't win this l
controlling us. You can't make me stay or Billie care abo
you by giving her your last name or putting her in your wi
That's not what matters. It's the people. Us. You. Me. B
lie. Love us. Let us love you. That's how we'll make
work."

He turned away, but not before she saw the fear in h
eyes. He couldn't, she realized with a sense of panic. F
couldn't do it without the control. To him that's all he ha
She'd grown up while she was gone, but he hadn't learne
that love without trust, without freedom, could never su
vive.

"Oh, Adam." The tears fell. She didn't bother to brus
them away.

He looked at her then. "No," he said coldly. "You're n
going to run this time. You're not taking Billie away fro
me."

She shook her head. "You don't get it. That's not wh
this is about. It's about letting yourself love somebody, a
trusting them to love you back."

The front door banged open. Billie ran in.

'I'm hungry, Mom," she called. "When do we eat?" She
ne to a sudden stop and glanced up. "M-mom?"
ane reached up to wipe her face, but it was too late. "I'm
:," she said through the tears, then turned and fled up the
irs.

3illie stared after her, then swung her gaze to Adam.
'You made my mother cry!"

\dam felt as if he'd taken a sucker punch to the gut.
illie, I didn't mean—"

'Why'd you do that? I hate you."

5he ran at him and began punching his thighs. The blows
·e too light to cause damage, but they hurt him as much
f she'd stabbed him with a knife. Every touch of her fist
s a dagger to his heart.

'Billie! No! Stop, please! This isn't what you think." He
·pped to his knees and grabbed the girl's hands in his. She
iirmed to get away.

'I won't let you hurt her. I won't!" she cried.

'Hush, Billie. Listen." She tried to twist out of his grasp.
lease. Just listen."

Iis quiet voice finally got through to her. She stopped
ving and stared at him. Tears rolled down her cheeks.
r nose was red and her hat askew.

'I didn't hurt her on purpose," he said, taking the chance
l releasing her. "I'm going to go up and talk with her, but
t I need to make sure you understand."

'You made her cry," she repeated stubbornly, wiping the
:k of her hand across her face.

'I know and I'm sorry. Sometimes it's easy to hurt peo-
we care about even though we don't mean to. Have you
r made your mother cry?"

5he stared down at her feet. "Yes." Her voice came out
a whisper.

'Do you remember how it made you feel?"

'Bad."

"That's how I feel inside. I'd never hurt you or yo
mother on purpose. I'm going to apologize to her. Do ye
understand?"

She nodded without looking up.

"Billie?" He touched his index finger to her chin. Sl
raised her head. "Are we okay?"

"Yeah."

"Promise?"

She gave him a watery smile. "Yeah. We're okay."

"Can I have a hug?"

She hesitated for a second, then flung herself at him. Sl
spoke so softly that he couldn't hear the word at first. The
it sunk in.

"Dad."

She'd called him Dad. The coat of armor he'd bee
building ever since Jane had barreled back into his li
cracked a little bit more. He was losing ground fast her
First with Jane and now with Billie. He couldn't sto
thinking about keeping the two women in his life. But
what price? Billie had just shown him that her temper cou
easily explode. What happened if she decided that she didr
want him as her father anymore? What if Jane refused
listen to his plans for the future? How was he going to kee
them from leaving?

He held Billie tighter, as if by hugging her close, he cou
hold the world at bay. He was losing a war and he didr
even know who the enemy was.

He felt her ease back, then kiss his cheek. "I'm gonna g
outside till dinner, okay?"

"Okay. I'll go talk to your mom."

She ran out the front door.

He rose to his feet and turned to go upstairs. When I
reached the landing, he paused. He couldn't lose them. N
now. What was he going to do?

A thought burst into his mind. He ignored it at first, then began to wonder if it wasn't true. Perhaps the reason he was going to lose this war was that the enemy was himself.

Jane knocked on Charlene's door. When the older woman called for her to come in, she stepped into the living room and laughed.

"I can't believe you're going to need this much luggage," she said, looking at the suitcases open around the room. Clothes stood in piles on every available surface.

Charlene sighed. "I'm not a light traveler, dear. I always think of something else I just might need. So I pack it all."

"I've come to say goodbye."

Charlene raised one auburn eyebrow. "I assume you mean because I'm leaving in the morning."

"Why else?"

Charlene didn't answer. She folded the silk nightgown she was holding and laid it in the nearest suitcase.

"Oh." Jane grimaced. "As opposed to my leaving because everything here has gotten so awful."

"I *was* going to ask about that, but now I won't."

Jane cleared off a space on the floral-print sofa and dropped down. Charlene handed her several camisoles. She began to fold them. The older woman's small house provided a haven for all of them, Jane thought. Billie had stayed here. Who knows how many times Adam had run here, and now she was doing the same. It was better than being home.

She sighed as she recalled Adam's stiff apology for making her cry. He hadn't said he was sorry for what he'd wanted to talk about, though. She'd noticed that distinction. And then dinner had been strained and awkward with Billie talking to the two adults, but them not talking to each other. When he'd offered to read to Billie and put the girl to bed, Jane had gratefully accepted and had fled to Charlene's.

"There are problems with the adjustment," Jane said. "It would have been foolish to assume otherwise. Still—"

"You were foolish?" Charlene smiled.

Jane shrugged. "Let's just say things are about what I should have expected if I'd thought this thing through."

"What exactly does that mean?"

"He's still the same. He's still trying to control people by controlling the circumstances."

"In what way?"

"He wants to talk about changing Billie's last name, putting her on his health coverage, adding to her college fund. That sort of thing."

The older woman nodded. "I understand perfectly. I can't *believe* he'd be so self-centered. I hope you put him in his place." She took back the camisoles Jane had folded and packed them next to the nightgown.

"I told him—" Jane looked at her. "Wait a minute. That didn't sound completely sympathetic."

Charlene winked. "You always were a bright girl."

"What are you trying to say?"

Charlene shrugged and headed for the bedroom. "Nothing, really."

"Sure," Jane muttered under her breath.

"I heard that."

Jane chuckled. "Okay, go ahead. Say what you're thinking."

Charlene returned with an assortment of lingerie. She shook out a long, pink, gauzy gown and smiled. "Are you sure you want to give me that much license?"

"Speak."

"You say that Adam hasn't changed, but maybe you're the one living in the past. You've had over eight years to get used to being Billie's mother. Adam has had three days. Under the circumstances, I'd say he's acting pretty decently." She sighed. "The Barrington men have always been strong. I remember when his mother was first dating—"

"Charlene! Could we please stay on the subject?"

"If you insist." She picked up another negligee, this one black, with more lace than fabric. "Have you considered the possibility that you're overreacting to his very normal concerns about his child? Wanting to make sure she has medical insurance and a decent college fund hardly seem like offenses that deserve your outrage."

"Maybe." Jane leaned forward and rested her elbows on her knees. "I hadn't thought about that. He came in with his list of things to change and I—"

"Reacted. Sit up straight, dear. That position does nothing for your posture."

"I'm twenty-eight, Charlene. I can sit how I like." But she leaned back, anyway.

The older woman smiled. "Very pretty. Now, about Adam." She shoved aside a pile of caftans and settled on the arm of the couch. "If you could have seen him that day at the church, when we found out you'd left. He was very hurt. I remember thinking it would have been kinder if you'd shot him."

Charlene spoke in a matter-of-fact tone. It took several seconds until her words sunk in. Jane blanched. Shot him? Was she kidding? But the older woman shrugged.

"He loved you, Jane. You abandoned him. Why are you surprised that he might feel that pain?"

"Did he love me?" She folded her arms across her chest. "Did he tell you that? Did he say those exact words? I've thought about it, you know. Tried to remember everything from the past. He never told me."

"What?"

She looked up. "That he loved me. Not once. Not even when he proposed. 'We're well suited,' he said to me that afternoon. Then he kissed me and promised he'd make me happy. He didn't have to try hard. I worshiped him already. But he never said 'I love you.' Did he to you?"

"Don't be silly, Jane. Of course he cared." Charlene began to bustle around the room, picking up toiletries and tossing them into a smaller carryon bag.

"But did he say the words?"

"Not those exactly, no. But you mustn't read too much into that."

"That's what you told me when I first came home. Maybe you're wrong, Charlene. Maybe I was just a convenience. Maybe Adam can't love, maybe he can only control people."

"He didn't have to say the words," Charlene said sharply. "I watched him suffer. He lost weight. He couldn't sleep." She blinked several times. "He begged me to tell him why. When I couldn't answer, he told me I was never to speak of you again. And we never did. But I saw it in his eyes. Perhaps he controls his world because without that barrier, it hurts him too much." She turned away. "That sounds like a man who loved very much. To me, at least. But then I'm an old woman. Feel free to ignore me."

"Charlene, don't." Jane rose and walked over to her. She reached out to touch her arm, but Charlene shrugged her off.

"Besides, what about what he's done for Dani and Ty? He raised those two on his own. He worked for them, gave up his dreams about learning banking somewhere else."

Jane stared at her in surprise.

"Oh, you didn't know about that, did you?" Charlene asked. "Adam hadn't always planned to come straight back to Orchard. Before his parents died he'd been considering doing an internship in one of the big cities. Maybe working there for a few years and returning to Orchard when he was older." She leaned close to Jane and pointed her finger. "What about the dreams Adam has had to give up? Who cares about that? Who's taken the time to find out what he's suffered? You? Did you bother?"

"I—" Shame flooded her. "No. I didn't find out. I never thought to ask."

"I love you, Jane. You're family now. But don't ask me to choose sides. I can't take a stand against you, but I won't take one against Adam, either. If you don't like how he's handling the situation, tell him. But before you go complaining about the man he used to be, maybe you should take the time to learn about the man he's become."

Chapter Fourteen

"I really appreciate this," Jane said as she stuffed a few more papers into her briefcase. "I would have made other arrangements, but with Charlene gone this last week—"

"Hey." Adam reached out and touched her arm. "It's okay. You didn't know the meeting was going to continue this evening. Billie's my child, too. I'm happy to look after her for a few hours. We'll be fine."

She nodded. "I shouldn't be too late. Nine o'clock. There's just a couple more things that need to be discussed."

He leaned back against the kitchen counter and grinned. "Stop explaining. I've said yes, I've said I understand. What else are you looking for?"

He'd meant the question teasingly, but Jane looked at him so seriously, he began to get uncomfortable. He held her gaze for a couple of seconds, then let it wander over her face and body.

She always wore dresses or skirts and blouses, so her out-fit didn't surprise him. She'd pulled a blue jacket over a white dress cinched at the waist with a belt the same shade of blue. Sensible low-heeled shoes gave her an extra inch or so, but she still stood well below his eye-level. Her hair—long and silky, smooth and perfect—had been pulled back in one of her fancy braids. If he concentrated, he could re-call the feel of those strands in his hands, against his chest, stroking him as she had— He shook his head to dispel the thoughts. They weren't productive. He shifted slightly to conceal the rapidly growing hardness between his thighs. All right, they *were* slightly productive.

Her hazel eyes met and held his. What was she searching for as she looked so intently, he wondered. Her mouth, wide and soft, shaped to looked innocent, but designed for pleasure, trembled at one corner.

"What are you thinking about?" he asked softly, not wanting Billie to hear. The rain trapped the tomboy inside and she had reluctantly settled down in front of the TV.

Jane glanced down at the papers she was holding. "Nothing important." She stuffed them into her briefcase. "Just remembering something Charlene told me about you."

He grimaced. "I'm not sure I want to know."

"It was all good."

"I doubt that."

She straightened and shoved her hands into her jacket pockets. "Adam, if your parents hadn't died, would you have come back to Orchard after you graduated from col-lege?"

"No."

She smiled, but didn't look especially happy. "Just like that? You don't have to think about your answer?"

"Why would I? I'd already started making plans." He shrugged. "I wanted to try a big city. New York, Chicago. Dallas."

"Dallas?" She raised her perfect eyebrows. "Really?"

"Don't you think I'd make a good cowboy?"

Her gaze swept his body. Her attention was as tangible as a touch, and heat flared inside. "You'd look great in jeans."

"Thanks," he said wryly. "That's always been a priority in my life."

"I'm serious," she said, looking up and smiling. He saw the laughter lurking in her eyes.

"So am I." He moved closer to her, stopping when he was only inches away. Her chest rose and fell in time with her breathing. "Why all the questions?" he asked.

"I only asked one."

"Today." A strand of hair had escaped the confines of her braid. He tucked it behind her ear. "Over the last few days, you've done nothing *but* ask questions."

She stared at his shirt collar as if it were the most fascinating thing she'd ever seen. "I don't know what you're talking about."

"Liar." He grinned.

She made a fist and tapped his arm. "Don't call me names."

"So why all the questions?"

"I'm taking Charlene's advice."

"Now we're in trouble."

She shook her head. "She told me to get to know you. That's what I'm trying to do."

Get to know me in bed, he thought, but didn't speak the words. Since the evening he'd made her cry, they'd slept apart. In separate rooms in separate houses. He longed for her as a thirsty man longs for water. He thought of nothing but her. But he wouldn't ask and she didn't offer. He wanted her to get used to him, to them. He'd apologized and she'd accepted that apology. Now they were feeling their way through a mine field of emotions. It would have been easy, he thought, seeing the need on her face. But he wanted her to be as hungry as he was. In the past, he'd pushed her far-

er and faster than she was willing to go. He wasn't going
o do it again.

"Why?" he asked, stepping back.

"Why what?"

"Why are you getting to know me?"

She lowered her eyes. "Because I'm not sure I ever did."

he picked up her briefcase. "I've got to run. Billie should
e in bed by eight-thirty. She'll probably hassle you."

"I can handle it. Drive safely."

"I will."

Jane offered him a tentative smile, then escaped out the
ack door. The rain pounded on the roof of the house. He
aited until he saw the headlights of her car sweep down the
riveway and disappear.

"Adam, this TV show is dumb," Billie called from the
amily room. "Can we play a game?"

"Sure," he answered. Something physical, to tire her out.
What did you have in mind?"

"Hide-and-seek?"

She appeared at the doorway to the kitchen. The once-
hite T-shirt had been stained with an assortment of col-
rs. Despite being trapped indoors all day, her shorts were
qually dirty. He'd seen her first thing in the morning and
new that she'd started out with clean clothes.

"How do you do that?" he asked.

Billie frowned. For once, her hat had been left in her
edroom. Her brown hair, exactly the color of his, hung
round her face. "Do what?"

"Get so dirty."

She glanced down at herself and shrugged. "I'm a kid."

He picked her up and swung her in the air. She laughed
nd clung to him. "More!"

He continued until they were both dizzy. "All right, kid.
'm going to count to twenty."

She rolled her eyes. "Twenty! How about a hundred?
ive me some time to hide."

"Thirty-five," he countered.

"Fifty."

"Forty."

She wrinkled her nose. "Forty-five."

"Done." He closed his eyes. "One, two—"

"Don't peek."

"You're wasting time. Three, four—"

With a screech, she ran out of the room. Adam contiued to count. She was an indescribable joy. He'd bee blessed many times in his life, but never with anything li her. He regretted the time lost, he acknowledged. When was alone, usually late at night, he hated what Jane had d prived him of. But the emotion decreased slightly each da and had recently become tinged with sadness.

Some part of the blame was his. He had underestimate the needs of the frightened young woman he had asked marry him. Instead of a relationship, he'd offered maint nance. She'd left him, yes. She'd been wrong not to tell hi about Billie, but he shared some of the responsibility.

"Forty-five!" he called out loud, then gave her a coup of seconds for good measure.

He'd heard her go upstairs, but had then heard a sc whooshing noise. Had she slid down the banister to tri him? He crept along the hallway, stepping on the edge of t carpet to avoid the creaking boards. In the parlor, checked behind the sofa and inside the armoire. A slig breeze blew in from the rainy night. He stepped closer to t window to close the shutters. A flash of white caught h attention. She'd tucked herself in the corner, behind t wing chair. He took another step toward the window. Bill huddled deeper into the shadows and kept her eyes close as if her not seeing him would mean he couldn't see her.

He was about to speak her name, when he realized would spoil the game if he found her so easily. He closed t shutter, turned his back on her and walked out of the roor

Several minutes later, after combing the house, he called out to concede his defeat. Billie emerged from the parlor.

"You walked right by me," she said triumphantly. Her brown eyes glowed. "I was in the corner."

He pretended dismay. "I thought I heard you go upstairs."

"I did, but then I changed my mind." She covered her eyes. "Okay, your turn."

They continued to play for almost an hour. Adam called it quits and started to fix cocoa. Billie turned on the TV in the other room. He'd just taken the milk off the stove when there was a crash. He set down the pot and sprinted toward the noise.

Billie stood in the hallway. Beside her, a small table lay on its side, along with the smashed remains of a vase. He crouched down beside the mess. On top of the broken china rested her softball. He picked it up and carefully wiped away the glass. Now what? He wanted to go get one of his child rearing books and read the chapter that covered this, but there wasn't time.

"It wasn't my fault," Billie said, thrusting out her lower lip.

He raised one eyebrow. "I don't see anyone else here."

"I wasn't *throwing* it. It slipped." She planted her hands on her hips. "I'm *not* in trouble."

"Are you allowed to play with your softball indoors?" he asked, knowing the answer.

"Yes."

"Billie?"

"No." She hung her head.

"You knew the rules and you broke them."

"You gonna tell my mom?"

"Yes." Why couldn't Jane be here now? What was he supposed to do? He couldn't bring himself to spank Billie. So how did he punish her? A vague thought passed through his mind. Something about time-outs and— "I want you to

sit in the corner for twenty minutes,'' he said, hoping he wa
doing the right thing.

She stared up at him, her expression outraged. ''No way.

''Yes, way. Now.'' He took her by the shoulder an
guided her to a corner in the dining room. He pulled out
chair and slid it behind her.

''Sit.''

''I'm not gonna stay here. You can't do this. You're nc
my mom.''

Her words hurt, he acknowledged, but that didn't chang
a thing. ''You're right. I'm your father. You've disobeye
and now you must face the consequences.''

''You can't make me.''

He looked at her. Slowly Billie lowered herself into th
chair. He pushed it until the edges touched the wall. Sh
bounced her feet on the rung. ''I'm not going to stay here.

''Then you'll have to be punished for that, as well. It
your choice.''

She turned her head away from him.

He left the room. His heart pounded in his chest and hi
palms were damp. Was he doing the right thing? Was h
scarring her for life?

He cleaned up the glass then put the milk back on th
stove. The time passed slowly. He heard Billie hitting the to
of her athletic shoes against the wall. He wanted to tell he
to stop, but wasn't sure of all the rules for a time-out.

When the twenty minutes were up, he walked into th
dining room. Billie sat hunched in the chair. ''You may ge
up now.''

She slid the chair back and climbed down. Her dark eye
accused him. ''I thought you were my friend.''

He wanted to be. But more than that, he needed to be
parent. This was the fine line those books he'd read ha
talked about. The reality of caring about someone enoug
to do what was best, even if it made her unhappy. ''I'm you
father.''

"I don't want you for my dad."

He'd seen it coming, but that didn't stop the pain. "I'm sorry you feel that way, Billie," he said quietly. "Come into the kitchen."

"Why?"

"You're going to write a letter to your mother explaining what you did and that you're sorry. I'll give it to her when she gets home."

Billie followed him silently. When he placed a sheet of paper and a pencil on the small table, she sat in the chair without saying a word. He poured cocoa and set a mug next to her. She ignored it.

He wanted to say something. But what? She deserved the punishment. Didn't she? His chest ached from the hurt inside. It seeped all through his body, making him feel beaten. It was happening, just as he'd feared. He cleaned up the pot he'd used and put away the ingredients. Behind him, Billie wrote on the paper. Her pencil scratched slightly with each letter. He heard a sniff. He turned around, and she was brushing away her tears.

"Billie?"

She didn't look up. God, he wasn't ready for this. Before he could decide what to do, she pushed back the chair. "I'm done."

"Fine. Would you like—"

"I'm going to bed." She wouldn't look at him.

"I'll come up and tuck you in."

"No!" She raised her head and glared. "I hate you. You're not my dad. My dad would never do what you did. Go home."

With that, she marched out of the room.

He'd lost her, he thought grimly. He'd had her for less than two weeks and now she was gone. "I hate you." The words repeated themselves over and over in his mind. He could see the tracks of her tears, hear her voice, see the rage in her small body. He'd lost his child. If he'd ever had her.

Was it all an illusion? Jane, Billie, the chance to be part of a family—his family? Everyone left eventually. Why hadn't he learned that lesson? Billie was gone; Jane wouldn't be that far behind. He took Billie's untouched mug and poured the cocoa into the sink. He couldn't let it happen, he realized. He couldn't let Jane go. He had to hold her with him. Being left a second time—he shuddered—he would never survive.

He turned off the lights in the kitchen and walked toward the parlor. There was only one way to convince her to stay.

Jane arrived home a little after nine-thirty. Adam heard her car in the driveway.

"Hi," she said, as she swept into the kitchen. Drops of rain glistened on her smooth hair. "It's still raining."

"So I noticed." He smiled slightly and wiped the moisture from her cheek. "You should have taken a jacket."

"You sound like my mother." She wrinkled her nose. "Besides, it's too hot out there. I won't melt." She set her briefcase on the counter. "Is Billie asleep?"

"Yes. I just checked on her." He didn't mention that he'd spent the better part of an hour sitting in the dark and watching his daughter sleep. She clutched her teddy bear so tightly to her chest. Was that her normal position, or was she still traumatized from what had happened before? He knew *he* was. His stomach clenched tight as her words again echoed. "I hate you."

"How was the meeting?" he asked.

"Great. I really like several of the programs they have here for the students." She slipped out of her jacket and hung it over one of the chairs, then sniffed the air. "Coffee?"

"Decaf." He motioned to the pot. "Want some?"

"Thanks. Anyway, they have a real commitment to education. And a few surprises. I heard about the Barrington scholarships."

He walked over to the cupboard and pulled down two mugs. "So?"

"So? It's wonderful. You're offering ten scholarships to kids who otherwise wouldn't have a chance."

"It's no big deal."

"Of course it is." She moved to stand next to him. Even more hairs had escaped from her braid. They drifted around her face and tempted him to touch her. Her hazel eyes glowed with admiration. "Ten regular students. Not the most athletic, not the brightest, just ten kids that have the grades but not the money to go to college. I think it's terrific."

He shrugged off her praise. "Super smart students get academic scholarships and jocks go on athletic ones. I wanted to help the students that fell in between. Like I said, no big deal."

She leaned closer and kissed him on the cheek. "I don't care what you say, I'm impressed."

Her scent enveloped him. It was late in the day and the fragrance should have faded by now, but it hadn't. Her hand, resting on his shoulder, provided a warm connection between them. He turned slowly until he faced her. Behind him, the coffeepot hissed. He ignored it. Hazel eyes, wide with no hint of blue, met his. Her mouth curved up at the corners. Lipstick stained the sweet flesh, darkening the color to a deep rose.

He had forgotten. All the time she'd been gone, all those years, he'd let himself forget. The work, his responsibilities, the women who came and went without touching past the first layer of skin, had allowed him to pretend that it didn't matter anymore. To have come so close a second time and then to have lost it all. How was he going to survive?

"What is it?" she asked, smiling up at him.

"Nothing."

She swayed slightly, toward him. He read the invitation. He wasn't sure she knew what she was asking. He'd promised himself not to push her, that he'd let *her* say when. But could he wait? Could he risk it all?

No! Not if there was a chance of tipping the scales in his favor. He reached up and placed his hands on her shoulders. Slowly, so that she would know what he intended, he lowered his mouth to hers. She didn't back up or pull away. Instead she rose onto her tiptoes and met him more than halfway.

He'd planned a gentle kiss. His partially formed idea had included seducing her with soft touches and gentle words. Instead, the moment their lips touched, he lost control. He had to have her. All of her.

His mouth angled against hers. Without asking, he swept forward with his tongue. Instantly she parted her lips to admit him. Instead of shying from his assault, she counterattacked with her own plunges. They began a different sort of hide-and-seek with pleasure being the prize for both players.

Jane strained against him. She wrapped her arms around his waist and pulled him toward her. Their bodies touched from chest to knee, but it wasn't enough.

He reached for her braid and yanked off the ribbon. The elastic band quickly followed. Raking his fingers through the long silky lengths, he combed her hair free. When it was loose around her shoulders, he buried his hands in the warm satin. It tickled his skin and aroused him. His groin already throbbed with painful readiness, and the feel of her hair slipping through his fingers, trailing along his arms, made him grind his hips against hers.

She pulled back slightly and looked up at him. He read the questions in her eyes.

He could lie. He could confess his fears. He could even tell her what had happened with Billie. Each would require more explanation than he could provide right now. He released her hair and stepped back. A voice inside said that she must come to him of her own free will. If he didn't allow her that, all would be lost.

"I need you," he said simply.

She bit her lower lip, then smiled. "That's all you ever had to say." Lacing her fingers with his, she led him out of the kitchen and up the stairs to her bedroom.

In the darkness, with only the sound of the rain to distract them, he undressed her. When her clothes fell to the floor, he lowered her onto the bed. He touched each inch of her. His fingers traced the delicate skin on the inside of her elbows and behind her knees. He tickled her insteps until she begged her surrender. When her hands reached to caress him, he captured them and held them above her head. This was for *her*.

Still holding her arms up against the pillow, he plundered her mouth. When her tongue chased his back into his mouth, he gently bit on the pointed tip. At her gasp, he sucked on her lower lip. She grew limp. He pressed his leg against her secrets and felt her ready moistness.

Before he reached for his own clothing and removed it, he took her twice up to the edge of passion and caught her as he fell. Only when she had cried out his name over and over again did he allow himself to be buried in her waiting warmth. And not until her third release rippled around him did he give in to the need that pulsed within him. With heavy-lidded eyes and a satisfied smile, she moved her hips in a way designed to reduce his control to ashes. As the fire consumed him, as he reached the pinnacle and prepared himself for his own flight, he wondered if he'd indeed won.

"I'll have to leave more often," Jane said as she settled back against the pillows. "I like how you welcome me home."

Adam didn't respond, he just continued to hold her close and pray for a miracle.

"Why now?" she asked.

"Why not?" It was avoiding the question and the truth but what else could he do?

"I wasn't sure." She snuggled closer to him. Her hair fanned out over his chest. One of her legs rode up against his and her arms held him tight. "After the last time. You never said anything about doing it again."

"I wanted to give you time."

"Oh."

He looked down at her. "*Oh?* What does that mean?"

She shrugged. "I knew that it was better that we try to get used to the arrangement without complicating it with, you know, sex, but—" She shrugged again.

"Jane." He touched her chin and forced her to look at him. "What are you saying?"

Her eyes, dark now in the stormy night, refused to meet his. "I wasn't sure you wanted me again."

"You're kidding?"

She shook her head.

"Why would you think that?"

"I wasn't very experienced." She rested her head on his shoulder. "I wasn't sure I pleased you."

"Do you still have doubts?"

He felt her mouth curve against his skin. "No. You took care of them nicely, thank you."

If only you could take care of mine, he thought. They continued to hold each other. His hands stroked her bare body, loving the feel of her skin. Warm living satin, he thought. He couldn't leave her. He didn't deserve to stay.

"I had a problem with Billie tonight," he blurted out.

"What happened?"

"She played with her softball inside and broke a vase."

Jane groaned. "Which one?"

"The one in the hall. On that little table. It was completely shattered. There wasn't anything to save."

"That little— I've told her and told her. What did you do?"

He closed his eyes against the memory. "Gave her a twenty-minute time-out and had her write you a letter of apology."

Jane squeezed him. "Welcome to the world of parenting."

"Did I do the right thing?"

"Yes. I especially like the letter. It's a nice touch. I usually take her ball away for the rest of the day, but seeing as it was so close to bedtime, it's no big deal."

He nodded. At least he hadn't scarred Billie for life, he thought grimly. "She said she hates me."

Jane raised herself up on one elbow. "What?"

"After I punished her. She told me I wasn't her father, that she wanted me to leave. And that she hates me."

"Adam, I'm sorry."

"It's not your fault."

"Don't take it too seriously. She's a kid. She's just reacting to the situation. You've gone from being a friend to being an authority figure in a very short time. It'll take some getting used to."

He turned away. "What if she doesn't get used to it? What if she decides to hate me forever?"

"Billie's attention span isn't that long."

"This isn't humorous to me."

"Adam." She touched his cheek. "Are you upset?"

"Of course. What did you think? That I'd take this lightly? My God, Jane, I've known her two weeks and she already hates me."

"She doesn't. I promise. Billie thinks the world of you."

"It's not enough."

He stared into the darkness. There had to be a solution.

"Adam, please. She's just a little girl. She often says things that she doesn't—"

"Marry me."

"What?"

He hadn't meant to say that, but now that he had, it felt right. He leaned over her and brushed her lips with his fingers. "Marry me, Jane Southwick. Live with me in the big house. Be my wife."

He hadn't planned the proposal enough to have formed thoughts on her reaction, but he never expected her to jump out of bed and glare at him as if he'd suggested something disgusting.

"How dare you?" she asked in a low cold voice. "That is the cruelest thing you've ever said to me."

"I asked you to marry me."

She walked over to the closet and pulled out a robe. After slipping it on and tying the belt tight, she clicked on the lamp on the nightstand. Her hazel eyes flashed with fire and something that might have been pain.

"Why?" she asked. "Why do you want to marry me?"

"Because—" He paused. "It's the right thing to do."

"No!" Her hands closed into fists. "Damn it, no! Not that, Adam, please. Tell me you love me. Tell me you can't live without me. Tell me—" She sighed and collapsed onto the edge of the bed. "Tell me anything but that," she whispered.

"I do need you." He moved behind her and took her in his arms. "Please, Jane. You've got to understand. All of this. It's too—"

"Too what?" She spun out of his embrace. "Too scary? For me, too. I'm terrified. It's almost like those nine years never happened. We're still connected with each other. But those nine years are real. I'm not that frightened girl who ran away. I'm all grown up. I know what I want."

And it's not you. She didn't have to say the words; they echoed loudly enough already. He'd lost. It didn't matter how or why, but it was over. He rose and walked to the window. Keeping his back to her, so she couldn't see how much it hurt, he asked, "What *do* you want?"

"You."

He couldn't have heard her correctly.

"Then why—"

"I love you, Adam. I've never stopped loving you. I had to leave to find out everything I needed was right here at home."

Hope flared inside of him. He turned to face her. "Then—"

"No." She shook her head. "It's not that easy. You don't trust me."

"That's crazy."

"Is it? You want to marry me to keep me from running away again. And I'll bet it has something to do with forcing Billie to be with you as well. That doesn't sound like you trust us very much." She stood up. Her gaze traveled from the top of his head to his feet. He stood naked before her and prayed that she would find him enough. She didn't. "I could probably forgive you for not trusting me, if you loved me."

"I—" He couldn't say the words.

"See." Her smile was sad. "You never told me then, and you can't say it now. You won't risk loving me, because it's the final risk. Everyone you've loved has left you."

She walked over to him and touched his chest. "Here, in your heart. This is where I want to be. But you won't let me in. You won't trust me enough to stay. You won't love me enough to give me the chance to prove I'm not going anywhere."

"You're wrong."

"Am I?" She smiled sadly. "Tell me you trust me."

"I trust you."

"Tell me we can stay together without getting married."

"Why won't you marry me?" he asked in frustration. "What's so wrong with that?"

She shook her head. Her long hair swayed back and forth on her shoulders. "You don't get it. Look me in the eye and tell me you trust me enough to stay without the commitment of marriage."

He couldn't. He didn't.

"Adam Barrington, I love you. It's taken me nine years to figure that out. I'm going to prove it to you, too." She folded her arms in front of her chest. "I'm going to live next door to you. I'm going to love you. I'm going to tempt you into my bed. When you can risk my leaving enough to confess your feelings—when you can tell me you love me, I'll marry you."

Chapter Fifteen

Adam sat on the old wicker chair in the corner of Jane's front porch. He should go home, he told himself. But he couldn't. Not yet.

It wasn't the rain that kept him in place. The storm had passed, leaving only a few sprinkles. It was his personal band of demons that kept him close. He couldn't bear the thought that, in a matter of hours, he'd lost them both. The pain, a hollow emptiness inside that seemed to be sucking in his soul, grew with each breath. He felt as if he would disappear in the void. He leaned his head back against the chair and sighed. The truth wasn't that eloquent. He wouldn't disappear. He'd keep on going, day after day, knowing he'd lost the two people he cared about most.

He shouldn't have proposed. He realized that now. But he'd panicked about Jane hating him as Billie did. Marriage had seemed an easy solution. Jane had seen right through him.

He shook his head. Damn, she'd grown into a beautiful woman. Not just on the outside—as much as he adored her body close to his—but in her heart. She'd become independent and capable. Those fears about losing herself in another person wouldn't matter to her anymore. She'd conquered them. And him.

Give me strength, he prayed silently. And then asked—for what? How did he want to be strong? Did he want to walk away and not regret what he'd lost? Or was he looking for the power to follow in Jane's footsteps and conquer his fears?

The front door creaked open. Adam half rose from his chair. But instead of Jane's willowy form, he saw Billie stepping cautiously on the damp porch.

"Billie?"

She turned to look at him. The lamp above the door cast a harsh pool of light. The child looked pale and drawn.

"Adam? Is that you?" she whispered.

"Yes. What are you doing up?"

"Oh, Adam!"

She ran across the wooden floor and flung herself at him. He grabbed her as she leapt and pulled her next to him.

"I'm sorry," she said, then sniffed. "I'm sorry I was mean."

"Hush." He held her tightly, her small head nestling against his chest. Inside, the pain around his heart eased some, allowing him to draw a full breath. She felt warm and soft in his arms, and smelled of sleep and little girl. He shut his eyes as a burning began behind the lids.

"I kept waking up," she whispered, then tilted her head to look at him. "I had a dream that you really went away. I woke up scared. That's why I came to find you." She wrapped her arms around his neck. "I'm glad you didn't go home."

"My home is with you," he said thickly, touching his cheek to hers.

"I don't hate you."

"Thank you for that."

"Are you mad at me?" Her lower lip trembled.

"No, Billie."

"You won't go away like in my dream?"

"No," he said, recognizing that they shared the same fears. "I promise I'll stay with you."

"Forever?"

It was like looking into a mirror, he thought, staring into eyes that were so much like his own. "Forever," he answered.

Her arms tightened around his neck as she clung to him. "I love you, Dad."

His heart filled with gratitude. "I love you, too."

As he spoke the words, he knew they were true. She was his daughter; how could he not love her? He kissed her forehead and waited for the wave of fear. He'd said the words; now it was just a matter of time until she left him.

He held her until she fell asleep, then he picked her up and carried her back to her bed. After tucking the worn teddy bear under her arm, he pulled up the covers and whispered, "Good night." She didn't even stir. On his way out, he passed by Jane's door. He thought about knocking, but she might be asleep as well. Certainly she wouldn't want to see him. He crept down the stairs and out the front.

It wasn't until he reached his own house that he realized there was no fear. He felt wonder that this child was his, and gratitude that he had the chance to be with her now. But no fear.

He stared up at the sky. Clouds drifted by, exposing the beauty of a starry night. He held on to Billie's words, repeating them over and over like a prayer. "I love you, Dad," she'd said with the sincerity of one who still believes. It gave him hope, he realized. Hope that there might be a way out of this after all.

* * *

Jane stared blurrily at the coffeepot and begged it t hurry. Her night had been long and sleepless. She'd doze off for a short time, then had spent the rest of the predaw hours staring at the ceiling.

Had she pushed him too far? Was she asking more o Adam than he could give? Could she settle for less? Sh shook her head. No. Not for herself or for Billie. She coul handle his fears if he would meet her halfway. All sh wanted was to know that he loved her. Easy enough. Wh didn't she just go ahead and change the tide while she wa at it?

Billie came bouncing into the kitchen. She'd alread dressed herself. Her softball bulged from its usual pocket.

"How are you?" she asked, remembering what Adar had told her about the previous night.

"Fine."

She bent down to receive Billie's kiss. "Fine? That's it What about the vase?"

"Oh, that."

"Yes, that."

Billie shrugged. "I've already been punished." Sh grinned. "And I wrote a letter." She thrust it at her mother

"What about Adam? I understand that the two of yo had some words."

Billie laughed. "He's fine. I talked to him last night."

"When?"

"After I'd been asleep. I had a bad dream that he wen away because I told him to." Her smile faded as she re membered. "I was sad when I woke up, so I went to fin him."

Jane frowned. "You left the house in the middle of th night?"

"No. He was outside. On the porch." She put her base ball cap on her head. "You know, on the chair out front We talked."

"And?"

"I 'pologized." She wrinkled her nose. "He said he'd always be my dad. I told him I love him. Is that okay?"

"Yes, honey, that's fine." Billie was growing up so fast, Jane thought sadly.

"Good, 'cause he loves me, too."

"I know he does, Billie, but sometimes people aren't comfortable saying the words."

"What words?"

"I love you."

She shook her head and skipped toward the door. "He said 'em. I'm going over to see Adam for breakfast. Bye." With that, she slipped through the back door and headed toward the hedge that separated their property.

He said them? "Wait," Jane called after her, but it was too late.

He said the words? Adam Barrington said "I love you" to his daughter? Was it possible? Jane poured herself a cup of coffee and sat at the kitchen table. She smiled to herself. Maybe, just maybe they were going to get through this.

Adam stared out his office window. Give it up, he told himself as he tossed his pen onto his desk. He wasn't fooling anyone. For the last week he'd existed in a fog; going through the motions of his life, but not really participating. He wasn't kidding anyone. He shook his head. That wasn't true. He *was* kidding everyone else; he wasn't kidding Jane.

He thought about the routine they'd slipped into. Billie appeared at his house for breakfast. He went over there for dinner. They spent the evening as a family, but as soon as Billie went to bed, he returned to his own place. As Jane watched him leave, she asked him silent questions. He still didn't have any answers.

She'd threatened to tempt him into her bed. So far she hadn't tried anything, but that didn't mean he wasn't

tempted. It only took a look, a brush of her hand against h
arm, or the scent of her perfume and he was hard and reac
to take her. So far he'd managed to resist. Not out of an
moral strength. Rather it was a feeling of self-preservatic
and the sensation that he was on the edge of a great disco
ery. He just had to hang in a little longer. He hoped.

The late afternoon had turned hot and muggy. Despite th
air-conditioning in the bank, he felt uncomfortable. H
swore out loud. He couldn't stand it anymore. Rising fro
his seat, he grabbed his jacket, then headed for the door. H
met his secretary in the hallway.

"Mr. Barrington?" Edna asked as she stared at him.

"I'm leaving."

"Now?" She sounded scandalized. "It's only thre
o'clock."

He grinned at her. "I know, Edna. Why don't you tak
off early, too?"

"I couldn't." Her heavily painted mouth formed a mou
of disapproval.

"Your choice."

He walked through the bank and out the back door.

The trip home took about ten minutes. After opening
cold beer, he loped up the stairs toward his room. Once he'
shed his suit, he felt better. The house was oddly quiet.
was because Charlene was gone, he told himself. Eve
though she didn't actually live with him, she was in and ou
enough for him to miss her. He wondered what Greec
thought of Charlene Standing of *The* Carolina Standings.

He pulled on shorts and a polo shirt and picked up h
beer. But instead of going downstairs to his office, he turne
left and continued down the hall. One of the small rooms a
the very end, in what used to be the maids' quarters, house
a few of his boxes. There were his sports trophies from hig
school. Some old clothes, his letterman's jacket. His luck
jersey and a football helmet.

He pushed open the door and stepped inside. He wasn't
interested in anything from high school, or even college.
Adam crouched by a small box tucked in the corner. He set
his beer on the floor and touched the white cover. Taking a
deep breath, he lifted it up and stared inside.

White roses. They still carried their scent, he thought as
he inhaled the sweet smell. Two dozen, in the shape of an
oval. Yellowed ribbons circled the arrangement, and it all
sat on a cloud of tulle. Jane's bouquet.

He sat down and picked up the flowers. They'd dried
perfectly. A couple had crumbled at the edges, but other
than that, they were exactly as he remembered.

It had been after the guests had been told there would be
no wedding. He'd stood in the back and watched them file
out. A couple had walked over to him to offer condolences.
He'd been too numb to respond. Jane's mother had approached him last. Her hazel eyes, so much like her daughter's, had avoided his. Without saying anything, she'd
pressed something small and hard into his hand. The ring.

He looked into the box and saw the velvet jeweler's case
in the corner. He'd taken the ring and held it tight. When the
last person had left, he'd walked through the church. There
had been so many questions. Why had she left? Why hadn't
he said anything? What could he have done to keep her?

Then he'd seen them. The flowers. She'd left them on a
chair by the church's side door. He'd picked up the bouquet with the intent of throwing it into the garbage. In the
end, he couldn't. He'd stared at the flowers every day for
two months, until they'd dried up and he'd finally packed
them away. With the ring.

He set the flowers on the floor and picked up the velvet
box. Inside a two-carat solitaire diamond winked at him. A
ring fit for a princess, he'd thought when he'd seen it in the
store window. He'd bought the ring months before he'd
proposed because he'd known it was perfect for Jane. He'd
practiced what he'd planned to say. The romantic phrases

had sounded silly, so in the end he'd told her they wer
suited.

Suited. He shook his head. *Not* that she drove him wil
with her smiles. *Not* that he wanted to watch her grow larg
with their children and raise them together. *Not* that h
dreamed about building a life with her for years to come
Not that he loved her. Because he couldn't say the words.
he loved her, she would leave him.

She'd left him, anyway.

He snapped the box closed and took another drink from
the bottle. So the system had its flaws. Nothing was per
fect. Nothing was forever. Nothing was guaranteed. H
could make it easy or he could make it hard. In the pas
he'd chosen the difficult path. By listening to the voice in
side, by giving in to the fear, he'd lost the only woman he'
ever loved.

And here he was again. Damn close to losing her. He wa
supposed to be the smart one. When was he going to learn

He rose and walked over to the small window. He coul
see Jane's house from here, and her yard. Her car stood i
the driveway. She was right there, he thought. All he had t
do was reach out and take what she offered. A single step o
faith. Three small words. How much easier could it be?

Jane stared in the refrigerator. There wasn't anything de
cent for dinner. Maybe she should suggest that the three o
them go out to eat. Not a good idea, she thought, swingin
the door closed. It had been awkward between her an
Adam lately. There would be enough gossip without spec
ulation that their undefined relationship was already fal
ing apart. She glanced at the clock on the wall. There wa
still time to go to the store before Billie came home from he
day camp. Maybe a nice roast.

Someone knocked on the front door. She walked throug
the house and pulled it open.

"Adam?"

She stared, not at him, but at what he was holding. She recognized the dried flowers and crumpled tulle. Her bouquet! She'd wondered about it. Her mother had saved her dress and veil, but had told her the flowers had disappeared. Had Adam kept them all this time?

She looked up at him. His brown eyes gazed warmly at her, but she couldn't tell what that meant.

"Can I come in?" he asked.

She stepped back. "I don't understand."

"About the flowers?"

She nodded.

"I kept them." He set the flowers on the table in the small foyer, then shoved his hands into his shorts pockets. They were standing so close that she had to tilt her head to look at his face.

"Why?"

"At first they reminded me of what you'd done. They fed my rage. Then I kept them because I couldn't bear not to. They were all I had. The flowers and this."

He pulled his hand out of his pocket and held it out. Automatically she raised her palm up to take what he offered. She gasped. Her ring.

She stared at the circle of gold, the sparkling diamond. Tears burned, but she blinked them away. What did it mean? Her heart thundered in her chest.

"Adam?"

He touched his forefinger to her chin and nudged her until she raised her head. He stood so tall and handsome. A special man she had loved her whole life. Just him, she thought, knowing she would accept whatever he offered. She had no choice. There would only ever be Adam.

His gaze caressed her face. He brushed his thumb across her lips. "I love you," he said.

She stared, mute, not able to believe.

"I love you, Jane. I've always loved you. Even when you were gone and I told myself I hated you, I couldn't let go of what we'd had together." One corner of his mouth lifted "You don't have to marry me, but will you come live with me in my house? The two of you. Can we be a family?"

"Oh, Adam." She flung her arms around him. "Yes love, yes. I'll live with you. I'll even marry you."

He clutched her upper arms and held her away from him "Really?"

She nodded.

He leaned forward and kissed away the tears she hadn't felt fall. Then his mouth captured hers. Warm and prob ing, his tongue swept her lips before plunging inside. Sh gave herself up to him, clinging to his strength, knowing tha her world was at last complete.

A gagging sound broke through her passionate haze Adam lifted his head.

"You're kissing," Billie said, sounding more disguste than unhappy. "Gross."

Jane held out her hand. Billie shuffled forward, but re fused to be drawn close.

"I don't like this kissing stuff," she said.

"You will." Jane smiled at her. "We're—" She glance at Adam. "You tell her."

He took her hand, the one that held the ring. He slid it o her finger and kissed her palm, then crouched in front o Billie. "Your mother and I are getting married."

"Really?" Billie grinned. "So we'll be a real family?"

"Yes," Jane said. "And we even get to live in Adam house."

"With the island in the kitchen and the banister? Cool. She looked up. "I won't slide down the banister, of course.

"Yeah, right." Adam rose and tapped her nose.

Billie tugged off her cap and frowned. "Does this mea there's going to be a wedding, like when Auntie Jolie mar ried Uncle Brad?"

Adam looked at her. Jane smiled. "A friend of mine back in San Francisco. Yes, Billie." She glanced at her daughter. "But a lot smaller."

"I'm not wearing a dress," Billie announced.

"Where?"

"At the wedding." She frowned. "No way."

Jane kissed Adam's cheek. "There's still time to back out. She's a handful."

Billie held out her arms. Adam bent over and picked her up. Jane wrapped her arms around his waist. "I wouldn't change her for the world," he said.

"Good." She leaned her head against his shoulder. "Because I want four more just like her."

He coughed. "Four?"

"Yes. Do you have a problem with that?"

"No. Four is a nice round number."

"All right!" Billie pumped her arm. "Four. Enough for an infield."

Adam groaned.

"I warned you," Jane said.

He shifted Billie so that he could support her with one arm and hug Jane with the other. Pulling her close, he murmured, "I can handle it."

"Brothers," Billie interrupted, just before his mouth touched Jane's.

"What?" Adam asked.

"I want all brothers. No girls."

Adam smiled at Jane. She felt her insides start to melt. They were going to make it, she thought, feeling the happiness flood her heart. They were going to make it just fine.

Adam looked at his daughter and winked. "Brothers? I'll see what I can do."

* * * * *

Silhouette
SPECIAL EDITION

It takes a very special man to win
That
SPECIAL
Woman!

She's friend, wife, mother—she's you! And beside each Special Woman stands a wonderfully special man. It's a celebration of our heroines—and the men who become part of their lives.

Look for these exciting titles from Silhouette Special Edition:

August MORE THAN HE BARGAINED FOR by Carole Halston
Heroine: Avery Payton—a woman struggling for independence falls for the man next door.

September A HUSBAND TO REMEMBER by Lisa Jackson
Heroine: Nikki Carrothers—a woman without memories meets the man she should never have forgotten...her husband.

October ON HER OWN by Pat Warren
Heroine: Sara Shepard—a woman returns to her hometown and confronts the hero of her childhood dreams.

November GRAND PRIZE WINNER! by Tracy Sinclair
Heroine: Kelley McCormick—a woman takes the trip of a lifetime and wins the greatest prize of all...love!

**December POINT OF DEPARTURE by Lindsay McKenna
(Women of Glory)**
Heroine: Lt. Callie Donovan—a woman takes on the system and must accept the help of a kind and sexy stranger.

Don't miss THAT SPECIAL WOMAN! each month—from some of your special authors! Only from Silhouette Special Edition!

TSW3

Take 4 bestselling love stories FREE

Plus get a FREE surprise gift!

Special Limited-time Offer

Mail to Silhouette Reader Service™

3010 Walden Avenue
P.O. Box 1867
Buffalo, N.Y. 14269-1867

YES! Please send me 4 free Silhouette Special Edition® novels and my free surprise gift. Then send me 6 brand-new novels every month, which I will receive months before they appear in bookstores. Bill me at the low price of $2.71 each plus 25¢ delivery and applicable sales tax, if any.* That's the complete price and—compared to the cover prices of $3.50 each—quite a bargain! I understand that accepting the books and gift places me under no obligation ever to buy any books. I can always return a shipment and cancel at any time. Even if I never buy another book from Silhouette, the 4 free books and the surprise gift are mine to keep forever.

235 BPA AJH7

Name	(PLEASE PRINT)	
Address	Apt. No.	
City	State	Zip

This offer is limited to one order per household and not valid to present Silhouette Special Edition® subscribers. *Terms and prices are subject to change without notice. Sales tax applicable in N.Y.

USPED-93R   ©1990 Harlequin Enterprises Limited

Silhouette®

SPECIAL EDITION®

MORGAN'S MERCENARIES

by Lindsay McKenna

Morgan Trayhern has returned and he's set up a company full of best pals in adventure. Three men who've been to hell and back are about to fight the toughest battle of all...love!

You loved Wolf Harding in HEART OF THE WOLF (SE #817) and Sean Killian in THE ROGUE (SE #824). Don't miss Jake Randolph in COMMANDO (SE #830), the final story in this exciting trilogy, available in August.

These are men you'll love and stories you'll treasure...only from Silhouette Special Edition!

Silhouette®

SPECIAL EDITION®

WILD RIVER TRILOGY

by Laurie Paige

Come meet the wild McPherson men and see how these three sexy bachelors are tamed!

In HOME FOR A WILD HEART (SE #828) you got to know Kerrigan McPherson. Now meet the rest of the family:

A PLACE FOR EAGLES, September 1993—
Keegan McPherson gets the surprise of his life.

THE WAY OF A MAN, November 1993—
Paul McPherson finally meets his match.

Don't miss any of these exciting titles—only for our readers and only from Silhouette Special Edition!

Premiere

Silhouette Books has done it again!

Opening night in October has never been as exciting! Come watch as the curtain rises and romance flourishes when the stars of tomorrow make their debuts today!

Revel in Jodi O'Donnell's STILL SWEET ON HIM—
Silhouette Romance #969
...as Callie Farrell's renovation of the family homestead leads her straight into the arms of teenage crush Drew Barnett!

Tingle with Carol Devine's BEAUTY AND THE BEASTMASTER—
Silhouette Desire #816
...as legal eagle Amanda Tarkington is carried off by wrestler Bram Masterson!

Thrill to Elyn Day's A BED OF ROSES—
Silhouette Special Edition #846
...as Dana Whitaker's body and soul are healed by sexy physical therapist Michael Gordon!

Believe when Kylie Brant's McLAIN'S LAW —
Silhouette Intimate Moments #528
...takes you into detective Connor McLain's life as he falls for psychic—and suspect—Michele Easton!

Catch the classics of tomorrow—*premiering* today—
only from ❤ *Silhouette*

If you've been looking for something a little bit different and a little bit spooky, let Silhouette Books take you on a journey to the dark side of love with

SILHOUETTE *Shadows*

Every month, Silhouette will bring you two romantic, spine-tingling Shadows novels, written by some of your favorite authors, such as *New York Times* bestselling author Heather Graham Pozzessere, Anne Stuart, Helen R. Myers and Rachel Lee—to name just a few.

In July, look for:
HEART OF THE BEAST by Carla Cassidy
DARK ENCHANTMENT by Jane Toombs

In August, look for:
A SILENCE OF DREAMS by Barbara Faith
THE SEVENTH NIGHT by Amanda Stevens

In September, look for:
FOOTSTEPS IN THE NIGHT by Lee Karr
WHAT WAITS BELOW by Jane Toombs

Come into the world of Shadows and prepare to tremble with fear—and passion....

SHAD3